Praise for *Mrs M*

'Australian journalist Luke Slattery's bea[...]
is told through the eyes of Governor L[...]
Elizabeth. It's a vivid recreation of Sydney as a penal colony and a
convincing portrayal of a feisty, passionate woman. The love between
Mrs Macquarie and the Architect (a character loosely based on Francis
Greenway) is fictional, but no less moving for that. A richly evocative
piece of historical fiction' — NICOLE ABADEE, *Good Weekend*

'It is, at its core, the story of Slattery's most extraordinary creation:
Mrs M, whose real-world counterpart was the wife of Lachlan
Macquarie, fifth governor of the colony of New South Wales ... There
is a kind of clarion certainty to her, both in how she understands
things as well as in how she is presented ... I think readers will be
swept up by this creation. The sensuous descriptions of her Scotland
and her Sydney — as well as her own inner world — rise off the page
with a poet's perfect pitch' — ASHLEY HAY, *The Australian*

'In this moving, intricate novel, Luke Slattery does more than reveal
these multifaceted historical figures — Macquarie, Elizabeth and
convict architect Francis Greenway — and the complex vectors of
love between them. He brings to life the radical moral largeness at
the founding of Australia. Every love story has at its heart a vision
of inherent human worth in the beloved; Slattery's achievement is to
render, subtly and powerfully, both a human love story, and a love
story to the nation' — ANNA FUNDER, author of *All That I Am*

'A remarkable early nineteenth century heroine comes alive for us
in this story: we share Mrs M's thoughts and feelings in almost
uncanny fashion. Luke Slattery's debut sets new standards for the
Australian historical novel' — NICOLAS ROTHWELL

'A loving ode to architecture — poignant and totally engaging.'
— GENE SHERMAN

'Saul Bellow says somewhere that in fiction sentences should be "charged" — something should quietly beat through them. When one begins reading, this is what you should listen for — imaginative confidence, a sense of sureness. This applies to historical fiction as much as any other. You don't ask, "Is this true to history?" You ask, "Is this true to itself?" Luke Slattery's *Mrs M* is imaginatively true from beginning to end' — BARRY OAKLEY, *Australian Book Review*

Luke Slattery is a Sydney-based journalist, editor and columnist whose work appears in *The Australian*, *The Age*, *The Sydney Morning Herald* and *The Australian Financial Review*. Internationally he has been published in *The New Yorker* online, the *LA Times*, the *International Herald Tribune*, the UK *Spectator* and the US *Chronicle of Higher Education*. *Mrs M* is his fifth book, and his first novel.

LUKE SLATTERY

MRS. M

FOURTH ESTATE

For Madeleine and Carla

Fourth Estate
An imprint of HarperCollins*Publishers*

First published in Australia in 2017
This edition published in 2019
by HarperCollins*Publishers* Australia Pty Limited
ABN 36 009 913 517
harpercollins.com.au

HarperCollins*Publishers*
Level 13, 201 Elizabeth Street, Sydney NSW 2000, Australia
Unit D1, 63 Apollo Drive, Rosedale, Auckland 0632, New Zealand
A 53, Sector 57, Noida, UP, India
1 London Bridge Street, London, SE1 9GF, United Kingdom
Bay Adelaide Centre, East Tower, 22 Adelaide Street West, 41st floor,
   Toronto, Ontario, M5H 4E3
195 Broadway, New York NY 10007, USA

A cataogue record for this book is available from the National Library of Australia.

ISBN: 978 1 4607 5767 3 (paperback)
ISBN: 978 1 4607 0901 6 (ebook)

Cover design by Hazel Lam, HarperCollins Design Studio
Cover images: *Aleurites moluccana*, candlenut tree, by The Natural History Museum /
Alamy Stock Photo; Woman by istockphoto.com
Author photo by Renee Nowytarger, courtesy of *The Australian*
Typeset in Sabon LT Std by Kirby Jones
Printed and bound in Australia by McPherson's Printing Group
The papers used by HarperCollins in the manufacture of this book are a natural, recyclable product made from wood grown in sustainable plantation forests. The fibre source and manufacturing processes meet recognised international environmental standards, and carry certification.

For we are, all of us, small men.
But in this new world we may become giants.
Jonathan Swift, *Gulliver's Travels*

There's an old story ... which may or may not be true.
Euripides, *Helen*

PART ONE

CHAPTER ONE

I paid the boatman with a bag of fresh cherries this morning. I picked them myself from the sloping orchard beside Loch Bà. I need not give at all. He knows. Knows that I am married — was married — to Macquarie of Mull; that since his death last year there has been nothing from the crofters, not that there is ever very much.

The English butler left on Boxing Day with a tight smile and a portmanteau of suspicious heft and now there is just me and the young footman. The rascal drinks away every spare shilling and returns with an awful clatter each night to the cold house at Gruline lying deep in the shadow of Ben More. I am very near done with him.

The island of Mull is large and muscular, not entirely beautiful, though not easily forgotten, and the islanders clannishly tight when they are not at one another's throats. They have all heard of our journey to Sydney Cove, so full of promise, and the calamity — at the very least the indignity — suffered there. They shook their heads at the journey out; doubtless they shook them again at news of our return and our ruin. They must think me cursed.

And yet I am born too high for their sympathy and their eyes cannot meet mine for long. The women turn away, or lower their gaze, as if I have suddenly become disfigured, which manifestly I have not because the men — the married men mostly — offer a dark, direct look: testing and very bold.

Not the boatman, who is to row me the short distance across the Sound to the little island of Ulva, my husband's birthplace. He is at peace with whatever it is that I am, or have done, or have endured. He takes the milk-white cotton satchel plumped with cherries — a few crimson stains mark the underside where the split and wounded fruit have pressed. Stepping stooped and splay-legged to the head of the rocking rowboat, he tucks it under the gunwale and returns for me. Taking my hand, he leads me to the varnished bench opposite his own. He bends to take the oars, straightens as he pulls.

'Apologies,' I am about to say. 'There is no coin about the house.' But the words dissolve under his mild gaze.

Instead it is the boatman who speaks: 'It'd be two hundred yards across. Not far enough from one shore to the other to raise a sweat, even on the warmest days.'

A crumpled grin spreads across his unshaven outdoor face as he tugs on the oars. 'If I'm delayed for any reason — the nets, the crab pots, visitors to the boathouse — you need only whistle for Ben and he'll take you on his back,' he says. The smile broadens.

'I would think the old labrador might take some convincing,' I return. 'He enjoys the sun — when there is sun.'

'Aye, he does.'

A glass of port wine with this man at the Ulva boathouse, a wedge of cheddar shared between us, a few slices of warm bread, and these splendid cherries taken into the mouth one by one — the unyielding fruit tasteless before the crack of the flesh and the burst of juice. What bright conversation there would be!

'I am grateful,' I offer. 'I will be finished by mid-afternoon.'

A final heave and we nudge the Ulva pier with a sweet hollow knock, quite musical. He tethers the boat to the bollard. Again, he takes my hand in his.

I join him on the pier. He pulls a weathered old parasol from beneath his arm, gives it a shake and opens it for me as we walk past the crab pots and the mounds of seaweed drying in the sun.

'The kelp burning season,' he says apologetically. 'The wife,' he shoots a glance at the boathouse to the right on the low rise, 'she calls it the scent of summer.'

'You must,' I say firmly, 'return the sunshade to her.' I extract a light bonnet from my pocket.

'It is kind of you ma'am. She will need it for the journey.'

'What journey?'

'No matter,' he says and looks away.

The boatman's hair is drawn back from his broad brow and worn at an unfashionable length. Age has him in its grasp. And yet the grey — a full head of it — is no dull absence of colour but a bright weave of charcoal, steel and mica. He wears a moss-coloured waistcoat and the billowing sleeves of his once-white shirt are long, unbuttoned, a little frayed at the cuffs.

We stroll towards a fork in the path. 'You still know the island well enough for this?' he inquires as we pause beside the track to Ormaig. 'Alone, I mean.'

'Yes, of course. I have walked this path with Macquarie, and walked it alone. Do you not recall? I plan to walk it every summer until age renders me lame, halt or blind. Or until the house is sold.'

'Surely it will not come to that.'

'Already I have several bidders, or so the attorney from Oban tells me. He suggests I slice the Macquarie estate into portions, as if it were a wedding cake, and sell it — well, this is how it seems to me — for little more than such a cake would fetch at market.'

The sea breeze stirs. I reach for my bonnet.

'Then he is not acting in your interests,' he says, with a rasping rub of the chin. 'They'd be hoping you'll walk away. Start again on the mainland somewhere.'

'And they expect me to leave with little more than my sorrows?'

'It is enough that ...' He pauses. 'Well, it angers me. You know a commission will come his way.'

'Most likely. He is of the new dispensation. A speculator.'

'The age,' he mutters. 'Surely it is out of kilter.'

As I take my leave a dark inward look steals across his agreeable face. There is something he knows, or thinks he knows, about what is, or is to come. And yet he will not say.

His lips part, though nothing but a dull muffled sound, such as a mute might make, issues from them. I plead with my eyes but he lowers his, turns and walks away. I watch his heavy, even tread as he returns to the boathouse with his gift of cherries freshly picked.

CHAPTER TWO

The path through the heart of the island is firm and dry and the weather is fine. I tramp through a cool beech forest in full leaf, the treetops teased by a mild wind driving a few dry white clouds. I take my time.

Columns of sunlight plunge through the tree canopy, all apple green, dappling the grass below. The glistening shoots grow tall in the warming earth. Through them spreads a lovely filigree of purple wildflower.

At this time of year Nature takes as much pleasure in her own abundant beauty as she gives to her admirers. She is Flora, gorgeously attired, triumphant — Queen for a time and Queen for all time.

A thin brook trickles into a shaded pond lacquered at its rim with a black stillness. On that other island, so very far away, the skies are home to quarrelsome birds that screech and squawk, and others that roar with a laughter that would be truly diabolical if it were not so comical. Here the birds circling above flute sweetly. I have not heard true birdsong in a long time.

Higher up the forest gives way to a bare, almost ashen landscape of basalt and mountain heather. The path here twists to face the southwest and from its summit a view unfolds of a cold ocean very like that deep celestial blue of early evening. To the west lies a flotilla of islets scattered like chipped shillings: Little Colonsay, Inch Kenneth, and Staffa with its organ pipes of stone. I see how patches of ocean are scuffed by the breeze. The waves battering the rocks are a broiling acid green.

On the way to the village of Ormaig below, I pause to take in the sight of the sea reaching into lochs, sounds, narrows, channels and, finally, little rills veining their way across the marshes. Quite suddenly I am struck, swept up. Transported.

Here at the fringe of the island, with a fine view across Loch na Keal towards the cliffs of Ardmeanach, I could so easily be standing at the mouth of that grand Antipodean harbour flowing between one mighty buttress of sandstone and another, barely a mile apart. There is the same broad sweep of seawall, a land edge that will not surrender easily to the elements but rather rises proud and strong against them. The same pure lonely air.

Why has it never registered before, this echo of one world in another so far away? But I see it now. See it clearly.

I look about me for a place to rest. The stone wall beside the path is low enough to serve as a seat. Removing my bonnet, I turn towards the sun. I close my eyes.

I am standing on a bare headland in the New World gazing at a rippling sheet of sunlit sea. A man stands further out, towards the weathered ledge. He keeps a spyglass fixed to his eye. 'It is the French,' he says, lowering the instrument and turning to me excitably. 'See how quickly they sweep in.' The wind tugs at his shirt. He pays it no heed ...

The same man stands before me, visible yet dimly so in the gloom. It is wet. Cold. We are alone. He offers me his forearm. I take it, rolling the sleeve above the elbow, running my fingers over a red welt — serpentine, meandering — branded on the pale, tender underside ...

The taste of sea salt powdered on skin ...

I walk proudly arm in arm with my ageing husband, a tall man, though a little stooped with care, towards a meeting of natives. The air buckles with their chant. I comprehend nothing of its meaning. But this I do know: it is to two of these natives — one elderly and bearded, the other known to me by the plaited band about his crown — that I owe my life ...

I exchange pleasantries beneath a blazing sun with a small athletic Englishman whom I know to be an assassin ...

There is a subtle shift in the wind direction, and a quickening. The slight chill stirs me from my memories. How long have I been here, yet not here at all? An hour, I would guess. My left index figure has reached for my upper lip, pressing gently there as if sealing in a secret. I am not ready, I decide, for Ormaig. Now is not the time. So I raise myself from the stone wall, smooth my dress, and retrace my steps.

The boatman is waiting for me. He stands hinged forward from the waist, one foot planted on the bench beside a rough outdoor table of broad planks painted a cheering blue. In his right hand, forearm across thigh, he holds a pipe; in his left a wad of tobacco, which he rolls gently in his palm. He, too, is lost in thought.

9

'I see you have been busy?' I inquire as I draw near.

'You mean the bench,' he brightens. 'Yes, a few months ago with the first true signs of spring.'

There is time then for a cup of tea at the blue bench, even if the boatman's society is not as lively as I had hoped. Instead it is taken in companionable silence. Between drinking his tea and drawing on his pipe, he casts anxious looks towards the boathouse on the rise. I catch sight of a nimbus of blonde hair filling the kitchen window, spinning away sharply from my gaze.

How jealously his wife looks on.

* * *

When I step onto the rickety pier on the Mull side of the narrow Sound the boatman returns the milk-white satchel with the crimson stains.

I take the bag by the shoulder strap and, unable to resist the temptation, steal a look inside.

Yes, it is there!

The weight of the letter in its envelope is imperceptible, and yet I sense it as if it were a clay tablet or missive in stone.

'It is kind of you to return the bag,' I say, masking my anticipation with a bland courtesy. 'Of course — the stains. A little unseemly.'

'Not permanent,' he says with a deepening of those pleasing creases beside the mouth — a little like brackets — that a lean man will likely acquire with age. 'Nothing that can't be removed with a good scrubbing. And a little time.'

He is once again my old friend. But a friend with a secret. In this he is, I decide, much like me.

He takes his seat, picks up the oars, and gives a most solemn nod of farewell; quite unnecessary in the circumstances. Surely he

10

understands that I mean to return the next fine summer day. With the weight of only one the boat lurches with his first heave of the oars. They dig into the water, churn and stir. He is enjoying his power now; I am enjoying it, too.

I wave and loop the bag over my shoulder.

'We will see one another again soon,' I call as he glides across the narrows.

The boatman is silent for a few strokes and his answer, when at last it comes, is lost on the breeze.

He is Charon and he ferries me between the lands of the living and the dead. How handy would a coin have been, for that was Charon's customary payment. I shall return to him. I shall rejoin the living.

The black mare I have named Gooseberry after a fondly remembered notable of Sydney Cove stands contented beneath the thin shade of a willow, her fine head buried in a stand of long grass. As I approach she raises it, shakes her mane, stamps and snorts approvingly. Before mounting — they will think me wild and headstrong to ride astride her — I take the envelope from the bag. The word *Elizabeth* has been written in his distinctive hand, a lavish scroll beneath it.

CHAPTER THREE

There is such a thing as fine summer weather in these parts, though rarely does it last more than a fragment of any day. A mild dawn will give way to rain by mid-afternoon; a clear afternoon will succumb to storm by sunset. Today, by some providential magic, the weather has been golden from dawn to dusk.

I had laid aside my widow's garb this morning when I saw the sun and felt a little of its heat. Perhaps it was an error to step out in a sky-blue cotton dress over a pair of stout brown shoes. It will have been noticed, this want of plainness. But I felt drawn, summoned — stirred — by the warmth. And how long must this severity last? I was not made for pilgrim dress.

Now, with a twilight sky clotted by cloud and a sliver of moon hanging askew above Ben More, it is very gloomy in this house. I light the lamps and a candelabrum, of which there is one fewer since the departure of the English butler. And while there is no human warmth but mine within these walls, the hearths and the kitchen stove, at least, throw out a plush heat.

The footman is more like an errant son than a domestic; I never see him in the evenings. He returns between midnight and dawn, sleeps in and wears a complexion of parchment until mid-afternoon, when he takes his first restorative dram. It's only then that the colour returns to his cheeks. His greedy nights steal all the goodness from his days..But if I were to assert what is left of my authority over him I would, I fear, have no footman at all.

The woods wrap around one corner of the house, and it is here, in my bedchamber, that I have my walnut bureau. I call it mine, though it was Lachlan's a year ago. By day the window frames a view of a glorious green world: moss carpeting rock and trunk below, an arabesque of green leaf spreading and deepening above, and the air between as still and syrupy as a fishbowl.

Some of the trees have been allowed to grow too close to the house and on nights like this, with a north wind stirring the forest, branches scrape and tap their bony fingers on the windows as though soliciting entry.

My poor husband lies in the cold earth sheltered by a plain tomb of rosy sandstone — not Sydney stone but a good likeness of it — and a roof of slate quarried from Belnahua across the Firth of Lorn. I had work begin on the mausoleum as soon as I could muster the funds. Plans for this simple structure — in appearance much like a poor man's Gothic chapel — were delivered to me within the month. Stone was quarried, cut and dressed; labour hired; and the forest cleared at a place close enough to serve as a memorial, though not *too* close. The winter here is bleak enough. Work on the Macquarie mausoleum stalled in the hard months, resumed in spring, and hastens towards completion beneath this summer sky.

If he had died suddenly in the colony from disease or misadventure it was his wish that his body be packed in salt and returned to Mull for a burial such as this. And if not his body he requested that his heart be returned in its stead — a grim task that would have fallen to William Redfern, the colony's surgeon. In time I will lie here too, beside him, though I never really understood the fierceness of his feeling for this place above all others. His heart was always returning. My own heart, well, it has a tendency to wander.

On the journey out to Sydney, we lost a deckhand of just eighteen years from Cork. Young Benjamin Quinn plunged from the topsail and, cracking his skull, was dead in an instant. No stone mausoleum; we buried him at sea. A mute uncomplaining splash and his stiff corpse was plucked by the swell.

A dreadful thing an ocean burial. To end one's life as a ragged fish-pecked skeleton shifting indolently this way and that on the ocean floor. To be denied a simple plot and a bare headstone; a place to which some loved one, or even a childhood friend, might come with a poesy, or a few jewelled tears, and the benediction of kindly words. To not have such a place in death, a resting place, a marker to speak, however perfunctorily, to future generations — well, it's to have never lived.

Every few weeks a life was taken by typhus or dysentery or the meanness of the diet. Seven months at sea, three thousand leagues, thirty souls lost. At least Benjamin Quinn was dispatched to the next world with a tawdry ceremony; many a dead convict was discarded late at night with only a cold moon as witness.

By the time we appeared off the Heads with our colours raised the ship was pestilential. Later I would learn that the citizens of Port Jackson claimed to have caught our stench on the breeze that swept us in. They pressed their cotton kerchiefs, or folded napkins, over their noses. And they gagged and they laughed at the unfortunates rolling and pitching in their own filth. They were not to know that the source of their mirth was the transport that would bring their new governor. 'The Father of Australia' they call him now.

I gather in these spinning thoughts. Each night this past week I have dressed for bed, thrown a shawl over my nightdress, and sat with pen and ink by my side, staring vacantly at a book of smooth vanilla-coloured octavo sheets as one stares into a mirror.

In a week's time the priest will need the words for the inscription on the rose granite panel rising some six feet from the ground to the lintel. 'Just try to distil the essence of the man,' he tells me, 'and I will turn the phrases.'

No. The phrases will be mine. I will not have some clerical unguent poured upon them.

I live with this story — have lived it. I must now tell it and in the telling hope to find some peace, or at least a formula for it. So I will stand strong, as formidable as the cliffs of Ardmeanach or South Head, against the gusts of memory. I will let them come.

My hope is that when the storm is spent, the right words for Macquarie will be there, the fine public words, lying like cherries on the grass after a gale: precious, if a little imperfect.

CHAPTER FOUR

By birth I am a Campbell, a Hebridean at heart. I grew straight and tall from my tenth year and by my thirteenth had reared to five foot eight — a giantess for my age. I gained another two inches before the age of fifteen and then my growing ceased. All these years later I remain that proximate height: tall, for a woman, or statuesque, as I'm often called. A mystery, this precocious spurt of growth, like a brass tap turned on full in one solid wrench of the wrist and closed off again just as swiftly.

And when I began to flower again it took another form. The boyish girl had reached the verge of womanhood and, with one leap, vaulted right across. I could intuit from my side of a closed door when the conversation between adults had turned to the subject of my welfare. The two words I would most often catch from my listening place — words uttered always in a brittle tone — were *developing* and *maturing*.

At school in London I won the respect of my classmates, though not, I think, their affection. By temperament I was singular, held in and set apart. I craved the affection of my instructors and spent hours in the company of the French mistress, Miss Fullerton, at her small, cluttered apartment in Marylebone. She had lived in France — precisely why, with whom, or in what circumstances she never cared to divulge — and seemed greatly affected by that nation's tumult. She had seen, she said, the promise of the revolution fade into a cavalcade of death. She stressed, blinking as she told the tale, that she had really *seen* it. In consequence she was, I believe, as alone as I was in London: to both of us, in different ways, a foreign city.

She had a long face and a prominent yet finely modelled nose; a handsome rather than a pretty woman, with large restless hazel eyes. We would take tea in her drawing room before a window overlooking a green and leafy — almost rural — park. Gazing over the treetops and, beyond them, the roofs and chimney pots, we would drift into our private thoughts. When the silence was broken, we would converse in French. I was, in truth, more audience than companion. I was compelled to train my ear to the fluvial subtleties of French — a skill that has served me well on my journeying.

Airds, the Campbell estate on the mainland at Appin, sprawled from a two-storey temple front with Grecian pilasters. As the youngest of five children, I was oftentimes little more than an extra serving girl in that house. My three sisters married young and bred tirelessly. On their visits home with their broods I fell into the role of maid to mistresses who were my own flesh and blood. I believe I developed, at an early age, a powerful instinct towards flight.

On school holidays at Airds I would flee the stir of society whenever I could. I was very much alone. But I was never lonely — never that. I managed with a degree of native guile — a good Scottish trait — to orchestrate my absences so that they were noticed only when I had been a long time gone. I was forever tramping the high ground that hemmed the estate on three sides or combing the shore of Loch Laich when Connor, the cook's boy, was sent to reel me in, cupping his hands and calling in his clear silvery tones, 'Liiii-zzeeee!'

In those years I would ruin a pair of boots in a summer. But my pretty dress shoes I would outgrow barely worn at all.

My father, John, tall and thin, wealthy yet frugal, was a somewhat rigid man who on all subjects held the opinions of others. 'The child is destined for the Edinburgh Circus,' he remarked more than once to visitors drowsy with cake and biscuits. 'A proper monkey. She vanishes before one's eyes, materialises whenever food is set upon the table, and disappears along with the plates.'

I had a favourite place — what solitary child doesn't. It was a perfect little stone bridge thrown over a rill. In my wild imagination I gave it a Roman provenance — across the stone bridge tramped a legion bristling with standards and spears. And when I was told that no Roman legion ever came this way my fancy simply altered course. Over the bridge, in a procession of images possessing the vividness of memory, came knights in shining armour, riding richly caparisoned horses bound for a tourney.

The lichen-covered stones of various sizes were wedged haphazardly together and the masonry was so touchable, so varicoloured — almost alive — that the feel and scuff of it on my young palms has never left me. In winter the old arch was powdered with snow; flowers carpeted it in spring; drying weeds by late summer; fallen leaves in smoky autumn. Barely wide enough for a traveller and a dray to cross, and then only at their peril, it was rarely used.

From my earliest years I would spend lazy hours there in the gentle months, planted on the arch, legs dangling in the air as the glassy stream slid below, feeling as if I were striking roots deep into the crevices where the mortar had worn away. The shallow stream sliced over a bed of speckled stones, and always there was the companionable murmur of water over rocks.

When the weather was warm, which was rare, the stones on the arch were deliciously cool. On those days I would lie back across them, spread my arms, allow the sun to caress my pale skin and to heat my young blood. And when I returned to the grand house, which was designed to be above things, I felt most peculiar beneath moulded ceilings, niches filled with decorative urns, and chandeliers with their beads of false light. Having been high born, I knew that I would always live on stilts. But I craved the restless sky, the green fields and the chill breeze that swooped down from the bare crags. I loathed the very thought of stillness and torpor and desired above all things an adventure.

My mother, Jane, possessed an unfailingly sweet nature. Ever the diplomat, she cooled my father's bursts of rage and rouged the family's pallor. And when things went bad she somehow made them good again. As a cure for my solitary ramblings she took me, upon my coming of age, to the Continent. Father was unable to make the journey on account of an indisposition — gout, though not a fatal illness, is certainly an enfeebling one. Margaret, my elder sister, travelled with us in his stead. We stayed with relatives in Rue Saint-Honoré, and for a few weeks in Paris I transformed a capable knowledge of French into a genuine facility. When we left on the coach south to Lyon before the journey across the Alps, I was able to read tolerably well in French. But how grey was Paris, which I had always expected to adore but did not especially like; it paled beside the radiance of Venice and Rome — especially Rome.

My cousin Ronald Campbell, a merchant whose Glaswegian ships would leave Ostia with Sicilian Marsala and return with English twill, put us up at his three-storey villa on Via dell'Orso, close by his offices on the riverfront. It was a bachelor's residence wrapped around a small courtyard barely big enough for our coach. Cramped and restless on my first afternoon, I took Margaret's hand and made her walk the cobbles with me. We soon came upon the baroque Church of San Luigi dei Francesi. I assumed that the church's name betokened a French affiliation and hoped that French-speaking Romans, descendants of that ancient race of world rulers, might worship there. Surely there would be a young man — devout but not seminary bound — whose acquaintance I could make in the lavishly marbled interior. He might show me the city. Why, an attachment might develop.

The French affiliation was not a living thing, but ancient and half-forgotten; like much of Rome, I suppose. And the interior of the church was empty at that time of day but for a few kneeling figures gathered around the altar, one with a hacking cough that echoed disconcertingly around the gilded nave. But the paintings in the chapels held me fixed. One of them was a tender rendering of an aged St Matthew visited by a rather smug angel suspended in a swirl of drapery. It spoke of the angel's mystic beauty and the saint's aged vulnerability: the eternal spirit and the fallible flesh. Margaret broke the spell when she stole up behind me and whispered, 'But here, what is this clothed statue that stands before me, head as still as marble?' I clapped her lightly on the shoulder and we walked together into the soft powdery sunshine.

* * *

No sooner had we returned to Scotland than we learned of the passing of the elderly Murdoch Maclaine, Laird of Lochbuie. Mother took me aside before the funeral, to be held at Lochbuie House on Mull, a day's journey away. She settled herself on the divan and patted the cushion beside her as if summoning a favourite terrier. Defiantly, I took the seat opposite. Between us on the low table was a pot of steaming coffee, which she did not trouble to pour, and a plate of oatcakes, which she neglected to serve. Perhaps she was waiting for a wayward servant.

I would soon, she began almost girlishly, have an opportunity to make the acquaintance of a man I had greatly impressed. I inquired how it was possible that I had impressed a man I had never met and she replied, a smile easing across her plump cheeks, that she had sent the man a small portrait painted of me when I was but fifteen years of age. I roared with laughter and asked her to consider what would happen when this man came looking for a child and found instead a grown woman. My mother sharply reminded me that if he had met me at that age he would find me little altered now, as I did all my growing early.

'My dear,' she went on in an indulgent tone, 'you have lived your short life at such a sharp angle to the world that ...' Here she paused, lowering her tired maternal eyes. 'It is just that, well, it has been somewhat difficult to find a match your own age. Every time a young man walks through the front door you disappear out the rear.' She drew a laboured breath, let out a low sigh. 'Pressing you into the company of an appropriate suitor is like, well ... forcing an owl upon the morn.'

Mother was, despite her many fine points of character — though it seems churlish to make mention of it so soon after her passing — a ceaseless meddler. I had anticipated this turn of conversation, for it had been rehearsed in numberless small ways. It was a relief to have done with it.

'I thank you for your concern Mother,' I said. 'I fear that I have failed you. But I have not neglected to form an alliance out of some flaw of character. Or,' I shook my head emphatically, 'a lack of interest.'

I conceded that I had often seemed shy, and awkward, and somewhat solitary. 'The true impediment,' I insisted, 'is the world in which I was raised.'

I had been born in the midst of the American war and recall Father's rage — though I can't have been more than six years old — at news of its outcome. In the year I sat for the portrait that Mother had distributed to proclaim my readiness for marriage, the French murdered their king and their beautiful queen.

In a high and rather proud tone I said, 'Among the young men of my acquaintance I have heard talk of little else but bringing Boney to heel, clapping the Moghuls in chains, sending the Americans to the gallows. I can barely recall a young man whom you might consider eligible who has not purchased a commission, journeyed abroad to serve the King, and either failed to return or returned broken. The possession of a pulse means nothing in this age,' I huffed. 'The veterans are as ghostly as the dead.'

'I had been expecting some such asperity,' Mother sighed. 'I see your spirits run high today.' She waved her hand as if dispersing an odour and leant forward. 'In all seriousness, now, you must promise me that you will meet with him at the funeral. See he writes to us,' and here she reached behind her and retrieved a sheet of paper, the light returning to her eyes.

'Mother,' I said, raising a resolute hand and making to leave. 'No!'

'Stay, Elizabeth,' she urged. 'Please.'

And so out of respect — and a flicker of curiosity — I did.

'There are a few things I thought you should know,' she continued. 'The gentleman of whom I speak is Lachlan Macquarie.

22

His father is a relative of the sixteenth Chief of MacQuarrie; his mother is a Maclaine. You have never met — he has spent twenty years in the army — but you may have heard of him. He will spend some time at his estate at Gruline on Mull when he returns for the funeral.'

I had not so much heard as overheard tales about the man. He was by reputation a great traveller. 'I seem to recall that he has visited the Pyramids,' I said airily. 'I promise that I will look winsomely into his eyes and inquire as to the glories they have seen.'

Her voice dropped an octave and she went on in a grave tone: 'What you might not know is that he is recently widowed. He married a young beauty, Jane Jarvis, daughter of the chief justice of Antigua. The two met, it is said, in Bombay. There was a great romance and they were espoused within the month. She was in poor health — consumption. And it carried her away in Macau, poor child. The marriage lasted barely three years; but his mourning has gone on an age. The girl leaves him with a small fortune from her father, and a broken heart. He is a strong man from a good family to which we are warmly bound. Your father and I greatly desire that you deepen this bond. But, well, how best to put it: the wound he carries from a French sabre in the American war is not the only scar.'

My first thought when I saw his tall, uniformed figure across the room — standing stiffly in front of a bookcase that seemed to frame him — was that he looked intolerably old. Why, his hair was almost entirely grey! He was alone at that point but was soon accosted by the late Laird's son. The boy was laying siege with question upon question, to which he replied at length. When our eyes met there was a flash of recognition — so he knew the woman from the image of her young self!

He continued to entertain the boy, eyes all the while seeking mine. By my side were Mother and the rheumy-eyed James Campbell of Tobermory, some eighty years of age and straining to stay awake. Macquarie's feet, I noticed, were growing restless. He shifted from side to side. Eventually he laid a large hand on young Lochbuie's shoulder, stepped past him and strode determinedly towards me.

On reaching my side he breathed deeply, as if he had just bounded up a flight of steps. My mother made an artful withdrawal, taking the aged Campbell by the sleeve and tugging him, blinking and bewildered, behind her.

'I see the lad exhausts you,' I said to Macquarie.

'I will concede,' he smiled cheerfully, 'that he wearies me. I would not expect such a fierce interrogation in a courtroom. The lad dreams of India. He will not let the subject alone.'

'Of what, precisely, does he dream?'

'Its wealth.'

He held out his hand and squared his shoulders. In the instant I took his hand, which enveloped my own, I became conscious, as I had never been before, of a man's physical power. The broad-backed men in my life were blacksmiths, carpenters, coopers — crofters. Here before me stood a powerful man my social equal. I was drawn to him, as he seemed to know I would be.

I can barely recall our conversation that evening. I was giddy with a new sensation.

That night the family stayed at Lochbuie. The mood was sombre but the clear autumn sky above the island, dusted with whorls of starlight, was almost joyous. At dinner Macquarie continued to cast furtive glances at me from the other side of the table and, more out of curiosity than anything, I began to cautiously return them.

After dinner my mother insisted I perform for the group — she was incorrigible! — and a viola was produced. I played Purcell's 'Chaconne in G minor': the key of *tristesse* seemed right for the evening. There were a few tears by the time the last note faded into a long silence. Though I was urged to continue — Macquarie in particular applauded loudly — I excused myself by pleading the lateness of the hour and the sobriety of the occasion.

I retired to a first-floor room I shared with Margaret, and when I opened the curtains to the night sky I saw Macquarie standing outside on the lawns. He, too, was gazing at the heavens. This romantic gesture endeared him to me immensely; he seemed, despite the difference in our age, a man after my own heart. I would have dashed outdoors to join him if Mother had not been so keen-eyed and Father so easily provoked.

As the week rolled on after the funeral the gathered clan seemed to thin, and in the last few days it felt as if there were none in the world but us. We read: Boswell's *Life of Samuel Johnson* for me; Walton's *Angler* for him. We walked, fished and, on a cool morning, we rowed together across Loch Crinan through a light mist. It was very still on the water, hushed and soft and grey. I would not say that we were lovers; the love would come slowly. But it felt as if the match had been made, even that it was meant to be.

That day he was dressed rather handsomely in tan breeches, a waistcoat the colour of strong tobacco and a black velvet jacket; I should have known that this fine, manly garb betokened something of import. I sat on the bench before him and he rowed out. I asked if I could take the oars for a time and he, a little nonplussed, indicated that we should change places.

'You know, you are quite the heroine, Elizabeth,' he said as I pulled on the oars. 'You more than hold your own in conversation, you delight us with your playing, your skill with a fishing rod surpasses my own, and I see now that you can row after a fashion.'

I returned the oars to him. He held them at his side and let us glide on across the water.

'You know you would make an excellent sailor's wife,' he said with a nervous catch in his throat. He swallowed, paused and went on thickly. 'But I am convinced it is a soldier you shall marry.'

The smile that greeted me after the words were out was like a break in the clouds after weeks of rain. But instead of cheering me, it provoked a rush of worry: if I failed to bring things to a head this moment he might leave for another war, I thought. We would write; years would pass, and *it* would die.

'Is that a proposal of marriage?' I asked boldly.

'If you would like it to be, well — it shall be.'

'But do you intend it?' I pressed.

'I confess that I do.'

My nights from that moment were filled with dreams of places he would take me. I was readying myself for flight.

CHAPTER FIVE

Lachlan returned to India without his fiancée, distinguishing himself in several actions that he never mentioned by name. Nor did he speak of them in detail, except to say that he had seen six Indian mutineers blown apart by cannon, their heads flying into the air, the arms spinning away, the legs dropping to the ground in pools of viscera below the muzzle. On his return he recounted this dreadful story over lunch — we had the light-filled western wing at the Airds estate to ourselves — without seeming to realise that a tale of this kind should be withheld at such a moment.

India had hardened him. At the same time it had softened — perhaps the better word is sensitised — him. He had endured the loss of Jane Jarvis, had taken life, and seen life taken. He was in his forty-fourth year. He wanted to make his mark with something other than a sabre or a musket.

And then one morning, over a breakfast of perplexing silences a month after our marriage, he told me he had been offered the post — not exactly a coveted one after the rebellion against William Bligh — of Governor of New South Wales.

'A penitentiary!' I swallowed, aghast, reaching for the teacup.

My first thought was a practical one: how was I to break the news to my brother John, who was hoping to accompany us to India? And then there was the shame of it. I, who had seemed destined for Bombay, was now bound, along with a cargo of criminals, for Botany Bay.

Lachlan came to my aid, recalling New Holland's fame among botanical adventurers. 'It is reputed to be another Eden,' he said with an air of conviction. 'Nature at her purest. Here, then, is your adventure!'

'Indeed.'

'The world has been swept up by revolution,' he went on in rolling phrases that seemed to have been well prepared. His arms extended before him, elbows stiffly locked. Those large hands of his were firmly placed on the embroidered tablecloth in the manner of a man leaning on a lectern. He wore a white shirt and an oyster-grey waistcoat and looked, for some reason, like a block of marble. 'The American and French. And who knows what next. India, I believe, will cast off her yoke.' He paused and shifted forward in his seat. His voice had lost none of its masculine brass, but the cadence had changed. 'There is a great cause underway at Sydney Cove. You consider it a jail; I say it is an experiment, perhaps the greatest endeavour of our age. If criminals can be made into good citizens, why, society itself can be reinvented!'

It was a speech, a piece of intimate oratory ('Pass the toast and jam and may I tell you how things are with the world') designed to sway me to the fitness of the cause. On first hearing the news I was shocked; I admit that. But I required no soapbox sophistry to convince me. A deft reminder of who I was and what I most wanted from life and I would have followed him anyway. It was a measure of how little we understood one another that he was not to know.

I was desperate for adventure. And my new husband — was he not an *adventurer*? He had indeed seen Cairo; Bombay and Boston, too. He had fought against the French in America and helped to drive Napoleon from Abukir. He could describe to me the white cities of Arabia, the antiquities of India and Ceylon, the great pagoda of Canton. Where other men left these shores with a thirst for the fight, his passion was, as he put it, 'the great world and the works of men'.

That morning his grey eyes shone like metal. There was charisma in that fiery conviction; perhaps a touch of madness, too. But then we follow the mad. Follow them to war. Follow them to victory or defeat. Follow them to new lives in strange worlds.

'At Port Jackson His Majesty has deposited the land's poorest seed — felons and ruffians and rebels — in rich virgin soil,' he said, staring around me as if his sights were set on a receding landscape, not a woman barely six feet away, warm flesh and warm blood. His gaze was not so much directed as diffused.

I set my knife and fork on the china plate and pushed it forward over the embroidered tablecloth, somewhat ashamed of my appetite.

Silence.

'Already the convicts show signs of reform,' he continued in the same distant tone as if he were already there, in the Antipodes, the journey behind him. 'A highwayman marries a prostitute; he is possessed of daring, she of some allure. The past is never mentioned to their children. They acquire the parents' better attributes — his boldness and her ... her charms.'

'Might not the offspring inherit the worst of the parents' qualities?' I asked. 'Lawlessness on the one hand, wantonness on the other?' Desiring to question, yet careful not to oppose, I coated my phrases with a cordial smile.

29

'My Elizabeth,' he beamed warmly, his full attention upon me now, 'you have struck with that true aim of yours at the great question. Did the flaws of the parents issue from their nature, or from the desperate circumstances in which they have lived — that we have created? I am for creating another world.'

It was bold talk and I loved him then as much as I ever did. Although the thought did occur to me that he might have a tendency to bore.

'No more uprisings then,' I said as I pushed back the chair and went to join him at the other end of the table. 'But a rising up!'

'You mock?' he asked sharply.

'No my love, you *misunderstand*. I applaud you. We will be allies in this cause. If depraved convicts can become good citizens in that world, what might the deserving poor — given half a chance — become in this?'

I stood behind him and placed both hands upon his shoulders, which seemed to loosen at the first touch. I have no idea when the letter offering the commission arrived from the Colonial Office, but I suspect it was a week old and had been pondered deeply. He had prepared this oration in the belief that I would offer more resistance. But I was, I decided there and then, all for Sydney Cove. Remaining seated, and still a little distant, my husband drew me to him — a dutiful wife almost two decades his junior.

CHAPTER SIX

We left Portsmouth on a cool May morning. Men of the 73rd Regiment of Foot hoisted our trunks atop hard shoulders while I carried my viola in its case, not trusting them with such a fragile and precious possession. A drummer and a fifer led the way and our own servants followed behind. The *Dromedary* and her escort HMS *Hindostan* were docked somewhat apart from the other ships, beyond a dog leg of the wharf and a barrier of market carts heaped with hay. Upon this makeshift palisade lay several soldiers, tousled heads bare and muskets trained on the busy crowd. As I passed by I looked up at one of the young men. He shot me a game wink in return. Such boldness! I cannot pretend I was not, at the same time, a little thrilled. Macquarie walked a good stride ahead of me, oblivious, with the prideful air of a Lieutenant Colonel, permitting himself no distractions. I, in stark contrast, was hungry for sensation, even if a goodly portion of me wished contradictorily to shrink from the clamour, the filth, the heady odour. I was young. I had lived a spirited though small life.

At the taffrail of the *Dromedary*, Macquarie beside me, I took in the forest of masts and fixed rigging, so dense they crowded the sky;

the clutter of sea craft large and small; the wharves and walkways all tightly packed together. You could chase a thief from one end of the docks to the other and never wet your feet.

A bow-legged man with a thin, lined face and a balding pate came for Macquarie, introducing himself as the ship's master, Samuel Pritchard. His voice was husky and exotically accented: the inflection might have been American or Caribbean, or more likely a stew of many ports and places. He drew himself towards Macquarie, placed a hand upon his sleeve, and spoke with him most conspiratorially. I took little from the overheard conversation save for the words 'desperately' and 'provisions'. My husband excused himself. I was left alone.

Seagulls shrieked. The light breeze murmured among the lines. The boatswains barked their orders. Hawkers on the docks released their beseeching cries onto the green ocean air: *Today's bread! Sweet lavender! Pretty boxes for every need! The freshest farm milk! Pictures of remarkable places! The news, the news, all the news!* And from every corner of this boisterous theatre boomed a chorus of cursing and banter and song.

Above it all I caught the stuttering cry of cormorants in flight, familiar to me from hours spent along the rocky shores of my homeland. A flock of these plain black seabirds, perhaps a dozen in all, skimmed low across a flat plate of water in perfect formation. Such odd creatures when spied on land, hanging their tattered feathers out to dry, but in flight — quite majestic. They flashed brilliantly overhead, like beams from a black sun.

A crack of rifle fire — just the one shot — and a lone shag twisted limply away from its fellows, falling gracefully through the leaden sky. A triumphant cry went up. A soldier — the one who had cut me that game wink — leapt to his feet, his rifle raised in one hand and his black shako in the other. There had been no real marksmanship in the matter, and no endeavour at all: he had merely aimed into the flock as it streaked over the masts and the rigging.

I looked down at my pale hands. How fiercely they grasped the rail. That poor shag was not the only thing felled by the soldier's triumph.

As the flock of long-necked cormorants swept in it had seemed, for a moment, as if the Hebrides were calling to me. Calling me home? Or urging me on? I could not tell, for the memory came to me as a puzzle not a sign. In a flash I pictured a bed of tawny matted seaweed strewn across rock, beside it the grey ocean stirred by a high wind, and a squall brewing in the hills beyond.

A tall, thin soldier with black eyebrows a good finger thick bellowed in my ear that we would soon be underway. I asked him to direct me to the Lieutenant Colonel's chambers. I was alone, sick at heart, when finally we weighed anchor. I dozed. And when I woke we were at sea.

* * *

Macquarie was delighted when Sam Pritchard, later that night, reported the results of the first muster aboard.

'You will be pleased to know,' Pritchard said in a satisfied tone as he spread a ledger over a freshly painted table in our quarters, 'that along with the usual complement of Londoners tempted by the sight of a bolt of cloth or a silver teapot there are enough carpenters, masons, smiths, tailors and cobblers to build and serve a city. And you shall have the services of an architect.' He broke off with a hollow laugh, as if he thought some show of contempt was expected of him. 'An architect — and a forger.'

There was a pause as Pritchard laid the lamp on the white table. Its surface had been notched and indented in its time with some heavy blows from objects both sharp and blunt, and these had been painted over in recent weeks, in readiness for our arrival. He reached for a plain pewter tankard embossed with his initials and drained the contents. Macquarie fussed around in a crate packed with straw, the necks of several black bottles of port wine protruding like tubers sprouting from the earth. Stooping, he took a bottle, uncorked it, and poured for Pritchard. My husband hesitated, then poured for himself as well. Pritchard took another deep draught. 'This architect has been seen sketching from time to time in a tunnel of light from a starboard porthole, the only one on the lower deck,' he said, leaning forward into the glare of the lamp. 'It is said that a cloaked stranger purchased this indulgence on his behalf. It had naught to do with me! The hole in the hull is not much bigger than grapeshot, but it seems to suit his purposes. The talk is that he has a powerful patron. Some say the Duke of Norfolk; others Arthur Phillip himself. In any event he spends his days and nights filling a book of rough sketching paper with renderings of views.'

'You say he draws views?' Macquarie raised a tendrilled eyebrow. 'But there are none to be had from the lower decks.'

'Imaginary panoramas — antiquarian in flavour. For the most part he sketches some mighty buildings that are now little more than ruins but were glorious in their day. His name is marked on the muster.' Pritchard set down the tankard, ran a finger along the ledger. It came to rest two-thirds of the way down. 'Here. But to the prisoners he is known simply as the Architect. Rather grand, don't you think, for a convict?' Again there was that queer, hollow laugh from Pritchard, followed by a pleading look to Macquarie. When he failed to respond the laugh collapsed into a cough.

Macquarie muttered his agreement distractedly. 'For a convict — yes, I suppose.' Though I could tell he was not at all piqued. He was, in fact, delighted. The broad blocks of his handsome face arranged themselves into a barely suppressed smile. 'But then if he is indeed an architect' — he leant forward heavily in the chair and hammered his fist onto the table — 'then *let* him sketch!' he boomed. 'Give him paints if he asks for them. Procure them at the next port of call. No harm in that. No telling what he might devise on the long voyage.'

'This is a stroke of immense good fortune, Elizabeth,' Macquarie glowed when we were alone together that night in a ship twisting across the sea. 'I had requested a civil architect and the petition was denied. In time, I was told. Priorities.' He shook his head. 'Well now, a convict architect will do just as well, as long as the man has talent. It is providential, don't you see?'

He was eager for attention that night. And as he slept a satisfied sleep I went to the porthole. I was bored and restless and felt quite lost but the ship — how it moaned and hummed and trilled as it sliced across the swell! The moon had silvered a skein of sea foam on the crest of the nearest wave. It rose hugely towards the moon and the stars, seemed to roll beneath us as we, in turn, climbed the night sky. It was very beautiful. And very powerful.

A boat had gone down in the channel between Mull and Iona before I was born, and many lives were lost. I knew it as a story but Macquarie had lived it: as a young boy he had been called upon to comb the shore for corpses. But I was not particularly concerned for my own safety on the *Dromedary*. That strikes me now as a doughty attitude for a young woman on her first sea voyage, but I could not afford the luxury of fear; there would be many more nights such as this.

I sometimes wonder what would have transpired if Macquarie had at that moment caught a presentiment of the perils ahead. Would he have made the forger filling his sketchpad the ally of his dreams for the betterment of that lonely colony of criminals? I fancy he might have contrived to tip him overboard, for the moment the Architect's fortunes became our own, all things changed. For better, and for worse.

I had to that point never so much as sighted a felon; none, in any event, that had been apprehended. And during the first few weeks at sea my aversion to the grey mass below decks — more than 300 convicts in all — usurped my natural sympathy.

Father had warned me to expect the worst. On the last night but one before my departure from Airds, he tried to extinguish his fears and his sorrows with drink. 'Expect the kind of man who would draw a dagger on the streets of Glasgow if his nimble hands returned empty from a stranger's pocket,' he said with a raised and reproving finger after dinner. 'The type of woman who would sell her body for a tot of whisky.' It was the last thing I really needed so close to my leaving. I picked up a vinegar bottle, held it high, and told him most emphatically that the cast of his mind was as narrow as its neck. He reddened deeply, and I thought for a wee moment that he might erupt into a fit of apoplexy. But then he spluttered with relieving laughter.

It was one thing to inveigh against the 'convict filth', as Father had done. It was another entirely to set out across the seas with these miserable souls for company. The most vicious criminals — murderers and the like — had already departed this world at the end of a rope. I imagine many of the felons who remained, sentenced to terms of seven and fourteen years — some for life — had simply sought desperate remedies for desperate lives. Whatever their crimes, they shared the same sorry fate. Their days and nights were filled with low bass moans, orders from the deck echoing down angled steps, the creaking of timbers, the jangling of chains, the lazy stretching of rope, wails of pain, dying gasps. A convict transport on the open sea sings with a score of hideous voices.

Thereafter my thoughts towards those huddled below deck were ruled more — as in truth they should have been from the outset — by my heart. I observed how the women cared for the children who fell ill with the ship's motion, and how they suffered when illness spread below decks. Many died on that voyage — far too many.

After the first few months at sea the papists set up a small shrine to the dead — a roughly carved statuette of the Virgin Mary. She stood, I was told, in a wicker basket filled with scraps of paper on which the names of the departed and some lines of scripture had been scrawled. When I asked to go below decks to console them, Macquarie erupted: 'It is not the done thing, and it is a thing that will *not* be done.' He paused and his tone immediately softened. 'Think my love,' he went on, 'of your health! Why, I have already lost ...' and his voice trailed off as his eyes left mine for the memory of hers.

On the journey out I absorbed myself in the journals of our naturalists, explorers and keen-eyed observers — Cook and Banks, Collins and Tench — and those of the French who had taken such a keen interest in New Holland. In the trunk nailed to the floor beside the bed I kept a small collection of novels, both English and French, which I hoped to trade with the ladies of the colony (I would be sorely disappointed in this as so few of them read for entertainment). And then there was my copy of Boswell's *Johnson,* which I could always rely upon to nourish me when I hungered for high spirits.

More than once, in the depth of a dark night, Lachlan murmured *her* name in his sleep. I felt so sad for him. And so helpless. But it was my name that he cried during our raptures.

In the fourth month of the voyage, a fortnight after a break for repairs and fresh provisions in Rio de Janeiro, illness again broke out below decks. This time it spread like a blaze. I lost my appetite and became bilious. In the mirror I looked pale and drawn.

'You are not yourself,' said my husband as he tried to interest me in a bowl of thin broth.

'I am all at sea,' I quipped.

'Your smile,' he said with a grave air, 'is feeble. But your spirit — strong enough in the circumstances.'

I took to my bed. The next day Lachlan felt my brow, gave a puzzled look, and called for the ship's surgeon. Dr Crotty was surprisingly hale for a man who kept company with the sick and dying — it was said that he maintained his own pantry. He gave a wet smile, revealing a neat row of small yellow teeth, and informed me with perhaps more sadness than joy that I was pregnant. I sometimes wonder if men of his profession, who see so much suffering, realise how peculiar they have become — how deeply injured — as a consequence.

Crotty seemed blithe to my discomfort when he sat beside me and said, 'The child, if in fact it survives the voyage, will be born on colonial soil and for that — the better diet, the air — you may be grateful. But let us first get you,' he patted the sheets, 'to *terra firma*. I have delivered three new lives already to the convicts and all' — at least the smile had the courtesy to subside for want of conviction — 'were in too short a time food for the fish.' That he should offer such a tale to a pregnant woman!

I begged Crotty to keep news of my state from my husband for just a few weeks. He obliged by informing Lachlan that my indisposition was caused by the ship's motion and I would certainly recover in calmer seas. It was well that he did so for I lost that child a few weeks later, shedding all my tears alone. After a deeply unpleasant examination the doctor gave me news from which I would never recover, though my outward health was soon restored. 'Henceforth you may find that you can conceive,' he said. 'But I believe you may find it difficult to carry.'

It was time to tell my husband about our shared misfortune. I wept for the second time in a month, but he, dry-eyed and stoical, said that if he could not produce an heir he could at least leave behind some fine works. I believe the sad news steeled him for that great cause of his. But it unsteadied him, too.

* * *

By now the long journey was nearing its end. As we passed through new regions, not of land but of atmosphere — the humidity of the Torrid Zone easing off, the breeze quickening now, freshening, a touch even, of icy chill — I felt the anticipation building.

'Rock ahead,' came a cry from the crow's nest late one afternoon.

A group of prisoners was brought on deck for exercise like a catch hauled up from the deep. Piercing the air was a solitary white needle wreathed by gulls wheeling about in a great mist, their distant ululations rolling towards us on the gentle waves. It was a mere shard of rock frosted by the accumulated ages of avian ordure. There was great excitement on the deck and aloft in the shrouds.

I was able, as the only avid reader of our predecessors' chronicles, to explain all to Macquarie and a few officers of the 73rd Regiment drawn together on the quarterdeck by the excitement.

'Cook recorded the sea tower in his journals,' I told the company in the round voice of a town crier. 'It meant for him what it means for us. Landfall at last. Gentlemen, we have come to the Great South Land!'

Pritchard, of course, was well aware of the significance of this marker; he was busy consulting with the navigator, fixing our position and setting a fresh course north.

The mirrored waves in the late afternoon light seemed to welcome us, and bobbing about in the mild swell were three seals sprouting most gentlemanly whiskers. Their oily black faces stared with some remote and placid wisdom. And then they turned as one seeking the depths, dismissing us from their sight.

I thought at that moment of Noah and the Ark he had built sometime after his five-hundredth year: a wise man he must have been at that improbably advanced age! The Biblical Ark was designed to preserve from the Hebrew god's wrath every fine thing in the world — two of every kind. Our Convict Ark, by perpetuating all that is sorry and base, seemed to mock the words of Genesis. But perhaps it was, in its own way, a worthy addition to the Biblical theme of redemption — of renewal. I kept these thoughts to myself, for they were too bold to be uttered in that company.

CHAPTER SEVEN

Our last night, when we were forced by poor weather to heave-to outside the Heads, was hard on everyone. There were salty oaths from the sailors and a redoubling of moans from below. So close were we to our destination; almost upon it. A fire had been lit on the more southerly of the Heads to guide us in, a welcoming cannon fired and a flag run up a staff. Here were all the sensations of landfall: the ocean had visibly shallowed, lightened; crying gulls wheeled around the masts; scrags of seaweed drifted out on the swell. There was even a scent of eucalyptus on the air.

But the wind wheeled around to the southeast as we approached the Heads, and it stiffened by the minute. The waves soared to join it, and the sails with their damp muffled beat were trimmed out of fear that the *Dromedary*, after the loss of so many lives to typhus, dysentery and starvation, might after all this be swept in and smashed to splinters at the base of the great seawall ahead of us.

The decision was made to tack offshore before the storm reached its full strength. I felt as if I had been seated six feet from a table at which dinner had been served, only to find it snatched away.

Overnight the raging storm strode inland on jagged legs of lightning. When dawn broke bright and calm there was a soft breeze out of the northeast. For the first time in many months I saw the slow, steady rising and falling of ribcages. It was the breathing of men and women who have survived great peril and no longer fear the night ahead.

For its journey from the Heads to the Cove the *Dromedary* took on a white-haired pilot with a youthful sap and bustle about him, though perhaps his was simply the natural vitality of the unchained and well fed. He rowed towards us in a shallow craft with two solidly built oarsmen, who waited until he scaled the pilot ladder before returning to shore. He introduced himself as Jacob. Pritchard gave him a hearty welcome, wrapping his arm around the man's shoulders and inviting him below deck for a celebratory tipple. The pilot disappeared for a short while, then took up position beside the helmsman. He directed the *Dromedary* deftly through the Heads and she sailed downwind across the lovely waterway — a harbour like an outstretched hand. We soon spied, on our left, a town spread thinly over a north-facing cove speared by a small still stream.

I will long remember my first view of that distant shore. Humble, rude, unadorned — despite the loveliness of the setting. And yet ancient. So very old for a New World, while the Old World of recent memory seemed so fresh and green — so young. The mountain range behind the settlement, visible from the deck of the *Dromedary*, seemed a worn set of molars compared to the stark incisors of Skye.

A good portion of the New World's 'poor seed' — that was Macquarie's phrase — had gathered to welcome us on the Government wharf.

We arrived under a bright sun. The scented air was soft on the skin when the ship was in motion; painfully oppressive when we had come to rest. Phillip chose this site well. A large ship such as the *Dromedary* could anchor securely a short distance from the wharf. A regimental band was on hand to greet us. After the anchor had been cast, with that persistent grating rumble of iron links that never failed to set my nerves on edge, the band struck up a creaky rendition of 'God Save the King'.

Behind the band, clearly visible in the penetrating light, gathered women in trousers; sailors without shoes; would-be dandies in shirts with ruffs and frills, yet lacking the broad-lapelled high-cut coats needed to set them off to best effect. The natives clinging to the edges of the welcoming party were dressed like the dolls of neglectful children, in scraps of clothing that looked to have been found or handed down. The motley sprinkling of canary-yellow-clad convicts towards the rear of the group, dragooned to carry the heavy gear up from the ship, were in appearance much as I'd expected. Their bearing was not. Unbowed, they eyed the world on something like equal terms. One turned to another. There were sly laughs behind cupped hands. In open alliance, they viewed the disembarkation with knowing smiles. What, I asked myself, did they know? The smirks, I would soon discover, were those of anticipation. For we were about to be entertained — and instructed.

A tall thin native dressed in an admiral's blue and gold regalia — fraying epaulets, gilt buttons picked out by the sun — sprang onto the ship's deck as if capering at some sport. A face as black as cinders shaded by a preposterous cocked hat. Broad nose, broad mouth.

After the laughter ran its course the visitor declared, calmly, in a voice of some solemnity, 'Bung-a-ree.'

The native pointed to his chest. Gave a portentous nod.

Softly, compliantly, a few of the sailors murmured, as if bewitched, 'Bung-a-ree.'

He spread his arms. 'I am Chief — Chief of the Broken Bay mob,' he said in a soft fluttering voice that carried effortlessly on the air. 'The governors, they teach me English. I speak your language; you do not speak mine. I know the secrets. This here,' he gestured to a wall of eucalyptus rising on the northern shore, 'my land. This,' he revolved a full circle with hands outstretched in a gesture of complete dominion, 'my story.'

I was drawn to the sight of his unshod feet, pink on the underside, long and supple, and as he performed they danced lightly across the deck. He moved beautifully, this native.

'My people — first mob.' He knocked his chest with a clenched fist. 'You' — the hand was held flat now and thrust towards the audience — 'second mob. You come late.'

Bungaree pointed towards the south. 'One edge of the land far away is cold. People coming up from that place wearing possum skins. This way' — pointing inland now — 'very hot. From here' — he swung towards the east — 'comes the wind that brought you in.'

He paused to straighten his cocked hat, which had begun to tilt unsteadily on his nest of hair during the performance. With this done, he fussed about with his coat and as he opened his mouth once more to speak some wag offered a derisive round of applause.

Unperturbed, the native went on. 'The law says this: "Shoot the first mob and you will,"' — he ran a slashing finger across his throat — '"hang. If the first mob do the killing"' — he extended an admonishing finger towards the audience — '"they die too."'

Bungaree allowed a theatrical pause to settle over his audience. His last words were 'Remember the law!' The native chief executed a low bow and the moment his gaze slid from the audience to his bare feet the deck erupted in furious activity. Just as swiftly and mysteriously as he arrived the chief vanished over the ship's side, though not before thrusting a bottle of rum hurriedly into the capacious rear pocket of his admiral's uniform. A moment later a slender bark canoe slid out from beneath the bowsprit. The native wearing the cocked hat tugged at the water with paddles shaped like pudding stirrers, one in each hand.

I watched him arc across the harbour towards the northern shore a few hundred feet away. He pulled in at a pile of biscuit-coloured boulders from which small campfires sent up twisting pylons in the air.

It felt to me as if he had stepped briefly into the known world to impart a most noble teaching, then retreated behind a veil that concealed from me an unknown — and perhaps unknowable — realm. I longed to draw aside that veil — to fathom Nature's mysteries. But I cautioned myself to stifle my romantic impulses, and I recalled that the mysterious Bungaree had not, after all, neglected his lower appetites.

CHAPTER EIGHT

My first true companion was the natural world. As a young woman I would ride alone into the hills, buckled and spare, to gaze westward across Loch Linnhe and the Sound of Mull, with the jagged shard of Beinn a' Bheithir a coronet upon the northern ridgeline. On the heights I was — or felt myself to be — sovereign of a solitary upland domain. My poor parents, compelled to yield to my wild whims, regarded these adventures as the lesser of many evils that could befall a headstrong young woman.

More than once on those russet hills I glimpsed a crown of antlers etched against the broad sky and a buck — motionless, statuesque — regarding me with an insolent air. Solitude, I learned at a young age, offers passage to some mighty realms.

So it was inevitable that my dreams would run to the natural world of New Holland and its famed singularities. This would be *my* adventure.

My first footfall at the Cove was not, though, as I'd anticipated. In my naiveté I had expected some epiphany the moment I touched solid ground. I was, after all, at the far extremity of the Earth. I would feel some hitherto unfelt emotion; at the very least, have something memorable to say. Instead I stepped onto the wharf, with Macquarie by my side, and promptly sank to my knees. I had been so long at sea, buffeted by waves, that my brain now rebelled at the absence of motion. Macquarie reached for an arm. Out of the crowd dashed a slender young man, very fair with even features, to take the other. I heard gasps. A few marines stepped forward, raising their arms to ensure none in the crowd pressed too close. Macquarie looked up from me to the crowd with a stiff and slightly embarrassed smile.

'Shall we sit?' he said in a low voice, barely moving his lips.

'I am not entirely well,' I said as I rose. 'But I suppose I am well enough to continue.'

'Your colour has returned. It may have been the closeness of the air, the crowd — and the strangeness of the place.'

He made to move on and paused. 'A moment,' he said, holding out a hand to steady me. And then, raising himself to his full height he scanned the crowd for the fair-headed young man.

'You,' he snapped his fingers. 'Your name?'

'Currency,' the boy replied.

'Your parents named you Currency,' Macquarie laughed, turning to the crowd. 'Why, were they short of cash?'

'Your Majesty ...'

'I am your governor not your sovereign.'

'You see, your Governor ...' Currency continued as Macquarie smiled at his feet. Titters rose from the crowd. Guffaws from the soldiers. 'It's that my parents, being former convicts, and me being the first born free in our family, they gave me the name that all born in the colony do take. We are the currency. The currency lads and,' — he rose to the tips of his toes and indicated a group of tall young women — 'the currency lasses. Anyways, I am called Currency Jones.'

47

One of the soldiers motioned for us to hurry on, and as we strode forward he said to Macquarie, 'I am sorry to hasten you, sir. But with the delay at the wharf the first group of felons from the *Dromedary* is almost upon us. See.' He pointed to an approaching rowboat. I could make out a burgundy coat, a brown beaverkin, and a woman in a cream dress beneath a striped parasol. 'The so-called "superior convicts", sir. The lettered, the wealthy and the skilled.'

'Is the Architect,' I inquired, 'among them?'

'If there is an architect he will not be among the common convicts,' answered the soldier. 'We have here at the Cove a surgeon for healing the sick and a judge to make us honest. But we are badly in need of buildings that will not come down in the next storm.'

* * *

We are welcomed by the colony's acting Lieutenant Governor, Joseph Foveaux, a pleasing man with pastel-pink cheeks and a corpulence betraying his abiding weakness. Foveaux introduces the servants, gathered before the verandah. Six well-fed women of varied ages in fresh white pinafores over dresses of plain blue clasp their hands behind their backs and curtsy, smiling shyly. A young dark-haired and fresh-faced ensign with a reserved expression salutes his new governor before bowing to me. A tall butler, with greying centre-parted hair and ironical black eyebrows, stands behind the group and comes forward when introduced by Foveaux. His name is Edward Hawkins. Foveaux then introduces Mrs Ovens, the chief cook, and Miss Ringold, the chamber maid, before explaining to the assembled help that our own servants will come up from the *Dromedary* by mid-afternoon with our trunks.

'Might we survey the property before entering the home?' I ask Macquarie.

'But have you quite recovered?'

'I had lost my land legs after so long at sea,' I reply. 'But now, I think, they are found.'

He turns to Foveaux, who indicates that the ensign should lead us. Crudely cut clumps of black hair protrude from the lad's shako and his tanned face is glossed with youth. His fresh cheeks are full, adorned with a dimple on each side: a pretty boy.

The ensign springs forward with long strides and we follow his lead. Foveaux returns to the residence. A short while later I see him hoisting himself with some difficulty up the steps to the shaded verandah.

At the rear of the plain residence — white, rising to two storeys at the southern end, with a low verandah running along the front — we gaze out across a small vegetable garden. Beyond it folds of partially cleared land plunge towards a larger garden cross-hatched with avenues of plantings. I spy a figure hunched over a pail of water set down between rows of bright corn and leafy cannonballs of cabbage; carrots, too, judging from their feathery tops of forest green. Another figure, to the side of the ploughed and planted earth, stands idly beneath a broad misshapen hat smoking a pipe. A plume of smoke drifts from his shaded face. Beyond them, a fringe of trees along the shoreline and the white rim of a perfect little beach embroidering the harbour's edge.

It's then that I notice the famed kangaroo. A large male reclines on a shaded hummock just beyond the Cove.

'Can we approach?' I ask the young ensign.

'By all means. But quietly.' His voice drops to a whisper. 'They are — with good reason — extremely wary.'

I have read so much about this creature living on grasses and flowers, with its *mournful bleat* — that was Cook's phrase — and its young suckled in a pocket, or pouch, below its belly. Its renown has spread far and wide.

A large group, like a tribe or an extended family, has gathered beneath the shade of a spreading tree with thick palm-shaped leaves. At a sudden movement or drift of scent the largest rises slowly, head turning sharply, ears spinning like semaphores. And he is away, haunches heavy and muscled, bounding as gracefully weightless as anything I have ever seen, the others in his wake.

'That animal could outpace a greyhound,' I cry out to the young ensign. 'It looks to have springs in its haunches.'

'For all its speed it makes easy prey,' he replies with a sensitive note threaded into an Irish brogue. 'Shoot the creature and it looks in death like an overgrown mouse.'

Macquarie, who has been a few paces behind, reaches us. There has been little exercise for him on the *Dromedary* and his tread is a little laboured, his stride slow.

'I don't believe we have met,' I say to the young man. 'Lieutenant Governor Foveaux, who it seems has abandoned us to your care, did not bother to introduce us.'

'There are thousands in the colony and so many cause him trouble, ma'am. I am of no significance. He may have forgotten my name. But it is, as you were kind enough to inquire, Brody. My family hails from Connemara, though I left for Dublin when I was quite young.'

'I think,' Macquarie interrupts, 'that it is time we returned. The high summer weather, by all accounts, is changeable. And even now — look to the north — a bank of cloud begins to darken.'

We double back, encountering some native women along the way. I had seen one or two at the wharf and the dress of this small group seems much the same. They are garbed in rags tied around the waist or draped across the shoulder to help carry an infant or some other burden. Otherwise, they are naked. On one piece of cloth I make out the ghost of a floral pattern.

Two of the younger women, their breasts exposed, nod politely as they pass. 'How do you do?' one asks, in imitation of an English lady. And then, before I can reply, the same woman answers. 'Very well thank you.'

'It is as if she understands the form though not the meaning of the words,' I say to Brody.

'Either that,' he grins, 'or they are amusing themselves at our expense. They are very quick witted, these natives. Believe no one who tells you otherwise.'

'I was very taken with Bungaree, the native chief, who greeted us on the *Dromedary*,' I say as I take Macquarie's arm and stroll on to the residence, the young man dropping back a step or two behind. 'But I could not discern which elements of the performance were vaudeville and which instructional.'

'We will see more clearly when we get to know the man,' Macquarie replies. 'He is evidently not backward in venturing forward.'

'The natives are quickly stripped of pride when they abandon their camps for our settlement and our grog,' offers the ensign. 'But in their natural setting they are proud and free.'

'This is what Collins says, too.'

'Collins is well remembered here, ma'am. And in Van Diemen's Land.'

'And the native women ... you were saying?'

'Yes the women, who are much put upon in my view, are models of pluck and tenacity. They will give birth amid much wailing, attended by some of their own sorcerers and, moments later, they rise cradling their infants, dip them once or twice in the shallows, and return to their duties while suckling their bawling offspring.'

There was so much to know.

* * *

Even now, summoning memories of that strange world from the cold house in Gruline, I recall its terrors quite as much as its pleasures.

It is remarkable how swiftly the colonials, like men on the field of battle inured to the rain of bullets, had adapted to the perils around them. The townsfolk shook out their boots each morning lest spiders had lodged there, drawn by the strong scent into those damp caverns of rotting flesh and leather. The chain gangs attempted to disperse the snakes by pounding the earth with heavy sticks as they moved through forest and grassland. Some vipers, their instinct either protective or aggressive, refused to yield and instead reared up to strike. Many a colonial life has been saved in these situations by a shovel, rake or hoe — or a swift set of feet. In the *Sydney Gazette* I read how a girl in her teens, the issue of a convict sawyer and a dressmaker, had planted her bare feet onto a large brown serpent inert and coiled in the spring sunshine. The fangs struck at the girl's thigh and the poison sped to her heart.

The harbour, an enticing blue when not a lifeless grey, had claimed its share of victims. The natives sang to the fish feeding at the rocks and speared them from their slender bark canoes. Many times I saw them fish by moonlight and heard the cry of triumph carry across the laminate waters. I often saw the women wading out to collect oysters. Not the men.

All feared — and at the same time revered — the shark.

Guruwin. Shark.

I learned that name, and many others, from Bungaree.

CHAPTER NINE

The Governor's residence was dignified enough, for a penitentiary *en plein air* that had once been perilously close to ruin. A further six weeks without supplies and the colony settled on land claimed by James Cook for George III — perhaps compensation, one day, for that most peculiar monarch's loss of America — would have perished in its first year. Survival now seemed certain, though little else was guaranteed.

The colonists were wont to use the sentimental phrase 'mother country' when referring to the kingdom that dispatched them in chains. And yet there was nothing truly maternal about that unfeeling old crone. While the poor starved, the Prince Regent spent a fortune on champagne and cognac shipped across the Channel. He had, it seems, decided to punish the French for their revolution by drinking from their finest crus.

Macquarie was determined that this colony would take its colours from a different source. He was not a philosopher, was unable to amply express his ideals beyond a few speechifying phrases, sincerely felt though fragmentary, never amounting to so much as an argument. Instead he was a soldier, an administrator —

a governor — and he gave ideals concrete form. Equality for my husband was not an abstract thing; it was a fine street flanked by parks and gardens open to all, a school for the poor — particularly the poor natives. A grammar school for girls. A second chance. A place where men and women might become what they were meant to be. Build a noble place, and you create a noble race: this, at heart, was his philosophy. He was no radical, though his enemies often supposed him to be. Rather, he was a good Scot. He held some fine improving notions. He had a heart.

The residence, we discovered soon enough, was an incoherent jumble — each successive governor having added his personal touches — atop the crescent-shaped Cove's eastern rise. The industrious Joseph Foveaux had prepared it for our arrival.

It was Foveaux who managed through sheer force of personality to restore order after the upending of Captain Bligh and the seizing of power by the New South Wales Corps. The soldiers had made rum, the trade in which they enjoyed a monopoly, the colony's true currency. Foveaux simply stepped between the Rum Corps and Bligh, brushed each one aside, and brokered a peace. It is said that he favoured the rebels; I believe he favoured a return to normalcy. For that is what greeted us.

Foveaux it was who provided a measure of rural elegance with furnishings brought out from London and some gleaming white and blue porcelain pieces from the East. He took evident pride in beautifying Government House for us and, as he led us from room to room, wheezing a little from the effort, he drew our attention to features he expected would please.

In the long dimly lit corridor we were joined by Miss Ringold, a pretty woman with dark, almost black, hair and blue eyes — quite a Russian princess. She took us to our bedchamber at the end of the northern wing as Foveaux held back. It was large and clean, light-filled, though in no way luxurious.

The plain new curtains were sky blue; a nice match for the views of the waterway beyond. Miss Ringold lifted back the bed cover and retreated as I inspected the sheets. They were of coarse muslin, but brilliantly white. Next she motioned to the bedspread, which had been scattered for our arrival with fresh sprigs of eucalyptus blossom, slender grey-green leaves and scarlet flowers enclosing buds of bright yellow. I congratulated her on her good taste. 'T'were Governor Foveaux's doing, ma'am,' she blushed.

Foveaux rejoined us on the wide and low west-facing verandah.

'So it seems you have been appointed Governor,' Macquarie said to him in jest.

'Not at all sir,' he gave a slight bow. 'But I do govern in the *absence* of one. With your long-awaited arrival, I respectfully withdraw to the shadows.'

We followed him inside to the east-facing dining room, sparely decorated and blessed with a fine aspect. 'The walls here are kept bare,' he said, planting himself squarely before a large curved bay window. 'It's so that the natural glories will not be overwhelmed by the fine arts.' We looked towards the kitchen gardens and Farm Cove a short distance beyond.

Retracing our steps, we returned over slightly creaky floorboards to the front of the house.

Foveaux gestured with a plump white hand towards a wide reception room. Off that stood, to the right, an office with a handsome wainscoting of dark timber meeting a bottle green carpet and walls crowded with pictures, some painted in the colony's earliest years. 'Here you see drawings of natives clothed like Grecians in white robes,' Foveaux intoned. 'They much prefer complete nudity, which is not to say they aren't greatly amused by our' — he tugged at his waistcoat — 'vestments.' He paused for a laboured intake of breath. 'And here' — a foppish twirl of the hand before another picture — 'are the tangled eucalyptus forests that you would have seen as the *Dromedary* entered the Heads. The trunks of the most appealing species are lily white. They can seem cadaverous — certainly ghostly. But the shape' — he caressed the air with a fleshy hand — 'is very sinuous. Very beautiful.'

Extracting an embroidered kerchief from the pocket of his waistcoat, Foveaux smiled sweetly and mopped his brow. 'Here is the long-tailed hopping kangaroo, captured in a rare moment of repose. Next to it is a watercolour of a jellyfish, gossamer blue. Remarkable, really. The skill! We have the artist on the French expedition of 1802 to thank. It was a gift to, er,' — he raised a speculative finger — 'Governor King.'

The most beautiful room of all was a wood-panelled study behind Macquarie's office, facing south. The window was large, paned inexpertly with varied depths of glass, and the light seemed to buckle and warp as it poured into the room. Our host said not a word about this feature but merely bowed and threw out an arm. In one corner stood a pianoforte with its lid propped open and a sheaf of music leaning on the keys. Beside it, at a lazy angle, rested a violoncello.

'I believe,' he offered, 'that madam has an ear for music — and some talent for it.'

'I carried a viola on the *Dromedary* without once playing it, wary of the corrosive maritime air. And now …'

'You have the big sister too,' he beamed.

'But from where did it come?' I asked, quite lost for words. 'All this …'

'There are a number of fine instruments in the colony,' he explained. 'All we lack is the mastery of them. A man with money from the seal trade or the rum monopoly will have a pianoforte shipped out from London and spend half a lifetime admiring it without once troubling the keys. I had merely to requisition one.'

Macquarie shot me the tender look of a parent watching a favoured child unwrap a Christmas present. 'Already,' he addressed Foveaux, although I suspect the remark was more for my benefit, 'I note that there is more culture in the colony than any visitor, knowing its unique composition, would expect.'

'A salve for the isolation,' Foveaux returned, clasping his hands behind his back and puffing out his barrel of a belly. 'The death of a king, a revolution, famine, earthquake — a catastrophe on the scale of Lisbon — and we hear a muffled bulletin six months after the event. A letter, a dispatch: that is all.' He offered a half-smile, looking now at Macquarie, now me, with pale, watery eyes. 'We miss much and so long for connection with the world that we look always to the harbour. Much as the farmer looks to the skies, we keep watch for the signals from the flagstaff and the first sign of the sails that tell us we are not forgotten. And as soon as a visitor steps ashore we buttonhole him for news of the world.'

He took a step towards the pianoforte. Stooping a little he tucked one arm behind him, and with the other reached out to touch the inlaid work on the lid. He pressed a padded finger briefly onto the surface, leaving behind a humid impress. 'Why,' he went on, 'the women seize on the first signs of a shift in fashion among the few ladies to venture across the seas. And those with means equal to their aspirations collect leather volumes and porcelain from China — Tang, Sing or Ming dynasties, I'm afraid I'm never sure which. I am no connoisseur of chinoiserie. And, well, as you can see, it is thanks to this desire for connection with the world that fine musical instruments gather dust in some handsome homes like museum pieces until they are procured by a loyal official' — he tilted his head a little coyly — 'for a new governor and his musical wife. I had it polished just last week for your arrival.'

Foveaux made to move off, but Macquarie stepped forward. He went to the pianoforte and found middle C. The tone was, to my complete surprise, true. 'The one great absence — and this is no fault of yours, Foveaux — is that of dignity in the building. But that is easily remedied with the services of an architect. There is one such aboard the *Dromedary*, I believe.'

'Indeed, Your Excellency,' Foveaux replied in a tone as smooth as satin. 'Word of the Architect's arrival has reached my ear.'

CHAPTER TEN

I wake, dress, and step into a mild milky morning: my first in this curious New World. The air is sweet, soft, a little cloying. The harbour lies in gradations of shadow yet the sky is ripening quickly as the day comes on. I look up, astonished. A raucous troupe of parakeets, rainbow-plumed, careens through the air at the speed of musket shot. Its quarry is a four-square bird of prey with a beak like a dart. The air is momentarily splashed with colour — every colour there ever was. The birds climb, plunge and spin with stiff, rapidly beating wings.

Once beyond reach of its pursuers, the intruder, a robust type of kingfisher whose body resembles a fist with dull feathers thrown upon it, perches on the eave of a cottage adjoining the residence. From there it loosens an ungodly, quite uproarious, chuckle. If I had journeyed seven months under sail to this place of correction, and shipped back the very next morning, I would consider it a venture well worth undertaking for the sound of that laughter alone. But I would aim to distil the joyful sound, and bottle it. Returning home I would uncork it in time of need. There would be no need then for sloe gin or Highland whisky.

A soldier is stationed at the pretty white gate set in the picket fence around the residence. No movement yet so soon after dawn, but a stirring noise abroad: the discordance of a settlement rousing itself, like a village band preparing to play. I rush indoors to tell Macquarie about the sights of the morning. He is already at his bureau, quill poised.

'Come now,' I tug playfully at his sleeve.

'A stroll?' he asks distractedly, returning to his papers. 'By all means Elizabeth. But not for me. Be careful, now. Do not stray beyond sight of the guard.'

I had not allowed my parents to bridle me. Why should I permit my husband? I dash out the door.

The young Irish ensign with whom I spoke yesterday accompanies me along a straight path towards the shoreline. Leaving me there, he retreats to his post. The kingfisher has flown further towards the shore to perch on the chimney pot of a whitewashed cottage at the water's edge.

So entranced am I by the bird that I fail to hear the approach of an unkempt man with a piebald beard and a deficiency of teeth. Moving as stealthily as a shadow cast by a passing cloud, he gives me a start. 'Good morning,' I say. I look over my shoulder in the direction of the residence. The ensign stands stock still in his guard box. Evidently there is no cause for concern. I return my gaze to the bird. The queer old man watches, too.

'Koo-ka-burra,' he says, measuring out the harsh syllables like spoons of sugar. 'Native word. You'll get used to them soon enough. The birds, I mean. The natives will take longer.' I cut him a look. His eyes, hooded by age, blink rapidly. Leaning with a slight tremor on a heavy tree limb fashioned into a knotted cane, he turns to spit. The saliva does not entirely clear his whiskers. He wipes his mouth with the back of a hand as if he had drunk deeply from a tankard. 'Beggin' yer pardon ma'am,' he says, looking away.

I notice he is dressed in grey trousers with a patch on one knee and a faded dun-coloured coat. Not poor, but very poorly cared for.

'Mrs Macquarie, eh. The Governor's wife?' he goes on in those distinctive West Country undulations that will not leave vowels alone. 'Arrived on the *Dromedary*? More than thirty souls lost — from what we hear. If you'd been fed convict rations in chains on the prison deck then perhaps you too ...' He breaks off with a dispirited shake of the head. 'Of course I would not wish it.'

The eccentric tucks a wrinkled tobacco pouch into his pocket and draws on a clay pipe with a bowl modelled after the head of a moustachioed man. He turns to meet my gaze but quickly averts his eyes. He has the waxy skin of the unwashed — the odour, too.

'Your name, sir? You seem to know mine. You are out very early — the town, it seems, sleeps on beyond the call of dawn.'

'The iron gangs will begin to move shortly,' he says, scratching at his whiskers as if they harbour a flea. 'The muster has begun. But there is never any great haste — it is ugly work and only for the worst ...'

'But your name?' I press.

'You've seen Bungaree,' he goes on obtusely, ignoring my request for his name as if I had been addressing him all this time in Pekingese. 'All newcomers do ... before the muster ashore. Appointed himself King of the Natives. Hails from Broken Bay further north. Wait till you meet his —' he breaks off with a hacking smoker's laugh that begins in mirth and ends in near asphyxiation. He brings a kerchief to his mouth. I make to move off but he manages to rasp out the one word: 'Please.' And then, after a heaving of the chest, another: 'Stay.'

'Very well.' If it were not for my curiosity about Bungaree I would have turned and walked away. But the old man, he unnerves me. Spinning once more towards the guard I observe, to my discomfort, that he has disappeared.

'You will meet,' he starts up again, 'his consort Gooseberry. Queen he calls her. She has the magic, or so it's said. But there are many things said in this place.' His jaw flexes strangely. He paws at the whiskers on his neck. 'As a rule — and this I say to all new chums no matter what rank — it's best to disbelieve most of what a man says about his past, because it was never true, and all he says about his future, because it never will be.'

As he turns and shambles off, whistling a winding tune, a hand clasps my arm lightly at the elbow.

'Mrs Macquarie,' says the guard.

I cannot conceal my relief.

'We were introduced yesterday,' I say, 'and afterwards I heard you talk learnedly about the kangaroo and the natives. Ensign Brody, if my memory serves me.'

'It does indeed, ma'am.'

'Perhaps you can tell me how a young man with a scholarly cast of mind finds himself so far from the library at Trinity.'

His dark eyes blink and widen, blink again and narrow. I have confused him.

'A lucky guess,' I say.

'I was there only for a year,' he says, his tan deepened by a blush.

'Why so short a time, without graduation? Do you mind my asking?'

'Not at all, ma'am. 'Twas a family matter.' He looks away. 'A difficulty. I was forced into work. The Army — my parents are Protestant — took me on. My regiment — the 102nd — was sent to

Port Jackson. After Governor Bligh some, myself included, remained. Most of my earnings, you see, are destined for home.'

'Well, Ensign Brody. You are from the 102nd Regiment of Foot. And so I would greatly appreciate a walk to the town. Not too far — it is my first morning. Just to get my bearings. After the long journey, you understand. And that queer man ... I am curious.'

Brody cuts a glance over his shoulder towards the residence. And then, seemingly resigned to his fate, he leads the way. His stride is long. His arms swing at his sides. Now and then he slows for me to keep pace.

We stroll from Government House to the cove sweeping below us. Warehouses fringe the shoreline. Cottages mount the rise. I point to the promontory. The soldier anticipates my question.

'Dawes Point, ma'am. Named after William Dawes, a lieutenant in the marines. First Fleeter. You will often hear tales of his knowledge of the southern skies and his friendship with the natives. The harbour's narrowest point bears his name. At Dawes Point five cannon protect us. If an intruder were to enter the harbour we would make merry. Since the war with Bonaparte we mostly fear the French.'

The soldier swings around to Government House behind us on the eastern rise, as if to check it still stands, returning to face the harbour with a sigh of relief. 'Is all in order?' I ask.

'Yes ma'am. You see, I've abandoned my post momentarily but another sentry has replaced me now. Someone, it seems, is watching us and saw that I had come out to help you.'

Raising his hand towards the crest of the western ridge, he points with a proud air to the observatory and flagstaff. 'Below it The Rocks,' he says, with a dismissive swat, as if he means to clear the sight away. 'Convict quarters. Taverns. Cramped, poor and rather, er, wild ma'am. Not for you, I think.'

'Well, perhaps not this morning.' We stroll towards the shore. A rowboat with four oarsmen and a hulking, indistinct load pulls away to a ship lying at anchor. A horse-drawn cart rolls past, rattling and creaking dejectedly. Behind it follows a line of bedraggled convicts in leg irons. A sullen silence falls around them. From somewhere within the town the regular pulse of a hammer rises over the slow sweet rhythm of a saw.

'It seems an industrious little town,' I remark.

'It springs up quickly,' returns the soldier. 'Perhaps you hear the lumber yard ahead? Blacksmiths, tailors, shoemakers, carpenters, wheelwrights — all work there. And yet the town grows largely between Dawes Point to the west and Bennelong Point on the eastern side of the Cove.'

'Bennelong,' I say. 'A favourite of Arthur Phillip's. His fame has spread far and wide.'

'The place is named after a hut the native had there.'

'I remember hearing of his audience with King George. They met, as I recall, at the Theatre Royal, Covent Garden. I must have been fifteen or sixteen when I read the story. Such a curious tale: the native from Port Jackson in his London finery. Bennelong returned to these shores, I think. He still lives?'

'I believe so,' replies the soldier. 'Over the north side of the river, a little further west at Kissing Point. He has retired from the life he lived as an ambassador of his people and friend to ours. A great pity. We hear reports. It's said that he writes to old friends in London requesting some of the pretty things he acquired in Phillip's service — silk handkerchiefs, fine leather riding boots.'

We turn towards one another with mirroring smiles.

I catch something in the ensign's tone, something I have not heard for a long while: a calm and kindly intelligence. Poise. Macquarie would call it promise.

'Is it true the natives in their pure state want for nothing,' I inquire.

'Well, they want a good bath, but of course they'd not know it.' The lad gives a satisfied laugh and his pace slows. 'Is the town,' he asks, 'all you expected, ma'am?'

'More picturesque, certainly. And less — how to put it? Not the sensation I'd imagined.'

'From the early days the convicts have sought their own lodgings, ma'am. And they have been permitted to sell their skills — or merely their labour — outside the hours of assigned work. A man can earn enough to salt away — or drink away — by building a free man's fence or repairing his watch.'

'Tell me then, that ageing eccentric whom I encountered by the shore. Is he ... typical of the townsfolk?'

'A tragic tale, I'm afraid.' And here, his expression pained, he pauses. 'Are you sure?' he asks.

I nod. 'Do go on.'

'His name is Octavio Jewkes. He has been at work before dawn. It is the reason you see him at this hour, ma'am, strolling about the Cove at his leisure. He is a baker by trade. And this thriving little business governs him. He met with tragedy in his first years at the Cove and it is said ... well, some think him a little mad. Perhaps, after all, you would rather not know.'

'On the contrary, I would very much like to know.'

Brody relates the tale of Octavio's transportation for the theft of a loaf; how his wife, bereft, schemed to join him at the Cove by committing the very same crime. 'She pleaded guilty but the judge, learning of her intentions, dispatched the poor soul to the gallows.

66

It was to be, he said, "A lesson to all." There was not a dry eye in the court, I'm told. Both women and men held out their hands to her as she was led away. Octavio, when he heard the news, refused to speak. For months he was silent. Even now he is odd. He has lost the gift of civil conversation.'

I let out a deep sigh. 'I may have heard something of this story, though only in its generality. I had considered it a cautionary tale put about by a parliamentarian in a speech on the crime problem. "The deterrent value of transportation must be maintained," they are forever thundering. "For if it is not, the worst villains in the land will seek their tickets to the Antipodes by acts of brazen robbery." But to think … a woman lost her life for a loaf of bread. The life was taken from her to protect a policy.'

'This was some ten years ago and well before my time,' Brody continues. 'Octavio must now be in his mid-forties and he haunts the town like a living ghost. He never remarried. For some reason known only to him he became a baker after he had served his time. Perhaps he could think of nothing else. The business is a success; no man can do without bread. He accumulates money, and never spends it. He has become a wealthy miser.'

We stroll towards the heart of the town past a row of neat Government offices and stores. Through the double doors of a merchant's stone warehouse I spy figures weaving around one another in a shifting composition. Most seem respectably dressed — in light summer coats — and solidly shod. A large columnar man in a long coat, tall and dark-skinned, steps to the side of the hefty door, pauses to light a pipe, doffs a broad-brimmed hat as we pass. He studies me from lowered lids as he smokes.

'Campbell, the merchant,' Brody says under his breath. 'Paying a visit to Thomas Reibey. They do some business together.' A horse-drawn cart pulls up at Reibey's warehouse. Four men in convict motley — yellow jackets and knee-length trousers — ease a heavy table and leather upholstered chairs from the cart through the double door, while a fourth shakes out the blankets used to protect them. 'Careful,' warns an overseer wielding a baton.

Once we are out of earshot Brody again inclines his head. 'It's said that Reibey is in debt to him. A soured venture — there are so many.'

A little further on we come to a palatial three-storey stone house with a two-tier verandah — seven windows wide. It had been hidden from the verandah of Government House, which it rivals, by its position in the merchant quarter. 'The trader Simeon Lord's home, counting house and auction room,' says Brody as if making a formal introduction. 'Said to have cost fifteen thousand pounds. Across the road are his warehouses.'

'In what items does he trade?' I inquire.

'In what does he *not* trade! Exports sealskins. Seal and whale oil. Sandalwood. Timber. Coal. Produces glass, pottery, slop clothing. Imports tea and silk. He also acts as a public auctioneer.'

'And his crime? I presume he's a former convict.'

'Stealing ten pence worth of cloth — muslin and calico. He has risen so high that he is not ashamed to tell.'

Leaving the merchant quarter behind, we cross a narrow stone bridge over a stagnant, malodorous stream.

'It was once a brook of fresh water,' offers the soldier in a melancholy tone. 'Holding tanks were cut into the sandstone — hence the name: Tank Stream. But now it is not so much silted up as clogged.'

'I would have thought this a perfect Paradise when it was first settled,' I say, turning to look this fresh-faced young man in his dark eyes. 'But it seems we cannot avoid fouling it.'

68

Brody looks to the skies. 'It really is time to return,' he says. 'The sun gains strength with every word we utter. Even the morning rays will burn a pale complexion.'

'Such as yours,' he would surely have gone on to say if tact had not silenced him.

It occurs to me, when I part company with Brody at the guardhouse, that I failed to inquire about *his* years in the colony. It cannot have been many — he is still very young. He would have seen it rise from a dismal state, pass through the tumult of the Bligh rebellion, and emerge poised for advancement under a steady governor. I thought it a shame that a settlement in such a splendid environment should not — despite its constitution, and perhaps because of it — strive for a more dignified appearance. The dignity of the town might then confer dignity on the unfortunates who inhabited the shacks I could see spreading over The Rocks and westward down the disorderly main street.

It is mid-morning when I skip up the steps to the house and I head straight to the bedchamber. In the mirror I notice that my cheeks have reddened. The freckles that I have acquired on the journey will doubtless, now, multiply. I take off my bonnet and let down my hair, taking a towel to it so that it might dry. I change into a light summer dress and stride down the hallway, following the scent of freshly brewed tea.

The door to Macquarie's office was open when I left. But I see now it is slightly ajar. There are voices within. I knock. Macquarie calls for me to enter. It's only then that I notice my hair is loose. For a few seconds I retreat to the shadows and delay my entry. I bundle up my copper curls and secure them, before stepping into the room.

Before me is a man in a burgundy tailcoat, uncovered hair full of waves and kinks falling over his ears. He stands, a little stiffly,

69

before the imposing figure of my husband seated at his bureau. The visitor spins around sharply as I enter. There is a flash of warmth from a set of lively green eyes.

'Elizabeth,' Macquarie says genially as he rises from his chair. 'You must meet our Architect.'

CHAPTER ELEVEN

A smaller man than Macquarie, the Architect is broad shouldered, slim flanked and, as the French would have it, *bien fait*. His wide mouth, though not particularly well defined, is fixed in an expression of mild amusement. He has, I note, a disconcerting habit of tilting his head back, raising his jaw, and looking down his long thin nose in a manner that would seem supercilious in anyone, but in a convict appears unconscionably arrogant. Once or twice he runs his fingers through his thick locks, pushing them back from his brow as if clearing a path to a view. He has obviously been cared for on the voyage: extra rations, a little exercise, a touch of sun. Still, it cannot have been easy. The gentlemen convicts may enjoy better treatment, but it can hardly be said that they have evaded misfortune; they are simply less unfortunate than their fellows.

The Architect is tightly wound, restless on his feet. He has doubtless counselled himself before this, his first interview with the Governor, to reveal only what is required of him, to show due deference, and to offer his services with humility — an attitude that any modestly intelligent, certainly prudent, man in his situation would be sure to adopt. And yet his nature seems unwilling to accept the terms laid down by his situation. He is a little — how do I remember him at first glance? — unruly.

'I trust that you are comfortably installed in the cottage beside the Tank Stream,' Macquarie says from his high-backed chair behind the bureau. 'I had Foveaux make it available for you. It had been occupied, he tells me, by his aide-de-camp.'

'It is very comfortable, sir.'

As I step lightly towards Macquarie's side, he indicates with a reeling motion that the visitor should come further forward. He looks him up and down. 'You seem to be in surprisingly good health,' he says. 'I'm glad to see you suffered no harm on that dreadful voyage.'

'I suffered no real physical harm, Your Excellency,' the visitor says with darting eyes. 'On one occasion ... perhaps I shouldn't say ... a threat to inflict it. Though never fulfilled.'

'A threat. From what quarter?' returns the Governor in a voice rising steadily in pitch and volume. 'The convicts? Soldiers? An officer — surely not?'

'It is no matter. I am, as you see, alive and well.' He gives his hands a shake, as if to prove his vitality. 'And ready to begin.'

Macquarie rubs his cleanly shaven chin ruminatively as he turns to the window. There is a slow shake of the head. It is not in his nature to let such a matter rest. Only when I place my hand on his shoulder does he break from his thoughts.

'Quite so,' he says, returning to the Architect, who, I observe, has been turning this way and that with wide astonished eyes, taking in the paintings and sketches on the walls. 'What is an insult when compared with a life.'

Macquarie rises and strides heavily to a corner of the room, where he stoops to pick up a chair upholstered in midnight blue velvet with gold trim. He could have called the butler to do it, but that is not his way. Placing the chair beside him, he motions for me to sit.

To the Architect, who remains standing, he says, 'And you ... you kept your mind sharpened for the purpose I hope you will be able to serve by sketching — plans and the like.'

The Architect steps forward with a military crispness. He places a black folio on the Governor's desk, then returns to his former position.

He stirs my curiosity, this minor celebrity aboard the *Dromedary*, a floating world of criminals.

Macquarie leafs through the folio. 'Mmm,' he mutters in a warm bass. And then a little higher, 'Huh.' A few seconds later, 'Well. Well.' It has been an age since I have seen him this animated. 'I see you are fond of the classical orders. What else?' He continues leafing.

The Architect cuts me a covert look.

Macquarie motions for me to lean closer. 'Elizabeth, come look. The section here is titled,' he looks up quizzically as I lean over the folio, '"Plan for a Growing Town".'

We fall upon the work. This alert and rather bold convict has seemingly intuited our deepest thoughts. No. More than that. He has given them the shape and form we craved.

Here is a grand Government House crowned by a dome that would have made Wren proud, set in a garden of English trees; there a bridge vaulting from Dawes Point to the echoing northern shore. A keep buttressed by crenellated towers with arrow slit embrasures rises from a shore — harbour or loch, it is difficult to tell. As we turn the pages we behold dizzying wonders. A cenotaph rises from one of the islands we had passed in the centre of the harbour, pyramidal in shape, adorned with monumental sculpture. A villa spreads out

73

from a temple front, forested with statues of gods and goddesses, sibyls and muses.

Macquarie looks up from the Architect's folio. 'But how did you ...?' he begins. He looks at me with a puzzled expression. 'Incredible, don't you think?'

I intuit the drift of Macquarie's thoughts. How, with only a sketchbook on his knees and a porthole for light, did the Architect conceive of all this? Why, the man had not seen the colony until yesterday.

'Imagination,' answers the Architect, bouncing up and down on his toes. 'And inspiration. I studied a crude map of the settlement — Péron's from 1802 — and these ideas, they came to me. And of course I had seven barren months at sea.'

'Ideas,' I say. 'But also a vision for how the settlement might grow — if the wealth that it promises is ever to be realised.'

'I have made the study of cities — Rome, Byzantium, Damascus — my vocation,' he offers, addressing Macquarie, now me, now Macquarie again, his movements as precise as a mechanism. 'Permit me to return with more sketches. I have many.'

The visitor gives a small cough to punctuate the flow of his thoughts. 'Perhaps a decorative obelisk for the small triangle of park below the residence — the obelisk speaks of eternal Egypt and its mysteries.' And after a pause: 'Your residence here. If I may: more light perhaps. More grandeur.' His eyebrows shoot up as if to say, 'Yes. Really. I am serious.' And he goes on quickly, 'A portico befitting your authority. I would suggest Doric, the first and still most dignified of the classical orders, and, unless Your Excellency has access to a school of first-rate masons taught to handle levels, trowels, plumb rules, chisels and hammers, the easiest to fashion.'

Forgetting his station entirely, the convict steps towards the window with a view of the Cove. 'And the settlement itself,' he says with the hint of a West Country burr. 'It seems to seep inland from its origins between this rise on the east and The Rocks across the water. I see no plan in this arrangement and every reason for the streets to run broad and straight and the town be given,' he puffs out his chest, 'a chance to breathe.' He returns to his side of the desk and folds his arms, awaiting a response.

There may be some approving warmth in my eyes when he shoots a look in my direction, for he goes on eagerly, 'Why should the streets not in time be flanked by ornate mansions and terraces, flowering gardens, harmonious town squares? The settlement could be planned in one monumental sweep, terminating with a city wall opening onto Gothic tollgates in flamboyant filigree.' He places his hands firmly on the top rail of a chair reserved for visitors with a higher station than the felonry. And then he leans forward.

'In time — when I have trained some young masons in the craft — your squares and gardens will be given a classical air with Ionic columns. The Corinthian reserved for a grand processional way. Elsewhere, Doric. And ...'

'Enough!' thunders the Governor. 'You assail me with your schemes. I would counsel a little restraint! Men who have been in my service a score of years do not lecture me in such an unbridled manner.'

The Architect steps back from the chair and for a good three or four beats of a steady heart there is welcome silence.

'We are strongly pressed for a lighthouse at South Head,' Macquarie says coolly, 'and a male convict barrack to house those who now, Foveaux informs me, wander about the settlement without restraint, make mischief among the women, drink themselves senseless on a Sunday. The residence is contained by a mere picket fence; it will require one of stone. So will the Domain. The fortifications at Sydney Cove are clearly inadequate. We are far indeed from France but not so distant that we can escape her ambitions and stratagems if they should bend in our direction. For the moment we are at peace. But tomorrow? Who knows.'

'But you must,' I say, 'give no more thought than is necessary to your station — your crime. Consider this a new beginning.' It was not so much pity that was aroused in me as a feeling, a very primal feeling, of fellowship.

'That,' says Macquarie with a brisk wave as if dismissing a flunky, 'is all in the past. There will be no talk of it at this house. There is so much to do at Port Jackson that we must use men of ability irrespective of their ... their transgressions.' He breaks off and turns away. 'I sometimes think that for most men that damnable voyage is punishment enough.'

'I hope that I might serve as your accomplice in these grand schemes,' returns the Architect with renewed cheer. 'I possess a compliant nature.'

Macquarie, I see, is both affronted and amused and quite unsure which emotion has the stronger claim to him. 'I doubt you are truly the compliant type,' he says with an expression just shy of a smile. 'You earned your ticket on the *Dromedary* for, what was it, forgery, I believe? A canny crime, not so very far from craft — if not for our skill in copying we might never have progressed from the ape. And what, after all, does it mean to ape: to copy.

'But it is a crime nevertheless,' he goes on in a blazing tone. 'Robbery is one thing. But fraud is theft amplified by deception. And His Majesty's empire cannot run on counterfeited pounds, shillings and pence.'

A deferential nod from the Architect.

'What the Governor means,' I say in a mollifying voice with a pointed look towards Macquarie, 'is that your crime must not, should not, be entirely forgotten. But it is best regarded as a stain on the character, a blemish to be removed with a little ... a little scrubbing. And time. Eventually it will out. It is not a sin branded permanently on the soul.'

Looking down at his folio I turn to a page bearing a detailed sketch of an assembly building graced by a colonnade of Corinthian columns. 'The Corinthian order,' I say, only half in jest, 'rises to a crown of acanthus leaves. Let us conceive for Sydney Town an Antipodean order — eucalyptus in place of acanthus.'

The Architect's green eyes widen. He goes to speak but this time restrains himself. He merely tugs at the sleeves of his fine burgundy coat, puts on a serious face and awaits his dismissal.

I close the folio and return it to him. 'We are — both of us — extremely grateful,' I say. On close inspection I calculate that he is five or so years my senior. Some twelve years Macquarie's junior. This convict has reasons aplenty to be worn down by his ordeal, and yet he is not in the least bowed. He has shaved and washed for the interview. He is boldly dressed. But I can tell, too, that he is alone. A wife might have insisted on clean fingernails.

Though his crime is forgery, I tease him, surely he is also an excellent thief.

'For how else did you manage to pick the lock of my mind? The Governor's, too? We have talked of improvements to Sydney Town, but you have, it seems, done our imagining for us. We merely entertained notions. You pilfer our best ideas, returning them in a more refined state. You steal our stones and smuggle them back as jewels. A thief, but a kindly one!'

He lowers his head with an expression of gratitude and bows in a rushed manner that is not particularly elegant and not at all courtly. In the gesture there is more feeling — genuine feeling — than form.

I leave the office shortly after the Architect, closing the door on Macquarie and his papers. I resist the urge to pursue our visitor. Such an intriguing character. Everything seems quickened — brightened — by his presence.

CHAPTER TWELVE

The walnut bureau at which I write is wide and long and fashioned plainly to the needs of a figure of authority. Though of a robust disposition I feel hesitant in this seat. It is as if the piece of furniture craves something from me that I cannot return, requires a key that I have misplaced or, perhaps, never possessed. In time I will be rid of it. I will have something of my own.

The guttering candles cast a welcome glow around me, while the desk's extremities dissolve in the room's shadows. In the time it served Macquarie its busy surface was chequered with correspondence — official dispatches, private missives and reports. Tonight there is only the book of octavo pages, the steel pen and ink bottle beside it, and a filing box with a fine marbled paper surface. The file holds my own treasury — although the word does, I suppose, dignify this repository of papers, clippings, letters and artefacts. The precious letter I am searching for is from the Architect. One of his last and still his dearest — from a time when correspondence was our most intimate bond — it lies towards the bottom of the pile. I extract it carefully, guiltily, as if I am being observed, which of course I am not. It is my conscience alone that surveys me.

The note is written in his distinctive hand, with great attention to the forming of letters. Where for most a letter of the alphabet is merely a brick in the house of meaning, the Architect approached the act of writing with a monkish veneration for the beauty of written words.

Dear Elizabeth,
Do you recall our very first meeting?

I remember it well. An explosion of corkscrew curls —
rust and copper — at the half open door. And there you
were. Your head was lowered. Your elbows were raised.
Your face was flushed as you bundled up that rebellious
hair. Then you fixed it with a clasp.

'I do apologise,' you said stepping briskly into the
room with a lovely girlish sway of the hips and shoulders,
long pale arms swinging. 'I was quite lost in the view of a
flock of parakeets chasing a distinctive bird with an utterly
individual laugh.'

You were laughing, at that moment, yourself. It was
your first morning at Sydney Cove. Mine as well.

You ran your hands across your summer dress. You ran
them over your thighs. They pressed against the light fabric.
There, suddenly, was feminine shape and form. Such an
admirable form! You seemed oblivious to the impression
this milkmaid gesture might make on a visitor, especially
one as lowly stationed as myself.

The Governor spoke. I spoke a little too much. You
spoke very little. But I felt there was — even at our first
meeting — the beginning of a compact.

Almost smothered by the steady hum of my own nerves
was the impress of your individuality, your dominion

over yourself, your dignity. You seemed defined by a
bold contour. It was as if nothing else, in the short period
of the interview, really existed. There! I have described
an emotion as if it were an aquatint. Perhaps it is the
draughtsman in me. And yet if you had asked me to
describe the colour of your eyes as I sat an hour later, bent
over my sketchpad in the whitewashed cottage beside the
Tank Stream I permitted myself at that time to call home, I
might have answered: brown. Perhaps grey. No, blue-green.
In fact they were the colour of an Antipodean winter sky:
cold, pale, and pure.

And then there was your lovely voice — refined,
markedly that of a lady, with the added zest and vigour of
the Scots. Even when you were earnest, forceful, inflamed,
I never felt that laughter was far away. Yet there was
nothing light or trivial about your effervescence. It was not
the mousse of champagne but the force of a breaker. I was
caught by it, rolled, thrown, submerged. And then I came
up, exhilarated, for air.

For a brief moment, in my dark widow's house at Gruline, I, too,
inhale that wild air.

PART TWO

CHAPTER THIRTEEN

It is a still, silken autumn morning when we set out for the interior. The Governor squeezes his ageing form into a cream satin waistcoat and then, with even greater effort, contorts himself into a black parade jacket embroidered with gold. This decorous formality of dress, he feels, is eminently suited to the expedition's purpose.

Leading us out, a head taller than most of the soldiers, he cuts a fine figure. I feel a touch of pride as those few townsfolk watching our departure smile and wave — a mother reaches down to her sandy-headed child, takes his hand, and waves it for him.

Ah, but pride in the uniform is an old emotion, belonging to a younger self. A year in the colony and I am changing.

A detachment of ten men follows the Governor, sabres glinting coldly in the morning sun when they are drawn from their scabbards for a final inspection.

We march to the Government wharf, where the Architect, who comes from his cottage by the Tank Stream, will join us. I wear a white bonnet upholstered with my own sprung curls, and a light blue woollen coat to keep out the chill. On our way we pass a miserable chain of convicts trudging like oxen.

'To where is this group headed?' I ask Macquarie.

'By cart inland,' he replies matter-of-factly. 'They will leave shortly before us to fell timber. The trees grow taller there, and they are spaced well apart.'

There is a cry of pain followed by a distempered howl, more canine than human. The chains cease their clanking. I pause to look behind. The men have drawn aside from the path. One is down, doubled over. An overseer with a top hat crushed at the crown, as if it has been sat upon, stands in the midst of the group lighting a pipe. We move on.

'Are the irons ever struck from their ankles?' I ask. 'The poor men.'

'Pity is an indulgence I cannot afford,' he says, and leaning towards me, in an intimate tone, 'and nor, my love, can you. It is too costly.' He straightens. I offer silence, knowing that it will draw him out. 'Or, rather,' he goes on, as I expected he would, 'pity is a coin that must be used sparingly. I made it clear to all at the first muster. Good behaviour brings the richest reward of all: freedom. But there will be no quarter given for a return to crime. Severity is the only answer! Most of the men on the iron gangs' — he turns to regard the straggling group — 'have reoffended. Some tried to escape. One of these laggards walked into the bush and returned two days later jabbering like a madman. What's to be done?' He shakes his head. 'A rule of leniency is no kind of rule at all.'

'So the crimes of the past are forgotten but those of the present bring forth a punishment just short of death. I mean to say, what kind of life is it?'

'No kind of life at all, I'm afraid.'

The soldiers' boots grind the dry shale and pebble, though not in regular marching time. Too many empty hours wiled away at cards and they have lost their soldierly form — their regimental pride. Am I the only one to lament this absence of learned rhythm and discipline, to note it at all? It would help if there were a military band that could be relied upon to keep good time. Whenever I hear the band strike up I am reminded of a boat I had once seen sinking on Loch Creran: there is the same combination of helplessness and dread.

At the wharf, all is in readiness. The overseer of Government boats, Barney Williams, a stout red-haired fellow with short arms that pump the air furiously when he walks — and even when he doesn't — is on hand to greet us. He explains that the Governor and I will leave first, seated aft. Soldiers will ride at the fore, and convict oarsmen will take us down the river.

I insist that the convicts be unshackled. 'They will hardly attempt to escape with so many muskets about,' I say. 'And at Parramatta there will be a guard.' I give Macquarie a look and he returns it blankly. 'You say only the worst are manacled. Are these men of the worst kind?'

Macquarie inclines his head to Williams, a convict he had recently pardoned, and the men are released.

The longer I dwell at this vast distance from home, the more deeply I am struck by the insult of social hierarchy. I have learned more from my conversations with the native, Bungaree, and the convict architect, than from any of the braying officers of the 73rd Regiment of Foot.

We are headed inland to meet with a tribe of reconciled natives, lay the foundation stone of Spencertown, and survey its needs. If not for this last purpose the Architect would have been left to oversee the apprentice masons at the lighthouse. A sufficient quantity of excellent, though rather soft, stone has already been quarried and dressed, and the shapely tower has begun to rise. But he is needed on this expedition, the Governor tells me, for his gift of 'civic imagination', and a holiday has been declared on the lighthouse site.

I would have thought the colony's bard, Michael Massey Robinson, worthy of a berth on the boat to Parramatta; and the presence of the convict artist, Joseph Lycett, would surely be invaluable. Lycett, who has a good eye for the pastoral, could paint some of the scenery, or at least beautify what scenery we happen to find. But we travel light. One of Robinson's odes has been penned for the occasion and the Governor carries the verses in his pocket while their author stays behind. The Architect has been deemed by the Governor to be Lycett's equal with a brush; I pray that word of this insult does not reach the ears of that irascible artist.

'The Architect no sooner sets eyes on a place than he sees how to give it dignity,' Macquarie tells me. 'It's as if, for this work, I have the benefit of another set of eyes — another mind.'

He has begun to value the Architect's opinions, it seems, above all others. They speak to him of his great cause. To put down the foundations of a civilisation at this most unlikely place he cannot, he says, rely solely on his own and his wife's whims and fancies.

I have had placed by the window of our bedchamber a cylinder bureau used by our predecessors as a spare drinks cabinet; it's here that I read, correspond and store my small, yet growing, collection of colonial mementos. When this is done I will oftentimes find Macquarie and the Architect together in the study, along with George Howe, the printer of our *Sydney Gazette*, and Captain John Piper the naval officer. Each time I enter I am welcomed courteously into the club and directed to a comfortable seat. I remark on the pall of cigar smoke and the open bottles, and after I take my seat the conversation resumes. But I suspect it takes a different course after my entry; certainly there is a shift in the tenor.

I am the odd one out. I will never be excluded from these meetings and yet my presence, I sense, is not so much encouraged as endured. The Architect had vexed Macquarie at our first meeting by inundating us with his expertise. What a torrent he unleashed! Now it enchants my husband. He will come to me some evenings with talk of the Corinthian order and its origins, of triglyphs and architraves and the like. He is much like a student excited by his mastery of some esoteric branch of knowledge.

If I am to have some purchase on the business of improving this colony I will need to find a clear and direct path to the Architect. How interesting that he has become such a power in the colony. What is more he is, I can tell by his longer than absolutely necessary looks, desirous of a stronger bond between us.

As the boats slides along the Parramatta River, a cold dark-green jelly at this hour, there is only the rasping of the rowers' laboured breath and the rhythm of oars beating the water.

I'm reminded of how in late summer I would now and then take a small rowboat out across the pearly waters of Loch Linnhe and watch the lingering sunset in glorious solitude. Even if bad weather was on the way it seemed to courteously await the setting of the sun; as soon as it dissolved into the horizon, the wind and the water would stir and the storm renew its approach.

That life seems a world away as we push into the secret regions of this land that never ends.

We have visited the outlying towns before but on this occasion, Macquarie tells me, we may find ourselves in regions where no European boot has left its print upon the earth. I am thrilled and a little fearful.

In the inner reaches of the waterway there are no natives fishing in their slim bark canoes; or none to be seen through a veil of light mist. With every few yards the mist lightens. Quite suddenly it lifts on the breeze, departing like a wraith.

A flock of white parrots blushed pink on the underside bursts with a ragged displeased screech from a stand of mangrove.

Something heavy — a turtle perhaps — drops into the water as we pass.

A little later there is a thunderous crash in the forest fringing a wooded island rising to a conical peak.

'Widow maker,' gasps the closest oarsman. Noticing my dumbfounded response, he takes another deep breath as he draws through the stroke.

'Eucalyptus limb.'

A heave at the oar. Another syllabic gasp.

'They ... break ...'

Heave.

'And fall ... from high ...'

Heave.

'Worse than ... bleedin' ... snakes.'

Heave.

'Beggin' ... pardon ... m'lady.'

The boat pulls into Parramatta — a fertile open place, neatly settled, the soil of the garden plots black, blue hills piling up behind, and all around a dewy green pastoral aspect that puts me in mind of home. Macquarie orders the oarsmen onto the pier ahead of us while he waits, out of some unspoken regimental protocol, until the slower boat carrying the Architect and the rest of the soldiers is almost upon us. It's then that he nods to the men on the pier. They extend their hands to us.

I take Macquarie's arm and we move quickly to the horses tethered beside the old Government House; they are a little unnerved by the clamour, I can tell even from this distance. Built in plain Georgian style, the building has been often used by Macquarie on his tours of the growing settlement.

The soldiers stand in groups, packs on the ground, inspecting their muskets, attaching bayonets, giving their sabres one more admiring inspection. The Architect, in an olive-green hunting coat, stands alone, hands behind his back, waiting for an invitation to join us.

The Governor calls to him and extends a welcoming arm.

'The journey upriver with the soldiers for company,' he says. 'It went well?'

'Nobody spoke, at least not to me. In your eyes, sir, I am a professional man. In theirs, I will ever be a criminal.'

'Rise above,' the Governor says blithely, gesturing to the house.

'What do you say?' he asks the Architect, who has fallen in beside him.

'A fine example of a building of its kind, Sir. But I think you would not disagree with me — a little ornament to set it apart? A neat portico is easily done.'

The three of us — I am on the Governor's arm while the Architect stands at his left — turn from the house to regard the river.

'And the journey — your impressions?'

'The harbour is very beautiful at its sea mouth, sir. Blue and wild. But the interior reaches here are a little ... estuarine for my tastes.'

'You'll get no argument from me,' says the Governor. 'But the land is poor by the harbour. If the colony is to ever feed itself, it will need to work this good dark loam. Observe how tall and straight the eucalypts grow on either side of the road inland.' He gestures towards the low blunt hills in the west.

'I picture — if I may — the colony many years from now,' says the Architect, casting a hand before him as if he were sowing seed. 'I see it ornamented with buildings the height of these woods — higher. Solid dwellings of five or six storeys. The heights pierced by towers, domes and cupolas. All of it in golden Port Jackson sandstone.'

Leaning across Macquarie to eye the Architect, I add with a spirited air, anxious that I be given a voice, 'The city — if it is ever to become a city — will house its people in dwellings of timber. Not everyone can afford a house of stone.'

'Ah, but madam,' he returns, eyes alive with the pleasure of the contest, 'if I may. Only the brick and the stone will be remembered.'

Stiffening a little, I put in, 'Surely the only polis built entirely for posterity is ... a *necropolis*.'

'Ah!' cries Macquarie, raising his hand like a circus master. 'A draw.'

And then, after a paternal nod at each adversary, 'Now time for a truce. Time also' — he mounts, a little creakily, his chestnut stallion — 'to be on our way.'

A young soldier comes forward with a grave expression, lays his shako on the ground and helps me into the saddle of a spotted grey mare. We strike up an easy canter along the well-kept road heading west towards the hills, slowing to a walk every few miles to spare the horses. The detachment divides into a forward and a rear group bookending us; the Architect, a little subdued, rides behind Macquarie and me. We are hemmed in by the vaulting forest and diminished, despite our numbers, by it. At least there is a mild autumn sun above — its light scattered by a webbing of white branches — and a reviving freshness on the air. The perfect season for such a journey.

The tall straight trees lining the road are stockinged with frayed bark. I know this species from a few poor specimens close to the town. Most of the large stands near the settlement were felled in the early years for building material or, worse still, firewood. If we had a stand of trees this size at Airds then legends would have gathered around them long ago: a Gaelic champion might have climbed one to reach the clouds and smite a fiery dragon. By my reckoning at least fifty cabers could be hewn from a single tree in this old forest. I stop, dismount, and go to the nearest trunk. I rub my palms across the husk-like ribbons, pick at a red bead of sap like a devil's tear. I pull at a strip of stringy-bark and slip it into a bag on the saddle: a memento of the journey.

The earliest chroniclers gazed on these eucalyptus forests and pictured a vast and featureless arboreal ocean. I was inclined, at first, to see the landscape with their eyes. I now wonder if there is anything more beautiful in Nature — more resilient, for it endures both fire and drought — than the sinuous white trunks of the eucalypts in the Domain, branches like twists of silver when struck by the morning sun. I wonder at times if, while other trees are raised from seedlings, these are not forged in foundries.

There are few of that species out here. But all the eucalypts share a common feature quite apart from their reviving scent: it is their foliage. Raised into the air by those sinuous branches, the slender leaves join in conversation with the breeze. This is what gives the single eucalyptus its lack of definition and the eucalyptus forest its air of anonymity: it is all of apiece.

* * *

The night is spent at a property spreading for miles from a timber farmhouse girdled by a wide cool verandah. The land around the homestead has been cleared, although blue-grey forest still cloaks the hilltops. Smoke rises from a red brick chimney. The farmhands curse and shout as they come in for their evening meal. There is the yapping of dogs and the bleating of sheep as they pour into holding pens placed close to the homestead from fear of the native dog — the dingo. The sun has been claimed by these hills by the time we arrive, and a delicious fading light falls around. The luminous sky and the shadowed land seem, for a short while, to have divorced from one another: it is as if they belong to different worlds. But then the light begins to drain from the sky, it joins the earth in shadow, and the world becomes one again.

Our host, a weathered old Scot named Ogilvy, is unlike the Governor in all respects save blood. His wife is a soft and shy Irish woman named Mary, who craves the shadows. Her long lashes beat nervously when we meet. She holds my gaze with an element of discomfort. I note something veiled — fear or shame — in her aspect.

We take tea on the verandah. A maid with a white cap, lean arms and a full upper lip over crowded teeth, brings the pot along with three fine china cups, a tart of apple and a few slices of orange cheese on a plate. She bears her tray towards a side table of roughly planed timbers. There is a tremble of thin muscle as she sets it down. Serving Macquarie first, she seems to falter, perhaps from trepidation, though on reflection the pot may simply have been too heavy for her. There — she pours too much. The brackish tea spills over the cup's lip. Ogilvy berates the girl harshly. His right hand is raised, his palm open, as if he means to strike.

'It is no matter,' I say sharply. I hold his gaze until he lowers his hand. 'The Governor much prefers his tea without milk,' I lie.

There is such severity in Ogilvy's manner towards the servants — and the assigned convicts here seem little more than slaves — that

I am left to wonder how he must treat them when no visitors are present to judge. And what of poor Mary?

We reach Spencertown the next day, a miserable string of shacks too far from the fertile land we had passed to ever amount to much. A few families have gathered in the main street to welcome us. The young men have sullenly combed their hair for the occasion; the girls, without caps or bonnets, have tamed their tresses with plaits or pigtails.

'The rest of the settlers,' explains a sallow man of some thirty years, whose frame disappears into a bulky coal-black coat, 'have sold their land to John Macarthur. The wool baron owns half the district. More. Well, the land is suited to sheep, even if the natives have taken a liking to them. But then the natives take a liking to us Christian folk, too. Poor Perceval Chambers took up kangaroo shooting for a sport.' He turns to spit but catches himself. 'The natives soon made *sport* of him. We reckon they took him for a poacher. We sent out a search party. They came back with his bloodied clothes. ... Would the Guv'nor like to see them — the clothes?'

'No thank you. No,' I put in quickly. I look to Macquarie. 'Thank you for the offer, though.'

The Governor's hand reaches into his pocket. There is a rustle of paper. Presently he retracts it without Robinson's ode, shakes some hands, and asks that the ceremony be abbreviated as we are pressed for time.

Macquarie lays the foundation stone in a small park hemmed by an irregular picket fence, beside a low timber building with a thatched roof and a tattered flag hanging limply from a freshly painted pole. Afterwards the townsfolk join us in a rendition of 'God Save the King', their voices adding very little weight or depth to our own. We take tea in the shack flying the flag — its interior neat and tidy though very cramped — as the sallow man, whose name is John Few, and a gathering of thin and large-eyed townsfolk address us, not on the subject of the town's civic needs but its fears.

'A small detachment of men such as these,' Few implores, motioning to the soldiers waiting outside.

'I will give it due consideration,' says the Governor kindly.

'P'raps a small fort?' He pauses, licks his lips and goes on excitedly. 'Muskets.'

'Make a case and send it to me,' says Macquarie. He rises to leave and stoops to pass beneath the door.

It would take a civic imagination far more capacious than the Architect's to picture anything grand enough in this town's future to warrant the dignity of good design. I fear it will ever be a stepping-stone to somewhere else. When I voice this opinion to the Governor on the return journey he is not irked, not at all.

He rests a hand on the pommel and pivots in his saddle to ensure there are none within earshot. 'It sounded very fine as a proclamation, and was named, after all, for one of the few honest politicians of the age,' he says a little wearily. 'It looked even finer on a map of the district. But I agree it will take more than walls of sandstone and roofs of slate to entice settlers to venture this far from the protection of the main town.'

Soon afterwards he rides back to the head of the detachment and remains there, encircled by a few red coats topped with shakos. The soldiers turn now and then, like stiff puppets, to converse with one another. But the Governor seems aloof from their talk and somewhat lost: an ageing man with his disappointments. My husband.

It is a slow and dispiriting trek back to Parramatta. Sitting astride the saddle for this length of time, my legs tire and stiffen. Around mid-afternoon the party draws to a halt — there is a commotion of some kind ahead. Riders go forward to speak with two native men, almost entirely naked. They stand with spears and shields by their sides. Both men — an elder with wavy white hair and long beard and a young man with a plaited band around his crown — gesticulate with great animation in the direction we are heading.

They keep their voices low. Whatever they have to say, it is enacted rather than spoken.

When we set off again I spot a haze of flies hovering above a blackened mass in the long yellow grass to my left. A rancid stench hangs on the still air. My horse, unnerved, whinnies and breaks stride.

We are hardly an inconspicuous target — a slow-moving caravan, brightly coloured and elaborately dressed. At any moment, I imagine, a shower of spears might land in our midst. A soldier brandishing a musket while facing a native with a barbed spear or hunting stick has the clear advantage, though surprise will even the odds. I do not like our chances in the event of a spirited attack of the kind visited upon our soldiers in the American war by screaming Iroquois.

A mile or so further on we take a branch of the road. We cling to it for the remainder of the day, climbing into the foothills of a low range with a view over the plain below. The path is narrow, freshly cut but already furred with new foliage. The troops are wary. In the piercing silence I sense their fear.

Macquarie, with a redcoat on each side, falls back to join me.

'There is something afoot,' I say.

He raises a finger to his mouth.

We ride on slowly.

As dusk settles we reach the outskirts of the town. The spirits of the entire party rise at the sight of humble brick cottages held together with mortar of ground oyster — quite as reassuring, in the circumstances, as a Crusader fortress girded with a battlement six feet thick. There is much talk among the soldiers as we dismount and walk on beside the horses. That night Macquarie instructs the publican of a small hotel beside the river to serve the soldiers liberally from his cellars. For a while there is song. But then — and this is a surprise, as I had anticipated more revelry — that other great source of solace, sleep, falls upon them. Fear, after all, is a kind of energy, and these men are spent.

I learn from Macquarie that the two natives, members of a group quite reconciled to the colony, had come out to warn us of an ambush, or the threat of one, if we continued on that path. They joined us at a place where a longer route, though a safer one, cleaves from the main road.

'We have been fortunate indeed,' he says, lying in the dark yet quite alert with his troubles. 'The colony, too. If I had been killed or injured — or you, or indeed any of the party — there would have been nothing for it but to retaliate with a force not yet seen in this place.' I turn to my side, place a hand upon his chest, his strong heart. He places his own hand over mine. 'I fear we are,' he goes on, 'at war. And our instruments are but two: force and favour. There were already plans to reward this pacified group, but we will make a rare show of it now.'

The next day is a Saturday and at a small lozenge of cleared land in the centre of Parramatta the tribes gather by mid-morning. The natives seat themselves in a large circle. At the front of each group are the elders, propped up apprehensively on plain timber chairs as if they distrust them. In the centre is a table like a catafalque bearing a carcass of roast beef, the head of the beast still attached. Around it potatoes and bread rolls pile up in pale mounds. Encircling the feast are ten or twelve large bowls brimming — I catch the sweet, heady scent of it — with rum punch. The natives, doubtless bewildered by our use of the same word for an alcoholic beverage and a blow to the head, have their own word for punch: bull.

Before the feasting begins Macquarie and I stroll into the circle. A great cry goes up. Standing beside the table, he plunges his hand into a deep rattan basket and brings out a glinting half-moon plate of engraved brass. Like a Magus or an Inca high priest, Macquarie holds the first bronze piece up to the sky. It catches the sun.

'Whhhooahh,' booms a collective cry, bending the air.

The natives come forward to receive their breastplates. A soldier helps them to clasp the shining disks around their necks with a heavy bronze chain. They return to their places touching, caressing the trinkets, tilting them this way and that to catch the sun. The two men encountered on the road yesterday — the white-haired elder and the young man with the plaited band — step forward to receive their gifts. To think that loyalty can be purchased for such a pittance. Can it?

When the ceremony is over a group of Aboriginal children in white smocks, supervised by a tall, thin native with a beard neatly trimmed in the European manner, stands angelically before the gathering. Two of them recite the words of Psalm Eight: 'O Lord, our Lord ... how excellent is thy name ... in all the Earth! Who has ... set ... thy glory above the heavens.' The other children mouth the verses. All hold Bibles.

A young woman in a voluminous lime-green gown leaps up and shouts, 'Governor, that one — my pickaninny — she read better than them settlers.'

There is a burst of laughter from the natives, the watching soldiers, and Macquarie, who places his hands on his hips and rocks back. He stays in that pose for just a second longer than is necessary, staring up at the blank sky. The young woman, a trifle embarrassed, returns to her seat on the ground, tucking her long legs beneath her.

That evening, as the festivities roll on, the dancing begins. Feet pound the earth, hands slap thighs, ceremonial sticks go *click, click, click,* as if cutting up time, and in great surges of choral song I catch cries like bird call, shrieks and ecstatic cheers.

I ask the Architect if I might view the sketch he is making in Lycett's absence. Macquarie stands in the exact centre of the composition, holding one of his brass crescents to the sky, while the natives, gathered around, gaze at this object of veneration wide-eyed.

'But tell me, where is Bungaree in all of this?' I ask. 'Surely the man who is said to be King of the Natives would not allow himself to be absent.'

'I've put that question myself. He was last seen on a grassed strip above the beach at Middle Head, a large fish roasting on a fire and his women gathered around. He was not, I think, invited to this ceremony. He is loved by the Governor and by his own tribe. But that love is not spread widely. It does not seem to extend out here.'

We share a look of regret. He turns to me and shrugs. His green eyes are restless. I let him return to the work that calls him. Calls him, always. I retire to my room alone as the Governor feasts with his men. I sit on the corner of the bed in my nightgown, open the window to the sounds of the ceremony, and my thoughts drift to the absent Bungaree. He has become a ferryman, threading his way between two cultures, in neither one entirely at home. I wonder if I am not becoming, in my own way, a little like him — divided, distanced, unsettled.

CHAPTER FOURTEEN

A month later the Architect sends word that he desires an urgent appointment. Hawkins brings me his letter in the garden, walking across the lawn as if it were a sponge. He presents it on a silver tray, unopened. The gesture, I believe, is intended ironically, as the letter is from a convict; there is no need for such a formality. 'Delivered it himself, says it cannot wait.' Hawkins flexes an eyebrow. I remove my gardening gloves and open the envelope:

Dear Mrs Macquarie,
You may have been apprised of my journey north to the
Hunter Valley shortly after our return from the interior.
The Governor requested that I visit in order to survey the
town of Newcastle and plan a suitable port at the Hunter
River's mouth. In the process a fanciful notion suggested
itself to me: that the island called Nobbys standing barely
a hundred yards from the mainland be joined to it by a
bridge, and the highest point of Nobbys Island be crowned
by a lighthouse in the form of a Chinese pagoda. I picture
a procession of eaves — nine storeys in all — curling

gracefully upwards like the petals of the lotus flower. Why,
Nanjing built herself a Temple of Gratitude from gaily
coloured tiles. We are closer to Nanjing than London so let
us ship a thousand glazed bricks of white and blue!!!

I own that it is a fanciful notion. But I am convinced
it has appeal. I would dearly love to show you a sketch.
A belief in the power of architecture to raise the spirits,
enrich the impoverished; this is surely an interest that we
three share. I have an appointment with the Governor this
evening and would welcome an opportunity to meet with
you beforehand.

I re-read the letter with an eye to hidden, double — multiple —
interpretations. Certainly he means to share something of his
whimsy, and in doing so he risks censure. Why, I might laugh in
his face. But he knows that I will not. He calculates that I will be
receptive to his picturesque scheme and he means to make an ally of
me. But it is also an advance, if I'm not mistaken, and very subtle —
a sharing of his deeper self, his true self. I am certain that Byron
won hearts with the self-same stratagem — by spinning a web of
fancy with which to entrap those of a fanciful disposition. Ah, but
perhaps I study the words too keenly. His intention may be entirely
innocent and transparent and he may be simply writing to say he has
conceived of a Chinese pagoda at the town of Newcastle and would
like to have it built: nothing more. I caution myself not to involve
more of myself than is necessary.

I tell Hawkins to make time for a late afternoon interview
and request, as the weather is fine, that he prepare tea and cakes
to be taken beneath the towering Norfolk pine that stands sentinel
between the residence and the harbour.

The autumn sun has lost its heat by the time he arrives and we have a good hour before it dips below Observatory Hill. I hear him come briskly along the sandy path from the gate and turn, shading my eyes. The Architect wears his favourite tailcoat of burgundy velvet and loose cream trousers, but he has of late acquired, I observe, a pair of leather riding boots. I swear that transportation has not lowered his spirits in the slightest. It may be best described, in his particular case, as transplantation.

He carries with him the folio of sketches he is rarely seen without and a copy of an old leather volume. He takes a seat opposite me, rests the folio on his knee and the book upon the folio. I reach for the book as if to snatch it away, then pause, ashamed at my own impetuosity. He hands it to me with an indulgent smile.

'You know I crave a good romance,' I say, opening the supple leather cover.

'I'm afraid you will find no romance here. But you *will* find edification.'

I leaf through pages and pages of architectural diagrams. Before my eyes float floor plans and elevations of harmonious villas with pedimented temple fronts, rotundas capped by broad bosomy domes, grand loggias, statues of the gods and the graces. And, most of all — columns. Columns of every kind.

'Captivating,' I say. 'Though rather technical. My husband would feast upon it.'

'Palladio, the author, was an architect from northern Italy,' he replies.

I incline my head to show he has my full attention and he goes on: 'Equally well schooled, he was, in the architecture of Greece and Rome. And though he died more than two hundred years ago, his treatise on architecture is a treasury for one in my profession.

It came with me on the *Dromedary* and I promised the Governor I would show it to him at our meeting. To explain ...'

'A sort of pattern book and architectural bible combined?'

'If you like.' He shrugs.

While I spent my hours aboard the *Dromedary* reading about the New World, it seems the Architect was dreaming of the Old.

I offer him a seat, pour a cup of tea and pass a china plate with a fat wedge of crumbling lemon cake.

In the time it takes to pour and proffer he has grown impatient. The foot of one leg, draped over the other, bounces up and down, then oscillates from side to side. It puts me in mind of a river otter beating the water with webbed feet.

'There is something I would like to say,' he begins abruptly, looking down at his tightly clasped hands. 'Something about our earlier — our rather heated — exchange. You remember?'

'How could I forget?' I stiffen a little at the memory. It is not that I recall it as a fierce affray, but rather more that it presaged the obscure events of that short journey inland: the towering forest, the scent of fear, the native chant, the bewitching of the breastplate ceremony. 'But surely,' I go on, 'we are quite reconciled.'

'At least it is my hope,' he lays a hand upon his heart. 'I have been thinking about the issue at stake. You know I believe we were *both* right. An architect must build for eternity. But then a city is more than the sum of its monuments.'

'My point — the reason I felt provoked — is that, how to put it ...?' I rise from the chair, take a few steps towards the harbour, and wend my way back to my seat bearing the thread of a thought. 'My point is that a little stone bridge over a country rill can rival in beauty a mansion on a manicured estate. Wooden cottages with thriving gardens would make happy homes for hundreds —

thousands — of colonists. Architecture, it seems to me, is not only for the buildings to which we raise our eyes. The simple things for simple people are as worthy of your graceful designs as the memorials to future generations.'

He looks at me open-mouthed for a second or two before extending a hand. 'I am in perfect agreement,' he says. 'But I cannot pretend that I am deeply interested in the stone bridge or the wooden cottage when there is ...,' he turns to his folio and takes out a drawing, 'a Chinese pagoda for your consideration.'

Having politely ignored the offer to shake his hand I take, instead, his drawing.

'I don't suppose your friend Palladio was any help with this,' I say.

'None at all.' He shakes his mane — honestly, the man possesses a more attractive head of hair than most women in the colony. 'The model is William Chambers' nine-storey pagoda at Kew. It is a curiosity and a marvel. There is not a prideful Londoner who will not, on a spring day, suggest a visit to the gardens to view it.' He leans forward a little and taps his temple with his finger. 'Chambers' design — committed to memory.'

I have some bold notions of my own, I confess. I have raised them with the Governor but they, in truth, require some elaboration on paper before they can be taken seriously. I propose an exchange: I will support his scheme for a Chinese pagoda and in return he must pledge to speak on behalf of *my* designs.

He gives a volley of sharp, eager nods.

'Firstly, the Government House on the rise behind us' — I incline my head backwards as if following the path of a bird overhead — 'is as humble as ... this lemon cake. It is perhaps the best that could be done in the circumstances, with the available ingredients. It is plain.

It serves a purpose. But it is at the same time a little dull. And,' I prod the cake with the tip of the knife, 'see how it disintegrates.'

He smiles rather mischievously. 'It has been made poorly, then, by a country cook. You are in need, I think, of a professional.'

'As a matter of fact, I made the cake myself.' I throw his mischief back at him.

He coughs. I go on.

'I am warming to a point that is every bit as daring as your oriental pagoda. Could you, if given an hour or so, draw up a ground plan of a handsome and castellated residence for the Governor and me? Something built of stone — the best stone that can be procured. The residence has grown to answer the needs and the tastes of the four governors before us. It has no unity. It should be done again — harmoniously. The form of the new house, and the disposition of the rooms, will of course be left entirely to your own taste and judgement.'

He rears up a little, blinking rapidly with incomprehension. 'You say castellated? But I thought it was a cottage with a garden not a castle in an estate that you wanted.'

'Yes, yes,' I say impatiently. 'But I am talking about Government House, the heart of the colony. Surely you cannot object? To echo it, a Gothic fort at Bennelong Point. Then a handsome stable for the Governor's horses, carriages and stable hands, this also castellated and built of brick. We will fashion a romantic waterside precinct from Dawes Point to the Domain, where Nature will show her charms. When seen from the north shore the castellations and fortifications on their harbourside foreground will recall ... I dare not say it.'

'Please. You must.'

'Castle Stalker at Appin. A Campbell stronghold for a time.'

The next half hour is spent in a spirit of mutual congratulation as these bare ideas are fleshed, dressed and paraded before our eyes.

I find myself confiding to the Architect that Macquarie, when young, read many romantic histories about Alexander of Macedon marching to India, and Caesar conquering Gaul: great men who would let no mountain, no cataract, no force of arms, stand in their way.

'Well, his is a personality of comparable force,' the Architect offers with his hand raised to shield himself from the sun's last rays. 'He will not easily let Whitehall stand in the way of his improvements.'

It's then that I notice the true colour of his eyes: the silver-green of eucalyptus leaf.

'If you were to build one great — truly great — building in this country, what would it be?' I inquire. 'What drift would your ambition take?'

He shoots me a look of surprise, beams, tucks in his chin and cocks his head, as if to say, 'Here, now, is a chance to shine.'

After a contemplative pause comes the reply. 'Some measure the greatness of a thing by its size. The Colosseum — I know it only by drawings — is a wonder. But consider its purpose and the want of taste. We are not so very different, you and I. For myself I would prefer a summer house, elegant and simple, its ornament classical, and a garden all around: Mankind and Nature in harmony. Or a pergola to shade you from the sun at the place you like to read.'

Of course it is generally known that I have made the promontory between Farm Cove and Woolloomooloo into a sanctuary. But it is pleasing to me that I have been seen enjoying my solitude by this man. Am I often in his thoughts?

'There is already a natural pergola in the form of a spreading fig tree,' I say. 'I would much prefer a chair of my own beneath it.'

'Very well then. I shall chisel a seat from the weathered sandstone at the harbour's edge. And I shall happily carve an inscription at its base: "Mrs Macquarie's Chair." It would be an honour.' I feel a flush of warmth rising to my cheeks.

'You would ... you would undertake such labour to please me?'

'Why should I not? I spend my waking hours with measurements, proportions and designs. I have never lost my fondness for stone and the working of it.'

That the hands of this man, together with a few tools, could compel such an obdurate thing as stone to submit to his designs for a shaded seat beside the harbour! It is as if he has offered to domesticate a wild beast so that it could sit serenely at my side. I am moved by the ambition of it.

The last light fades from the western sky behind the observatory as Hawkins, with his strangely buoyant gait, comes towards us across the lawn bearing a tray to retrieve the tea and cake. 'It is time I went in,' I say to the Architect. 'And time, I believe, for your interview.'

'Do you know, I almost forgot,' he says brightly. 'I have been so swept away with our schemes.' He rises and smacks his coat and trousers to dislodge any fallen crumbs.

'You will not forget the pagoda,' he says with an imploring air.

'If you promise to remember the stables,' I return.

I watch him walk to the house, skip up the flight of steps and stride briskly along the verandah towards Macquarie's office, brightly lit with candelabras in preparation for the meeting. The clear autumn night falls, like a stone, from the sky.

When I recall that meeting in fading light beneath the Norfolk pine, I consider it the moment when things between the three of us stood firmly in a state of order and balance. The accord held for some time. But its terms — they would change.

* * *

Much later I realised that the Architect had circled around my question about his ideal edifice. He did eventually answer it in the most delightful manner possible: with a dream preserved in the aspic of art, not of one ideal building but many.

It is a panorama sketched in pen and ink for depth, detail and volume, and brought to life with gouache. The preliminary sketch may have been completed in the months after our journey inland, but the painting was finished only later, when he was very much alone, and I was lonely without him. His plans were outpaced by events and it was in the end not so much presented as left for me to discover.

I packed the work away with the other canvases and mementos for the journey home. And then, some months after Macquarie's death, I had it mounted and framed. For a few months it was in the dining room. A few months later it migrated to the hallway. It hangs now above the walnut bureau in my bedchamber. A little like the Architect, it has worked its way towards my heart.

A cobalt blue sea as placid as sleep reaches out to a shoreline, and above the pale cuticle of beach springs a wall of forest, lightly leaved, woven with structures from every age and place. An octagonal rotunda with a grey-green tiled roof stands in the foreground. On a promontory to one side sits a sturdy castle of Norman inspiration, as squat as a loaf of bread. A slender Ottoman minaret pierces the tree canopy as if launching itself into the pale air. A gleaming vermilion pagoda, nine tiers of uptilted eaves, never built though fondly imagined, commands a crescent-like bay. There is even a red and white striped lighthouse: a column free of ornament flanked at its base by a seaside pavilion with a shell-like dome on each side. The drawing bears a title, *New World*, written in the Architect's hand.

CHAPTER FIFTEEN

So the priest requires the words for the inscription on Macquarie's tomb; would that he had loaned me a church candle two feet high for this solemn vigil. Another hour and the flickering candles on either side of my desk will need replacing. I pray that the English butler has not departed with my box of spares. I swivel in my chair, yawn and rise. It is no easy thing, this conjuring act. I am in dire need of a tonic. There is not a soul to disturb or wake, but still I go quietly down the hall. I wrap myself in my shawl and rub my hands: even on summer nights the house is chilly and when the northerly wind is up, as it is tonight, it can be bleak.

At the kitchen stove I stir the embers, stoke the fire and fill the kettle. While I wait for it to boil I turn to the windows. There is little light in my bedchamber, sheltered as it is by the woods, but on this west-facing corner of the house the windows glow a cold steely blue. The long Hebridean winter nights, like sheets of black ice, have melted away and for a good three months in midsummer the glorious days are in full bloom. Between midnight and dawn a deep, and deepening, twilight settles over land, loch and sea. But it is not the kind of light that will illuminate a page on a bureau in a cold house enfolded by a forest in full leaf.

I place the teapot and cup on the rickety tray — a guttering candle too — and return to my room. The tea will sharpen my wits. But is that all I need? I require something else for these reveries to serve their purpose: I need also to *feel*.

In the kitchen I take down from a cupboard a bottle of whisky. The footman deceives himself into thinking it hidden. I pour, add some clear cold water, and taste. A little stronger perhaps. I add a few more drops of spirit. This is something I would not have done in my former life: a cup of tea and a glass of whisky in hot pursuit.

I sit down again to write of Macquarie, though not of him alone. I write that I might know my heart before my heart is called upon again.

I am a child of this turbulent age and I believe I grasp its laws — its lessons. Permit miseries to multiply and insurrection will surely follow. Hard upon the heels of bloody insurrection comes revolution; pressing close is the hell of war. Peace, when war's infernal energies are spent, comes as a blessing. But the moment of calm is short lived, for misery deepens when there is not food enough to feed the returning soldiers, and the cycle begins again.

Here there is clearing in the Highlands — the Hebrides, too — and despair in the smoke-stained towns. Great forces are at work, for good and ill. I am no meek observer of this restive world, surveying its drama from some lofty turret. I am it, and it is me. Driven by a thirst for adventure I married an adventurer and left with him for the end of the Earth. I returned home amid insult and indignity and in my arms I nursed a defeated — a dying — man. The bright promise and the blemished end: how it smarts! I have, at least, *survived* the great convulsions of the age. And while I have this past year been assailed by melancholic thoughts, creeping upon me like a lowland mist, my spirit has been strong. Often, craving the company of better times, I call upon my memories. I am like a circus performer with a brassy cry: 'Come! Roll up!' I put up my makeshift stage, take out my magic tricks and my castanets, and gather them in.

I am aided by my treasury of memorabilia. Not every memento is an ageing sheet of paper inked by quill or type. Since Macquarie's death I have had views of the harbour, and one rather brooding portrait of Bungaree, framed in town regardless of the expense. In a drawer of the bureau I keep a preserved lyrebird feather, fragile and delicately fanned; a dried rock lily, luminous yellow when plucked from its nest of green; a convict-made teaspoon stamped with the image of a kangaroo; and a brittle shred of stringy-bark stripped from that giant on the day we rode to Spencertown. I consider this private archive a shrine to the muse of memory. It is my Antipodean museum.

Here, then, is a copy of the *Sydney Gazette* from 1816, bearing a most important proclamation arrayed in three ragged columns beneath the paper's motto, *Thus We Hope to Prosper.* George Howe, the printer and publisher, was a large balding man with a high dome, a long jaw and a determined set of the mouth — he laughed without smiling and only ever smiled with his eyes — and a lean, powerful and determined walk. Mrs Ovens, if she knew he was expected at the residence, would declare that 'the shark' was calling by, and when asked to explain that marine moniker said the publisher's blank expression had suggested it to her. But I did wonder if there was another reason — Howe was rumoured to have a number of attachments around the town. The publisher, who had worked for *The Times*, had been transported for shoplifting. Once in the colony he had quickly earned a ticket of leave — his skills as a journalist and printer were invaluable — and he had been a free man for several years when first we met.

The little *Gazette*'s motto, printed on the masthead, hemmed an idealised woodcut of the Cove as Howe had imagined it on that March day in 1803 when he published his first edition. Ovoid in shape, it was much like a locket, and very pretty. In it a windmill, a keep and a citadel of some kind were etched against an empty sky. Picks and spades were strewn across the ground. On the right a farmer and oxen ploughed a field. On the left an imperious woman, in attitude a deity or an empress, was seated on pillowed bales of wool just as Britannia is envisioned upon her throne. Above her fluttered the flag of a ship at anchor. All in all, a remarkable vision for a colony in its infancy.

The charm of the *Gazette*'s woodcut is not the sole reason I keep a copy of the brittle paper, its surface foxed with age. It is the announcement that earns this fragment a place in my affections. For all but a few it will seem a piece of history; for me it is much more. It begins: 'His Excellency the Governor today unveils the Lighthouse at South Head, to be named Macquarie Tower.'

The words swim a little before my eyes, as if spied through another woman's reading glasses. I take a kerchief. I go on.

The edifice of handsome stone blocks, already a proud feature of the landscape, rises 65 feet from a wide rectangular base designed to house a small detachment. In time four cannon will join them. The lantern with revolving light atop the tower is in readiness for today's ceremony, to commence with the approach of night. Notice is hereby given that the light will be exhibited on each succeeding evening to aid vessels approaching the coast. It will be seen at an immense distance, and be an object handsome to behold from the Town of Sydney. The expense of raising the edifice will be defrayed by a charge, administered by Captain John Piper, on ships and vessels entering the harbour of Port Jackson.

The colony's poet laureate, Michael Massey Robinson, has composed an ode to the lighthouse:

> *And yon tall tow'r, that with aspiring steep,*
> *Rears its proud summit o'er the trackless deep;*
> *The recent care of his paternal hand*
> *That long has cherished this improving land;*
> *Thro' the drear perils of the starless night*
> *Shall shed the lustre of revolving light.*

As I read this proud proclamation, lightened by Robinson's verse, I picture Macquarie at his study, head bent over a sheet of paper. His hand moves rapidly in a pool of lamplight, the goose quill fluttering as if filled with the life that long ago left it.

Howe was a force of a man. The type he used to print his weekly gazette had come out with Arthur Phillip on the First Fleet. The travails of distance meant constant shortages of paper and ink. Howe and his readers were forced to adapt when a thief made off with a pound of type thinking it was of value simply because it shone like silver when cleaned. Replacement letters were carved of wood.

I recall the printer sitting opposite Macquarie that night, his long jaw cupped in his hands, one bent leg laid crossways over the other, quivering with coiled unspent energy. I caught the rasp of inked quill on paper. 'There,' said Macquarie, leaning back in his chair. 'It is done.'

The hour was late. A westerly wind, cold and thin, sent its probing shafts into the rambling house.

'Elizabeth,' Macquarie called out in a grainy voice as Howe looked up, sensing my presence at the door. 'The lighthouse. Announcement tomorrow. Am I well served by this?' He held out the paper. 'Does it round the thing out nicely — point firmly enough to the future?' He beamed with pride.

I return my eyes now to the desiccated sheet, for the words printed by Howe were those Macquarie showed me that evening:

> With the successful construction of Macquarie Tower our efforts will be harnessed to the completion of an ambitious building program designed to raise this settlement into a town the equal of any in the Empire.
>
> Work begins on a new convict hospital funded by three of the colony's most prominent citizens in exchange for a monopoly on rum imports. A male barrack at Hyde Park will follow; and a female barrack at Parramatta; in time there will be additions to Government House and a Botanical Garden beside it in the Domain; in the town itself street widening and alignment; a parsonage for the Reverend Marsden; new fortifications on Windmill Hill; an obelisk to record the distances to the main towns; a turnpike gate in Gothic style to mark the southern end of the township. The colony of Port Jackson henceforth becomes the City of Sydney.

It was a fine moment for the Architect, who was granted his conditional freedom with the completion of the lighthouse. It was also a landmark event for the Governor and the first of his many prideful marks on that largely unsullied landscape. His tormentors would later scorn the edifices, monuments, parks, towns and natural features Macquarie named after himself, believing it to be a gesture of supreme egotism. And yet it was not his own name that the Governor sought to glorify, preserve and aggrandise, but that of his diminished clan. A poor line now, the Macquaries of Mull — of that I am well aware.

The Hebrides seemed a dream to me on the days when I would sit beneath a twisting fig tree and watch the natives fishing. And how powerfully strange the natives and the fig trees seem to me now.

Nature's eccentric Antipodean garb has been studied from the time of Banks; and doubtless there are explorers of other nations — the Portuguese, Spanish, Dutch — who found it equally beguiling. But I sometimes wonder if the citizens of Jackson had not begun to dress themselves in the exotic colours of their curious abode. The skies at sunset swelled with the quarrels of those stiff-winged parakeets, the chuckling kookaburras, and the chattering bats; the folk of Sydney Town, raised on this cacophony, had become equally raucous. A native king dressed himself as an admiral in His Majesty's navy. His queen took the whimsical name of Gooseberry: would that Shakespeare had thought of it for his *Midsummer* comedy. The kangaroo is a kind of biological improbability. The crimes committed at the Cove were equally fantastic: convicts had been known to band together, commandeer a vessel and set sail for Batavia, never to be seen again. Others simply melted into the bush, lived for years with the natives and stumbled back into the settlement having lost possession of their wits. Then there was the story of Polly Barker, which ran in a single column on the front page of the *Gazette* on the same day as the proclamation of the lighthouse. No ordinary crime for her. The story read:

A self-confessed 'priestess of Venus', rumoured to have been a tambourine girl in a fairground before conversion to her religion, Miss Barker worked as a hostess at an establishment of The Rocks known as The Fallen Angel. Following her trial the *Gazette* can now reveal the facts.

Miss Barker had separated half a dozen drunken young men from their lives — and their savings — after luring them into a blind corner of The Rocks beyond closing hours.

There, in dark alleys filled with the smell of rum and the din of inebriation, she bludgeoned her victims with a stocking filled with stones (a near perfect murder weapon as it was, when emptied of detritus, returned to its former place on her oft-glimpsed thigh).

When finally apprehended she confessed all. Last week she strode to the gallows with head held high like Zenobia of Palmyra. She boasted to a cellmate that she saw life — hers and that of her victims — as a table game. She would win for a time, and enjoy her takings to the full, in the sure knowledge that she would eventually lose all. Let her short life be a lesson: there are NO WINNERS at the game of crime.

I wonder if Howe enjoyed this wicked juxtaposition: the fantastical tale of Polly Barker's crime and punishment, and the solemnity of Macquarie's proud moment.

If not for his crime, George Howe would have had the teeming city of London as his beat and its coffee houses for his amusement, but he would not in a lifetime have written the small item I have before me if he had not been banished to the Cove. The column below the masthead was given over to Government & General Orders, followed by Arrivals & Departures at the Cove, and below this lengthy catalogue of comings and goings ran a small advertisement for a spelling book — Howe was relentless in his campaign for better literacy. But the next column along, which I re-read now with undiminished wonder, recalls a sight that I, sitting on my stone seat, had also been privileged to witness:

This afternoon a flight of black swans from the southward, 40 in number, passed over Sydney in a direction for the ponds about Broken Bay. When over the channel that separates Dawes' Point from the North Shore, they divided themselves into two distinct bodies, and went off at angles, the one bearing N.N.W. & the other N.N.E. In their progress they were mostly in a line with each other; and from their size and number, formed one of the most pleasing spectacles of the kind that could be possibly imagined.

Nor did Howe restrict himself to reports of crimes, deaths by misadventure and world news — not so much a record of fresh happenings as a narrative of the events of the past decade. As the Governor's ally — it was the Government, after all, that paid his rent and kept him in ink — Howe sprang to Macquarie's defence in his occasional column of opinion, titled Pasquinade. This item, printed in the last year of our time in the colony, I have kept:

Without doubt much human misery could have been avoided if Britain was ruled by one such as our Governor. Instead it is led by a vicious conservative. Robert Jenkinson, 2nd Earl of Liverpool, is known far and wide as the butcher of the poor and the strangler of free speech. Hungry men and women at Tranent and Peterloo were cut down by Jenkinson's hussars and dragoons because they dared to gather in protest. The Governor of New South Wales, in contrast, works tirelessly to raise hungry men and women up in the world.

This provocation, like all the rest, was signed 'Pasquino'. But the identity of its author was an open secret in the colony.

Ah, my memories — how they run on!

By the end of our time in Sydney, the Governor could list two hundred public works he had commissioned and built. He established towns, fostered the arts, sponsored the first expedition across the Blue Mountains. I know, for I remember the scorching hot morning when he drew up a defence of his record and bound it with a blood red ribbon. But now it is gone; lost in the chaos of our transportation home, his decline — and his death.

I am determined that none of this shall be forgotten. And yet I am equally determined that some parts of this story shall be known to me alone.

CHAPTER SIXTEEN

I play a sarabande on my viola in the pure air of a Sydney spring morning. The sky is perfectly clear and hard, seeming so close that if I leap up I could touch it, returning to Earth with fingertips stained blue.

I play as I wait for the Architect with his folio of designs and his birl of ideas: a new formulation, or a caprice on an old one, every hour. The stately dance is for him; a gift of mine in return for his to me. He has been as good as his word. My promised chair is now complete. Rather more bench than chair, it requires a few cushions for perfect comfort, though nothing more than that. Commanding a fine view of the harbour, my retreat is shaded by a fig tree twisting into a parasol of dense dark leaves, some of which turn persimmon yellow in dry weather. I am not particularly desirous of company at this place. I entertain only notions there. And I read. Each time I raise my eyes from a book I am assailed by the beauty of my surroundings. And to think, this is a prison!

The Architect — and he alone — would be welcome company out there for he sees things much as I see them, or seems to. Unless he is a parrot habituated to mimicry, or a bounder skilled in the art of seduction, I read him as a man with a similar cast of mind to my own.

The sarabande will please him. I cannot imagine he would relish a piece of music that is not an invitation to dance. For he is apt to set things in motion.

Macquarie is in the dining room enjoying the morning sun and a view across Farm Cove as he takes tea with John Piper, whose position as naval officer permits him to collect excise. The taxation on visiting vessels, and the various goods contained therein — most especially those of a spirituous nature — funds the building and ornamentation of Sydney Town. Piper grows in importance, and he grows in wealth. I catch great gusts of his laughter over the lush chords of my viola.

The Captain's mighty guffaw, likely prompted by one of his bawdy jests, has barely subsided when I hear a knock. There is Hawkins' steady voice, followed by the creaking of floorboards. It surely is the Architect; he has arrived at the appointed time. A firm rap — in this colony the servants do nothing gently! — and the door to the study is eased open. The Architect steps forward with an easy roll to his stride; he is a regular enough visitor to enter without introduction. Does he pull the hair from his collar and shake it out before stepping forward? I believe he does.

As I continue playing I incline my head towards the midnight blue chair that I had placed here in expectation of his visit. He sits.

'The Governor will be some time yet it seems,' he says in a low vibrato as I play on.

I feel myself swaying to the jaunty tune. He taps his feet — I note a pair of buckled shoes at the end of his nankeen trousers. Surely, these adornments tell me, the Governor is not his only patron.

When I finish he rises, offering a flutter of light claps and a broad well-fed smile.

'What would you most like to hear?' I ask.

'I'm not learned in music,' he concedes. 'It was not a feature of my upbringing. I am from a family of builders, not a brood of players. I very much like what I have just heard. Something with a measured spring in its step.' He gives a little show to his words, throwing out his arms and shuffling his well-shod feet.

'May I suggest, your step having been suitably sprung, that we enjoy a stroll? It is a beautiful day.'

'I shall leave these designs then — your ideas for a new Government House and castellated stable. Shall I? Plans for the fort at Bennelong Point — they progress. But slowly. It is no easy thing to build an octagonal tower with ten embrasures and chambers for the twenty-four-pounders that will, at the same time, keep the powder dry so close to the shore.' He takes in a deep breath and exhales noisily. 'The more picturesque the structure — the less likely it will serve the purpose for which it has been designed.'

'But this is already splendid news!' I rub my hands together. 'No need to rush things. Leave these completed designs on the corner of the desk in the study. If a servant stops you, say that I permit it. Macquarie will notice them when he comes in.'

We take the path down to the harbourside fringe of the Domain. The first governors sculpted this botanical sanctuary out of dense bush and writhing ficus on the southeastern foreshore. Convict labour has been used to clear the gentle folds between two ridges of squat headlands raised above the harbour. I have made my own improvements: a bright green lawn; an ornamental lake like a melted coin; emus and kangaroos, black swans and lyrebirds; a botanical garden of native and introduced species.

Together we stroll down the gentle slope towards Farm Cove. All around us the wattle is in bloom, like a scattering of sunlight given mass and form.

We continue along the fringe of the harbour to which my predecessors gave the name Port Jackson. 'Jackson,' I offer in a peppery tone. 'It has such a sweeping, unparticular ring to it, don't you think? Why it could be at any corner of the Empire! Anywhere the Jack has been planted. How terribly lacking in romance. In imagination.'

'Can you think of a better name?'

'I could think of a hundred, though I might take Bungaree's advice on the most appropriate. If, that is, his advice can be relied upon. It is so very hard to tell when they do not write their place names down. I suspect the very idea of a place is foreign to them. They tell stories about places and how they came to be, but I wonder sometimes if the stories *are* the places — if you follow.'

'I'm not *entirely* sure I do.'

He presses those broad lips of his into a half-smile. I did not see that superior smile once in the first few months of our acquaintance, when he was as tightly wound as an automaton. How much more dignified — even a little proud — he has become. Responsibility, for some, is a weight borne on the shoulders; for my Architect it is a pedestal upon which to stand.

We are closing in on the botanical section of the Domain now and a banksia looms ahead.

'Named after Joseph Banks.' I gesture towards the shrub with bright, cylindrical yellow flowers like cobs of corn, brilliant against the blue of water and sky. I reach out to touch the spikes but draw back sharply at the sight of several bees whose suicidal instincts would doubtless be roused if I were to press ahead.

'You know, Macquarie persists in his vision of the place as a moral laboratory,' I say. 'Of course it is that. But we must keep the memory of Banks alive. We are custodians of a rare and wonderful land. It is fantastical.' I stride a few paces ahead and, turning to face him, walk backwards as he drives me on. 'It is faery-like.'

'Fantastical,' he concurs. 'And yet it grows more concrete, more material, with each passing month.'

I slow for him to catch me and when he reaches my side we turn together, as if of one mind, to regard the residence perched on the rise and the town thrusting behind it like a child clamouring for attention.

'I observe that Nature and art have combined here at your Domain,' he says, 'to form a most enchanting scene. It is a complete thing.'

'Yes of course we must have Nature and art in company; and then, quite apart from that, we must give Nature her head; permit her to paint her own scenes.'

'Your opinions are decidedly firm today,' he says drily. 'Not by any measure unsound, but so forcefully put. From where did this taste for the raw power in Nature come?' he goes on, turning to me with a penetrating gaze. 'I am sometimes bewildered by your enthusiasm for wild things.'

He slows to a pause. We face one another on the path. If we were anywhere else but the Domain — the Governor doubtless studying us as we stroll along this path beside the shore — I would lace my arm through his in a spirit of warm friendship. 'Perhaps it was a childhood in the Hebrides among wild folk,' he continues. 'You insist it was not a lonely upbringing. And yet I detect a keen — a most Romantic — instinct for solitude in those lone rides to the heights.'

'My parents, good sir, were not in the least bit wild.' I make a show of displeasure by stamping the path with my heel. 'That is a common misperception about we Scots. We are, in fact, very hospitable. But yes, you are right, the taste for solitude — it is not a new thing.'

Is that the reason I submitted to such a marriage, a marriage to an older man, a soldier, a ruler with a great cause? Were his long absences, and his self-absorption, a licence for my own?

I start at the touch of his hand on my arm. He is leading me forward with decisive strides. 'Emus,' he says forcefully. 'Almost upon us. Let us move on.'

'But they are quite tame.'

'Quite tame and quite insatiable. They will pursue us for hours to demand a morsel. If we fail to provide they will remove your bonnet and peck off our buttons ... We will be strolling back to the residence in our drawers.'

I laugh and give him a gentle slap on the arm. A firm arm.

We soon reach the stone chair.

With a deep — though slightly mocking — bow, he inclines his head. 'It is your throne,' he says. 'I insist that you be the first to take a seat.'

'If I am sovereign here, then I insist that we sit together.'

I am wearing a long dress of fine white muslin, and the stone seat is cold and hard. He notes my discomfort. 'Perhaps you could ...' He indicates my shawl, miming the action of rolling it into a cushion. I do as he suggests. 'A little better,' I say. We sit side by side facing the panorama and, at precisely the same moment, launch into conversation.

'Please,' he yields. 'You were saying.'

'No. But it was you ... You were speculating on my past. I am intrigued. Do go on.'

'Very well then,' he says. 'I see you clearly at, let us say, fifteen years of age, riding out into the hills, along the shore of some loch, copper curls flowing behind. But then ... the talent for music? And the fondness for repartee?'

I relate the story of my childhood and school days, my friendship with Miss Fullerton. I was, I confess, precocious in most things. I played the viola from an early age, though my father declared my first attempts a form of auditory torture that would have assisted his ancestors in their clan feuds by extracting confessions from enemies more readily than the rack. I had reached the brink of womanhood when my classmates still bore the frames of boys, and I could construct a Ciceronian argument before they had mastered their Latin declensions.

There were few volumes about the house and of those we did possess James Boswell's *Life of Samuel Johnson* was my preference. That book made its way into the home on the trail of Dr Johnson's fame. He had travelled with Boswell to the Hebrides a few years before my birth. Father claimed to have met the great bear of Fleet Street at a local inn. 'There is much wisdom in those verbal duels between Johnson and his opponents,' I say. 'And even more wit. Perhaps my immersion in those pages fostered a taste for raillery, not that it is a particularly admirable trait in a woman.'

He has been listening raptly for the better part of this story. Towards the end there is a shift in his mood, his attention wavers and his gaze moves to his hands, which he places together in a prayer-like gesture between his knees. I wonder if he is listening.

'Have you noticed,' he says a little flatly, 'that we do not speak of my past. Has my crime, and perhaps your discomfort in the presence of a felon — a *reformed* felon — made it an unseemly subject? I suppose it has.'

I lay a feather-light touch upon his arm. 'I think you mistake me. I would have inquired most certainly if I had ever felt you wanted it recalled. So many in this place desire only to forget. If you find yourself in an autobiographical mood, well, nothing would delight me more.'

He casts around him uncertainly, as if he expects to find scouts standing behind the trees, lying behind the boulders along the shore. 'In truth there is nothing much to recall,' he says. 'It is but a brief autobiography.'

'A fragment should be easy to relate.'

'I think, perhaps, that I wished to make a point rather than tell a tale. But,' he swallows, 'I will press on with it.'

'Well then. *Allez*.'

'At home in Bristol, my father a stonemason, and his father before him, I was neither of the first rank of masons nor the last. But my designs were admired by men of consequence. I was commissioned to build an assembly room in Clifton, three storeys high atop a basement, six Ionic columns wide, and crowned by a triangular pediment. My fortunes rose quickly in the heat of the war market and declined just as rapidly with the peace. While attempting to extricate myself from debt I made a grave error by appending a fictitious money order to a building contract and then forging the signature of a client who had, I am ashamed to say, served me well. Two hundred pounds: a sizeable enough sum to see off my troubles. And to arouse suspicion. Extremis was my only excuse; I was facing ruin. I was discovered, apprehended — arrested. You can imagine the rest.' The Architect's carriage is normally very erect, the plane between chin and neck almost horizontal. But as the tale goes on he slumps in stages until he is leaning forward on the stone seat, hands folded across his middle, eyes trained on a fallen leaf several feet away. He runs his hand through his hair, and begins to revive.

'The Governor describes it as cheating, trickery, worse by far than the simple crime of theft. More like foolishness in my case, foolishness born of desperation.' He breaks off, tosses his head back, and goes on in a lighter tone. 'It is curious to consider that I might not have risen to any great eminence in Bristol. But at Sydney Cove I am charged with making a New World.'

I inquire about his admiration for Palladio and he replies that all true artists require a master, a guide — a genius to follow in the years of apprenticeship, and in maturity surpass.

'And you aim to surpass Palladio?'

He gives a faint smile.

'As I see it, a mere builder ...' he says in a halting voice, 'a builder will erect a gabled roof to keep out the rain. A wall for the wind. A hearth. But there is something infinitely greater in an architect's gift ...' He rises slowly and looks up through the leaves to the hard blue sky, searching for the words. 'He forms ...'

'Go on. I am listening.'

'He creates the places and spaces that nurture memory. And there has never been a great civilisation that has not remembered.'

'Ah, but in this place,' I suggest, 'it is best to forget.'

'Seriously now,' he continues in the same earnest tone, but with more assurance as he moves from the abstract to the concrete. 'We think the great builders of the past — Ramses, Pericles, Augustus, Justinian — strode forward boldly facing a golden future that was already theirs. But no!' He raises a disputatious finger. 'They went forward while glancing, every few steps, backward. Towards the future, with eyes on the past. I hope to do the same — to build a future with old Palladio watching over me. So profound were his investigations into the past — so deep his knowledge — that he was never its prisoner.'

At the mention of that word 'prisoner' we lock eyes briefly.

I drum my hands on my lap before rising to leave. 'You, too, speak with passion today. But it is getting on.' I bend to pick up my shawl. 'And it is well that you reminded me of my husband, for he will be waiting, most probably pacing about the house. I should like to hear more of your story; what you have shared today is not so much an autobiography as an architectural treatise. Tell me, next time, a little more about yourself. If you do not tell me, I will have to resort,' I flash him a smile, 'to espionage.'

'My work is my life,' he says, rising and turning to me. 'It is, I fear, the best of me.'

'Well, no. I strongly disagree. The best of you is yet to come.' The remark was not made lightly, nor offered as a flourish to finish the conversation — although it did have that effect. I would not have shared such bold schemes with him if I did not think him talented enough to realise them, did not *believe* in him.

He is, I see, moved by this expression of faith. He steps towards me, leans close, looks into my eyes. His right hand begins to float up from his side. Is he about to straighten his coat? Or does he mean to caress my cheek? At the moment I suspect a gesture of tenderness, I pull away, turn anxiously to the residence. The spell is broken.

On the way back he seems unsettled. He concentrates on his feet, runs his hand once more through his hair. When the path narrows and we are forced closer, I touch the back of his hand. No, I caress it. He cuts me a look of shock and pleasure. I smile in return.

When we reach Government House I skip like a child up the stairs — one, two, three, four — and from the last step I fairly leap onto the verandah. The Architect trails a few steps behind. We are — both of us — laughing.

Macquarie steps from the verandah's shaded recess as if playing Hawkins' part.

'Do you mean to announce me to a waiting audience?' I ask, surprised and defensive.

He offers a feeble attempt at a smile, lips pressed tightly together. And his eyes: tight, defeated, the spirit gone from them.

'I took the trouble,' says the Architect, 'to deposit some plans on the desk in your study. For your perusal.'

'We shall consult on the morrow,' is all Macquarie says. And turning, he walks along the verandah. It is my duty to follow him in this instant, without delay. And to endure an hour or so of marital frost followed by a silent evening meal. With luck, I will manage to coax him into a better humour by bedtime.

We are all learning from each other. There are things, though, that we cannot — all three of us — enjoy together. The Governor shares my bed. But I have begun to wonder if the Architect does not share my mind.

CHAPTER SEVENTEEN

A good year later — long enough for work to begin on the castellated stables, a military hospital on the western rise, and the Gothic fort at Bennelong Point — I come to understand how truly fragile is our situation in the colony. I am midway through Boccherini's 'Cello Concerto in B Flat Major' when Brody charges through the door, ignoring protocol. His face is flushed and his mouth dreadfully contorted. I set the instrument down as soon as I hear the ensign cry out that the Architect has been badly hurt, is barely, indeed, alive. I must come quickly. I must follow him out to my stone chair.

Macquarie is at Parramatta, at least four hours away by carriage and two by riverboat. We cannot wait for him. I abandon my violoncello, leaving the sheet music open at the 'Adagio', and dash across the creaking floorboards of the hallway. Stirring up a storm as I rush out the door with the ensign I cry to Mrs Ovens, who is walking solidly up the path, that there is no time to lose. As she spins past me she looks shocked and confused.

We gallop towards the promontory on the Domain's eastern fringe. Brody leads the way, thrashing his bay Arab, its sweaty flanks splashed with gold in the slanting late afternoon light. I follow on my spotted grey. Just before we reach the road leading to the harbour, Brody takes a tight turn and plunges into a forest that soon enfolds us. He has already dismounted — the Arab's breath roars — when I draw up on my grey. The path is narrow. We tether the horses and dash forward on foot. I graze my hand on a broken branch, strike my foot on a rock, feel my dress catch on a spindly shrub to the side of the path. But I press on until we reach a clearing. There, ahead, is a native camp beside the shore of Woolloomooloo.

We both run, in the company of the first native to approach us, towards a figure lying prone beneath a fig tree with a trunk like carved stone. There is a bed of palm leaf beneath him, and around everything hangs a pall of smoke.

The Architect's hair is matted. His face is turned sideways as if we have stumbled upon him in a deep slumber. The high colour in his cheek is the only evidence of a still beating heart, and even then I am not entirely certain. Smeared over his back is a dun-coloured poultice giving off a stench that recalls the *Dromedary* on a still sea. On the pale underside of his forearm is a meandering weal.

A native woman rises from his side. She is extravagantly adorned with a necklace of shells and animal teeth that sways as she gets to her feet. In her massed hair she wears a tiara of small white bones. My eye is drawn momentarily to her skin daubed red, ochre and white. It's then that I kneel to inspect the figure before me. There is a pulse.

'Who did this?' I cry, rising to face her. 'Was it ...?' I point slowly, deliberately, as if taking aim with a pistol. 'You ... One of your ...'

'He has been flogged at the Cove,' whispers Brody, cupping his mouth and pressing it towards my ear.

'Not my people,' the native woman says shaking her head vigorously. The teeth of various kinds strung around her neck chime as they sway. 'Very sick. Lucky too. Bungaree and his mob find him — your place, the Cove. This here,' she bends to pick up a hollow shell filled with the thick brown poultice, 'blood medicine. Cool him. And we have stuff' — she points to a near empty bowl — 'make 'im sleep good. When'm sleep I take spirit out. Make better. Put it back. Let'm dream now.'

I am quite overwhelmed by the scene at the camp: the prone body of the Architect, the smoke, the smell, and the sound of a high-pitched chant laid over a sweet, sharp beat of ceremonial sticks.

It takes considerable strength not to succumb to a swoon.

'Elizabeth,' I say, holding out my hand. 'Governor Macquarie's wife.'

She takes it in her own. 'Yes, I know. Cora Gooseberry. Bungaree Queen.'

She is, at that moment, quite majestic.

CHAPTER EIGHTEEN

Brody gallops back to sound the alarm and to summon help; I follow at a steadier clip.

The Architect is transported by the swiftest possible route to the Cove, in a stringy-bark canoe paddled by a man especially chosen by Gooseberry. Thanks to God that he has drained her sleeping potion; if he had woken with a start and struggled, I fear the slender craft would have overturned.

Once at the town Brody makes for the home of Mary Reibey, close by the waterfront, to raise the alarm. She comes down in fading light to the Government wharf with her determined tread, surrounded by a gaggle of servants. That prosperous and kindly widow, who works with great vigour since the death of her husband Thomas, arranges transport for the victim to the new Rum Hospital in a cart laid with a bed of hay beneath a sheet of clean muslin. The Governor sleeps easily at the old Government House in Parramatta without any knowledge of these terrible events.

'Is it possible, ma'am, that he has incurred a gambling debt?' Brody asks later that night. 'I was told that the Architect had been flogged and was in the care of the natives. But I can't for the life of

135

me imagine what might have provoked it. Some in the settlement say he has fallen into old habits — used his talents to forge a contract or an order. Others, that he has enemies in the building trade. A provocation of that sort, it is supposed.'

I shake my head, exhausted.

On the frontier the natives and Europeans are skirmishing continuously. The free settlers complain that the natives have butchered their sheep, goats and cows and would take the horses if they could run them down. Why, they scarcely trust their own servants, who can all too easily vanish with the household silverware and exchange it at the docks for grog, tea and sugar. In my time at the Cove I have heard of untold crimes and their punishments, but until the injury to the Architect I have never known a man to be punished severely for no crime at all.

When the Architect regains complete consciousness a day later, his recollections are enough to plausibly identify a culprit who disports himself amongst us in plain sight. There is no need for further investigation.

Captain Edward Sanderson is a declared enemy of the Governor's. A good year ago he perpetrated some minor slander of Macquarie's reputation: a satire distributed to members of the regiment. For this he endured an old-fashioned dressing-down by the Governor himself at the Military Barrack on the Cove's western side. From that moment a clique of the Governor's opponents — their identities suspected though never proven to our satisfaction — formed around Sanderson in a violent alliance. Howe, with his ear to the Sydney shale, speculated in his *Gazette* about the cause of their resentment: the favourable treatment of convicts, as the rebels saw it, and the Architect the most favoured of all.

I can picture the rum-fuelled rantings of this indignant little group. Sanderson's hostility tips over into cold, hard calculation. He devises a cunning stratagem. This is how he came to instruct the Architect to design and build a frivolous Gothic addition to his regimental quarters; and when the Architect refused, as he was entitled to — explaining that he was employed on several building projects of some official importance — the Captain demanded that he at least pay a courtesy call to the Military Barrack. The Architect could hardly refuse this, and so he was trapped, alone, with a man who was an avowed and dangerous enemy.

* * *

I pay my first visit to the patient a few days later in the company of the Government surgeon, William Redfern, a slight and bespectacled man with a full head of baby-fine grey hair and a considered, unimpassioned — quite dry and scholarly — manner. The Architect has a small lamplit refectory to himself at the end of a long corridor of polished flagstones. It is a measure of his indeterminate status that he recovers here, in the convict hospital, in a room set apart from the convicts. Leaning against the doorjamb of raw timber is a guard chosen by the Governor to ensure no harm comes this way from the barrack.

At the unexpected sight of the surgeon and the Governor's wife the guard stands rigidly to attention, eyes fixed straight ahead.

Redfern pulls up a seat beside the patient. As he takes the Architect's pulse the surgeon says, rather stating the obvious, 'You are lucky to be alive, man. If not for Bungaree and whatever benign witchcraft was ministered by Gooseberry you would not be speaking to us now.'

I stand a little to Redfern's side, a few steps within the doorway, hands clasped before me. Redfern cocks his head to listen to the Architect's chest, regarding me sharply in the process. 'You will live,' he says, returning to his seat.

'The natives managed to rehydrate you — essential in cases of severe blood loss — and apply some disinfecting poultice of eucalyptus oil and God only knows what else. A somnolent potion, too, I would surmise. You have seen their men, and sometimes the women too, sporting ritual scarifications across their bodies. They have a deep knowledge of such things.'

'And Sanderson,' the patient asks. 'It was his intention to ...?'

'I believe so, yes,' he answers in a detached tone. 'The first strokes of the lash were laid on so heavily, the force so severe, that they burst through a large area of skin and lifted it quite off. Your back, when I first inspected it, was the colour of liver.' He asks the patient to turn over, inspects the state of the dressing, and clucks severely thrice.

I gasp at the blood-caked bandages. The surgeon cuts me an admonishing look. He goes on. 'You know there is some feeling among the soldiers about the punishments meted out to them in the barracks. Convicts receive a civilian lash, and it is as often as not laid on lightly. The soldiers receive the military cat, and it is a nasty thing. It looks to me as if this was the instrument. It was wielded ferociously. The ribs were exposed. Your enemies left you for dead and doubtless you would have bled to death if the natives and Mrs Macquarie here' — a slow swivel of the head and another analytical look — 'had not attended you in the first hours. Let us imagine you survived the initial trauma. Your wounds, if untreated that first evening, would have become infected. It would have been a painful death. Blood loss and trauma would have weakened your system. Suppuration and fever would in no time have finished you off.'

Redfern shakes his head and leans back in his chair. 'Macquarie, as your patron,' he goes on in a warmer tone, 'would have insisted on the most severe punishment of the Captain. If, I mean to say, you had died. His regiment would have resisted, protesting this as a misuse of power in support of one who had formerly transgressed the rule of English law. The colony would doubtless, once again, have been cast into a state of civil war.'

A week later, on the last evening but one of the Architect's lengthy convalescence in the Rum Hospital, I sweep aside a covey of nurses in their bleached pinafores. I take a seat beside the patient.

'It seems you were almost lost to us,' I whisper, reaching out to him. His hand is cold and limp. It frightens me. I return it to its owner, who says not a word. 'A less sturdy man might have died. You are still so ... pale.'

'I have barely moved for a week.'

On hearing hurried footsteps and alarmed voices, I swivel sharply. But the footsteps hurry on. The sudden movement has caused my unruly curls to cascade from my bonnet. I restore them to their proper place. And when I turn back again I notice how intently the Architect regards me.

I sense, though perhaps not for the very first time, that he might have begun to fall in love. For myself, I am brimming with feelings to which I dare not give a name.

I force a fragile laugh. 'It has to be said ... Captain Sanderson was not the wisest choice of enemy. I believe the blackguard has the Governor in his sights, too.'

139

A grimace — and the hand of the Architect gropes like a tortoise towards my own. This time it is decidedly warmer. 'It was not,' he says weakly, 'my choice.'

I lower my voice to a whisper. 'Things are delicately poised in the colony,' I begin. He signals with his eyes for me to go on.

I tell him all I know. That there are some here — Sanderson is not alone — who would have the colony governed with a much harder hand. There are calls for Macquarie's removal and a veritable reign of terror, though in the English not the French style. No guillotine in the square. No heads paraded in the streets on spikes. Instead it would be meanness and money and little else. Unless of course there was a protest from the poor — then it would be off to the gallows.

'What does Shelley say?' His gaze slides to the far wall as he searches. '"Leech-like" rulers.'

I raise a finger to my lips. 'Hush! Quiet now. You have had your "tempestuous day".'

I stroke the cool white sheet, careful not to touch the form within. 'Under the regime proposed by the Governor's enemies, convicts — even those with rare skills such as yours — would be little more than slaves for the clearing of the interior and shepherds to watch over the sheep. There would be no prompt emancipation such as you, my friend, enjoyed. No. None of that. The sentence of transportation would scar for life. Perhaps that is why he sought to scar *you*; if, indeed, he intended that you should live. The Governor in contrast wishes to liberate the convicts, once they have served their time or earned an indulgence. He dreams of a new world built by freed men and women and possessed — enjoyed! — by their sons and daughters. And you are ... you are ... the Architect of this dream.'

'Is that why I am so despised? The soldiers ...'

'And why you were a target for this viciousness. Yes.'

140

He props himself up.

'Water!' I call to the nurses. A girl comes with a pitcher. 'And something for his pain?' I inquire. 'Something other than rum.' The nurse lowers her eyes abruptly and scurries down the lamplit corridor.

The Architect is flagging. His bruised eyelids seem to weigh heavily and eventually they close. With a gesture of exasperation at his prolonged confinement he throws out a bare arm. Winding around his forearm is the savage snake-like wound I first saw at the native camp.

I reach out to touch but dare not. But then I permit myself. His eyes flutter and snap, brightly, open.

'Like a serpent,' I say, 'soldered onto the skin.'

'Just the one clean stroke of the tail,' he says. 'My hands ... they were ...' And then he breaks off, raising the bare forearm weakly.

I take a long pause. He is gripped by his pain, his humiliation. I am the stronger one at this moment and I must drive us both on from here. 'There is little time and much to do,' I say. 'Together we shall draw up a list of necessary buildings, train even more masons, and deploy those resources that come to the Governor through the trade in spirits and taxes on shipping to ensure that a fine city rises from this shore. We will make good on Macquarie's promise. We will realise what he has merely proclaimed. We will go further still. We will make a fight of it. And our weapons will be bricks and mortar and Sydney stone — and splendid timber from the forests.'

He nods in silence. Beads form at the corners of his weary eyes. I turn away, wiping my own eyes. It is not from sadness that I am forced to beat back tears but from the very opposite: a wild and fearful happiness.

A compact is formed at that moment.

And nothing is ever the same again.

CHAPTER NINETEEN

On the afternoon of the trial I dress plainly and steal away from the residence while Macquarie and Piper are discussing 'matters of commerce' — at least this is how it is put to me — at Henrietta Villa, Piper's splendid harbourside mansion. I have no wish to advertise my identity at the crowded courtroom; nor, for that matter, do I desire particularly to conceal it. I stand, dressed as I would for any other formal occasion, among common folk towards the rear.

Chief Justice Barron Field and Judge Jeffrey Bent share names lending themselves to ridicule, although they may not know it. I have heard numberless jibes about the 'barren field' of justice in the colony, while Bent is a particularly unfortunate name for a man of the legal profession. Chief Justice Field, neat-featured beneath his wig, presides over the case; Jeffrey Bent, his head large and spherical, his lips tight and thin, acts for Sanderson on the Governor's orders. The Architect has retained a portly Irish attorney whose famed eloquence is never put to the test as the facts, it soon emerges, are not in dispute. The questions are judicial: is it a crime for a serving officer to flog a former convict for the petty insult of insubordination? Does a former convict in this situation enjoy the same rights as a free man?

I am too engrossed in proceedings to register any glancing looks from the courtroom, though most certainly my presence is noted, speculated upon and discussed that very evening. Some days later it is drawn to Macquarie's attention. He says only that he wishes I would be more circumspect with my affections. I reply that it is not affection but curiosity that drew me to the spectacle. In this I speak the truth, although there is another truth that remains unspoken.

Sanderson is a tall, angular man, with closely cropped receding hair, a long leathery neck, lean cheeks and a quite rapacious appearance. He sports a pencil-thin moustache, which he is most fond of caressing. Standing upright in the dock, in full uniform, he is the very model of untroubled arrogance.

His gaze rakes purposefully across the crowded courtroom. In time it comes to rest on me. When I return it — this being a contest of wills from which I aim not to flinch — the pouch beneath one of those deep-set eyes appears to twitch excitedly. He is curious, sardonically amused. He pins me with his eyes. I am the first to blink. Evil, I tell myself, comes in many guises. This is surely one.

The court records reveal the following: after a rebuke from the Captain in his quarters the Architect had been seized by his shirtfront and forced to kneel. Asked in court if he had said the words 'You are here at my orders and to them you will submit. Fail in this matter and I shall shake the life out of you', the Captain agreed that he had most certainly said them and would again if similar circumstances arose.

The Architect had replied that he could not retaliate, and nor would he, as an employee of the Government, submit to the Captain's unauthorised request for alterations to his quarters. 'I may very well undertake them in good time,' he added, 'but on my *own* time — and for a fee.' Sanderson roared that it was high time the Architect received a lesson in humility. He reached him with one stride, tore the shirt from his back, and tied his hands to a coat hook.

And so the lashing began.

Sanderson, by his own account, had not intended to be so forceful with the Architect. 'I am afraid I allowed my contempt for the man to drive me on,' he confesses to the cheers of his supporters. He freely admits to laying some thirty lashes onto the Architect. His subordinates, rushing to the Captain's quarters when they heard the commotion, took it in turns to inflict twenty more.

Sometime in the following weeks I am reminded by Macquarie that Sanderson had come out on the *Dromedary*. I am usually quick to detect a wicked heart but the scoundrel had skillfully concealed his true nature from the Governor and me. Though not, I would later learn, from all.

Prosecuting a captain of the 73rd was a courageous move on the Architect's part. He was not yet in possession of an absolute pardon, so a failed prosecution would likely be deemed capricious. It would cast him back into the ranks of the common felonry. At best he might be clapped in chains and driven out to the forests to fell timber, at worse find himself working the mines at Coal River. This was a risk that he took and it is a measure of his audacity that he even entertained it. A humbler man would certainly not have.

Sanderson lost the case on the lone and reluctant testimony of a fellow officer who confessed that the Captain had premeditated his assault, boasting in the officer's mess that he would 'cut down the scoundrel and teach the haughty Scot a lesson about his patronage of scum'. The other witnesses either lied without shame or evaded court altogether. Sanderson was found guilty and fined the paltry sum of two pounds. He returned to England on the next transport home and in time made his way to India. Or so it is said.

CHAPTER TWENTY

On the day of the verdict, I keep to myself. I refrain from venturing to town and avert my eyes from the settlement; no easy thing as we command the eastern rise. Instead I spend the afternoon gardening. I insist that I do the weeding, pruning, planting and potting myself. A garden may seem a mere ornament but I find consolation in the nurturing of things as they sprout and flourish and die. I am midwife to the seeds, nursemaid to the shoots, and guardian of those that thrive. My work in the garden reminds me that while I hear the music of the angels I, too, am part of Nature — just like the aged St Matthew in the picture that had bewitched me long ago in Rome.

In the late afternoon Brody walks up from the guardhouse with a straight face that eases into a small smile when he is a mere yard away. I give a little clap — just the one. Things have gone well, though not as well as they might have done if Sanderson had been punished as a common criminal, not cautioned for overstepping regimental bounds.

I come in late from the garden, enter from the rear door and seek out the pretty Miss Ringold, who is in her room reading a letter — no doubt from a secret beau. She has already prepared a scalding bath for me. When it has cooled a little I slide down into the suds, close my eyes and allow my hair to float up around my face like a Medusa. After drying my hair and dressing for dinner I observe the light in Macquarie's office gleaming through the panes. I do not go to him, and he does not come to me. I eat alone. We sleep apart. At sunrise I wake, look for him about the house, and, failing to find any sign, step out in my nightgown to the verandah. Seated there in the gentle half-light surveying the town, he smiles weakly at my approach.

I tell him of the Architect's victory, but he has already been informed of it. In any event my husband seems more intent on the careful examination of my countenance for any telltale tremors of emotion than news of the trial. Accordingly, I report in a dry style. I withhold.

'We must reward Bungaree and his tribe generously,' I say in breach of the uneasy silence that has descended between us. I take on a solid voice — an insisting tone. 'And Gooseberry too. He calls her his queen. Let us treat her as one. Without her, I fear the Architect would have been lost to us.'

'I quite agree,' Macquarie concedes with a corrugated brow. I have touched on some source of consternation. 'There are other tribes I know' — a slight jerk of the head towards the vast interior — 'who would have filched the Architect and left him to die of his wounds. At this moment they would be attempting to fathom the purpose of the folding rule and divider he keeps in his coat pocket.'

'A rather harsh assessment.'

'Yet manifestly true of some. The point is to encourage those wishing to accommodate themselves to us.'

'And what of those with no such desire?'

He takes this in the spirit in which it was intended: as a question without an answer.

Later that morning Macquarie returns from the garrison with a small detachment. The soldiers go to the castellated stable, which hastens slowly towards completion. They take off their coats and join the convict labourers. They look hot and sullen. The sun is already stabbing through my parasol as I stroll in the garden and doubtless it boils the brains of those poor soldiers to a bisque. I come in from the garden and join him on the verandah.

'Work has slowed in the heat,' he says. 'I cannot afford to have Earl Bathurst countermand me before it is finished. I informed him I was building a dignified horse stable but the townsfolk, they call it Macquarie Castle. If he doesn't yet know — he soon will.'

He takes off his hat on the verandah, unbuttons his jacket, and frees himself a little from his cares. Before I can even be seated he springs forward, takes my face in his big hands, kisses me on the lips, looks deeply into my eyes. 'There are no secrets between us. Are there?' His eyes search mine.

'No, of course not.' I draw away. 'Whatever made you think ...?'

'Apologies, my love,' he says. He brings the chair to me. I sit across from him, hands folded contritely. 'It is just that,' he begins again, 'the colony talks. Remember that most of the cottages you see from here, and many that you don't, resemble your garden plants thirsting for water. They crave tittle-tattle and scandal and wither if it is withheld.'

He breaks off, rubs a hand sleepily through his wiry grey hair. 'You remember the day of the assault on the Architect,' he goes on with a heavy shake of the head. 'I was in the countryside and was told of the events a day later. It seems that you and Brody rode to him' — he raises his eyes — 'as if drawn.'

It is an unconvincing interrogation. Whatever suspicions he harbours, they are kept firmly in check. He cannot bring himself to voice his deepest fears; he can only hint at them. If he could peer into my mind he would find this very same seam of trepidation — the fear of betrayal. What had occurred between the Architect and me? Very little. And yet a large part of me is now given over to this man without my knowing precisely why or how. It is my unexplored self — the self not even known to me — that I most fear. This vein lies deep within, obscure to me and unseen by my husband. There is no hint of it in my demeanour.

'If we had not done so he might have died,' I insist coolly. 'Redfern agrees. And where would that leave your cause? Our work? Honestly, there is too much to be done in this colony for idle gossip.'

He studies his hands, turns them over, looks at the palms as intently as a soothsayer.

'I have a solution to the question of the natives' reward,' he resumes in a warmer tone. 'A land grant at Georges Head. A reservation. No need for them to wander — a gift from the Government, just as every settler and emancipist desires.'

I lean back, breathe easily, comforted by this sign of accord. 'Are you willing to endure the scorn of those who will declaim, "Not only does that beastly Scot favour the emancipists over the free, he now extends his favours to the heathens." Are you?'

'They will send their pernicious unsigned missives to Whitehall no matter what I do. The die, I'm afraid, is cast. It is said that I waste Government money on architectural toys and run a colony the likes of which Henry Hunt or William Cobbett would approve.'

'Your young wife approves. Is that not enough?'

'It may not be enough if these rumblings of discontent rise to a chorus.'

'Let us stop up our ears in the meantime. And sail on.'

I have always found my husband fortified by my boldness. But on this occasion he offers a brave smile that fades a little too quickly. Much of his former optimism — it ebbs now.

When, a few days later, Brody rides out to Bungaree's tribe to deliver the news of the Governor's gift, he finds that it has disappeared.

'It happens often that they will move with the seasons, the weather — even the tides,' he explains on his return. I ask him to sit but he prefers to remain standing. 'If a scout spots a school of fish at another shore they will follow. Well, I suppose' — he grins — 'there is little to pack.'

It occurs to me that the natives might not, in any event, consider this the magnanimous gesture Macquarie supposes it to be: the land, they no doubt believe, is not *his* to give. But that is an issue I will let Bungaree raise, if he is bold enough.

When contact is made with Bungaree he is enticed to attend a ceremony at Government House. He arrives in his admiral's coat and bicorne over a new set of pleated trousers. His feet are bare.

'I had to scour the colony,' Brody recounts, 'for a pair of breeches suitable for a tall, thin native, and then enlist a tailor to have them altered while I stood outside his door. For when I found Bungaree in town he wore none at all.'

'You mean?' I clasp a palm to my forehead.

'I'm afraid so. The top half,' he slices the air around chest height, 'the uniform and bicorne. The bottom half — a rag.'

We both laugh.

Macquarie has fashioned a second breastplate for Bungaree. 'This one,' he explains to the native, 'is no replacement for the kingplate — the one that declares you King of the Broken Bay tribe. This new one — and you must show it to any challengers —

confirms you and your people as owners of prime land at Georges Head. I have also provided a fishing net, and a fishing boat. All of this is given in gratitude for saving the life of the architect of the lighthouse.'

'I think we should also be able to provide a sow and some pigs — and some Muscovy ducks from our own stocks,' I say on a whim. Macquarie tucks in his chin and shoots me a look of surprise. Bungaree offers a broader smile at the news of this gift than he did when offered the land.

The native takes his new breastplate in his palms and rubs his hands over the engraving. 'Very fine thing indeed and I am profoundly grateful to Your Excellency,' he says with such a theatrical imitation of courtly etiquette that I confess I find it difficult to retain my composure.

And then, returning to his natural cadence, 'The soldiers teach me all the languages. Irish. Welsh. Scots. And one they call Posh.'

'We look forward to your rendition of Posh another time. But for now I have some duties to attend to. Do stay here and take a refreshment with Elizabeth.'

Turning to me before he flees down the steps, he says as an afterthought, 'The guards are close by.'

I offer Bungaree tea. He holds the cup between two fingers placed on the rim, sipping warily. 'Are you,' I ask, 'happy? The Governor has given you land — land for you and your people. Your children.'

'Will the land have a wall like this one,' he throws out a scarred hand. 'Before the stone here there was one of wood. And before that — none.'

'There will be no wall. I can assure you. Well, in time — who knows?'

'A lot of walls now. Whitefellas good in many things. Very good at cutting country,' he makes an axing gesture with his right palm, 'into pieces.'

'And your people, what are they good at?'

'Many things,' he says in a singsong lilt.

'Such as?'

'Good warriors. Good at secret things — dancing, singing, painting. Keep them old stories. Good at medicine — Gooseberry stuff. Healing magic. The women good at finding food, cooking; women sing the fish. The men good at hunting.'

'What do you like to hunt?'

'Wulaba.'

'Wallaby. Your word — a lovely word. Some others?'

'I teach words of the Sydney fellas,' he sweeps an arm from one end of the verandah to the other.

'Then teach and I will be your student.'

He leans back, regarding me suspiciously. After a brief pause he comes forward again. 'Warane,' he says, pointing towards the settlement. 'Your place now. You call it Sydney Cove.' He raises his right hand high and points behind and above the residence. 'Place you call Farm Cove — Wuganmagulya.'

'Wuga ... an ... ma ...'

'Long'un — that one,' he laughs softly.

'And the headland on which we have built the lighthouse?'

'Daralaba.'

'Some others. I'm keen to learn.'

'Baruwaluwu. You say, dolphin.'

'And shark?'

'Guruwin,' he says with a wide-eyed look of fear, extending his arms to their full span. 'Very big shark that one.'

I give an encouraging nod. 'Go on.'

He reaches towards my cap. 'Gabera — head.'

'Damara,' he holds up a hand.

Placing the hand on his heart, he pumps it firmly against his ribcage. 'Butbut.'

In the word itself I hear the heart's pounding. He nods and smiles with his velvety eyes.

'Burra,' he says pointing to the sky.

'And moon?'

'Yanadah.'

He returns his teacup to the table and raises his empty hands to the sky. 'Birrung,' he says. 'Whitefella say star.'

Then he takes a finger and, whistling through pursed lips, traces the trajectory of a falling object. 'Duruga that one.'

'Shooting star?' I put in, raising my hand. He nods with delight. His broad mouth spreads.

'Of course, kookaburra. Another of your words.'

'No.' He gives a firm shake of his stiffly matted hair. 'Guganagina.'

'Like butbut,' I say. 'The sound of the thing.' He throws back his head and performs that raucous unbridled chuckle with a perfect rising pitch.

'Try,' he says after my laughter subsides. I shake my head.

'So let us add mimicry to the list of things you are good at,' I say.

'Mimic?'

'Copying ... A talent with many uses.'

Bungaree nods thoughtfully and as he does so my thoughts fly to the Architect.

CHAPTER TWENTY-ONE

In time our Architect made a full recovery, although his scars remained as a daily reminder of the trauma he had suffered at Sanderson's hands. The most visible stigmata of all — the snake-like welt on his forearm — was regarded admiringly by the young apprentice masons whenever their master rolled up his sleeves. Some part of him, I believe, enjoyed the notoriety.

The colony continued to grow. A thousand disembarked in the newest of new worlds each year, many of them free settlers. The war with France was over and as the pulse of trade quickened — traders arriving from all quarters of the globe — the proportions of John Piper's harbourside mansion swelled.

The settlements in the interior grew and prospered; the colony began to resemble a well-fed man in a cheap coat. The Blue Mountains had been crossed. And the building program gathered pace.

Macquarie embraced my ambitions for Government House, though the Colonial Secretary, Earl Bathurst, did not. We had to make do with additions: three rooms and a new eastern wing rising to two storeys. Work on the stables continued and construction of the fort at Bennelong Point resumed after stone was found of sufficient mass to withstand the humidity at the harbour's edge. At Parramatta a refuge and workhouse for women was built and from it came linen, wool and wincey. I had a bedspread made of the wool spun by convict women after it had been finished by Simeon Lord at a mill he had built at Botany Bay. As for the design of the Female Orphan School established beyond the corrupting influences of the Cove, I can claim some form of authorship as I drew for the Architect a sketch of the estate at Airds and asked him if it might serve. Within days a finished plan for a little piece of my homeland on the banks of the Parramatta River arrived in a folio.

It was at this time that I began to detect worrisome signs of strain in Macquarie's temperament, as if it were thinning, wearing under the pressure of some immovable weight. I had once seen, on a ride into the uplands beyond the family estate, an ancient oak, barest of trees in that autumnal landscape, its trunk grown silvery and leached of life and sap, the few remaining leaves like twisting copper medallions in the breeze. It had been cleaved almost in two; one massive limb lowered itself towards the ground, as if in submission, while the other stood proud and unbroken. That melancholy sight returned to me as I witnessed Macquarie's struggle. He was nearing sixty years. He was weary of his labours. But he would not allow his enemies the satisfaction of an easy triumph.

When I recall his journey through the portion of his life he shared with me — as I must on this night of reverie — I see a man of the age just past rather than that beginning to take shape. Those of a strict conservative disposition have supposed Macquarie to be a modern for the simple reason that he sought to better the lives of the outcasts in his care and to beautify a place made by — and for — criminals. And what kind of man but a reformer favours such draff?

In truth he was shaped in the mould of the young George III. How the satirists had lampooned that sovereign's plain bucolic tastes — 'farmer George' they had scorned him. Macquarie was of that type, a leader with a feeling for ordinary people — a fine and rare fellow feeling. Once a year the convicts were invited to petition the Governor for their liberty. Macquarie applied himself with earnestness to the task, considering their pleas and summoning each spring his new class of emancipists to a ceremony on the lawn of Government House. And there he would forcefully proclaim, 'I have heard the arguments from each of you, had your respective masters interviewed by my clerks, weighed your degree of contrition and the practical contributions you might make to the future of the colony, and today you shall receive what you most ardently desire: your freedom!' Each year the words were much the same; and each year they brought forth precisely the same response: a cry of jubilation and a flurry of hats and poesies launched upon the air.

In this business my husband was the good king; ruling over a tainted kingdom, admittedly, but a king nevertheless. Why, he was freeing the slaves just as a pharaoh might have done to remind all — subjects, vassals and enemies alike — of his power and benevolence. As time went on, and Macquarie's frustrations mounted with each countermand from London, I observed jarring signs of the contrary disposition: that of an isolated tyrant, small of mind, raging and pacing in his keep.

The good king lost his lustre when he had two convicts flogged — ten lashes apiece — for trespassing on the Domain. I read of their crime in the pages of the *Sydney Gazette* before it was discussed between us.

* * *

Returning late from a regimental entertainment — a dinner at the Military Barrack from which even wealthy emancipists were expressly excluded — he settles into a chair before the glowing embers of a winter fire, insensitive to my protests.

'And what would you have me do?' he says, raising an arm and bringing it down loosely on his thigh. 'Allow vagabonds to cut corners whenever the desire takes them and trespass over my — over our — reserve? To wander across one of the few sanctuaries of civility available to us, as if it were a common in some Midlands market town? Why these rascals pulled down a portion of the stone wall while clambering over it. Did you know one of these men, named Tallis, was transported for armed robbery; the other, Wilkins, for stealing a pig from its sty and butchering it. And if they had approached you at your ... your harbourside chair ... as you consumed your novels' — a satiric snort — 'or gazed upon the splendid view before you? What then? Would you have made polite conversation with these ruffians? Invited them to sit beside you? Encouraged them next time they happened to pass that way to bring friends and family?'

I lean forward, a hand braced on each of the chair's solid arms.

'No!' he erupts. 'Do not rise and pace about with that high fiery spirit of yours. Sit! Your look is haughty; it should be contrite. These two men will be punished so that none in the future will pose a risk to your wellbeing.'

'You have been drinking,' I say, springing up against instructions. 'Drinking to still your fears? It demeans you. Men can smell fear, especially fear that needs dousing in a night of port wine. And you have been imbibing with the men of the regiment. Was that why you went to them? For the comfort and succour of their prejudice?'

'You will sit when I address you!' he roars.

'I'll do nothing of the sort. I am not your chattel. And I mean to protest. The lash should not be laid upon men who meant no harm and caused no harm, who in all likelihood wandered drunkenly across our garden after a few too many tots of rum. But of course you return home in a four-horse carriage because you could not walk without doing yourself a damage. If not for a man to open the door, guide you to your seat and bring you here, you might be wandering as lost as they. You,' I raise a scolding finger and with it my tone, 'talk about the company I might have kept if they had assailed me. And what of the company *you* have kept this very evening? Those blackguards of the regiment. Yes. Blackguards! In what manner are the men of the regiment, snobs and greedy speculators, superior to men and women who toil in your colony? You express these sentiments oftentimes yourself, and yet this evening you speak as another. I have always heard you advocate for the poor in this argument of the age; you now argue for the wealthy. You have become contradictory!'

'Watch your tongue woman! It runs on. The men of the regiment, whom you consider idle, take the fight to the natives. And remember: it is to check others who might not be so mild that I ...' It is his turn to rise. He does so slowly, his unbuttoned coat falling open to reveal on his white shirt a claret stain the shape of an oak leaf. 'Severity is, on rare occasion, a necessity,' he proclaims as if he were speaking to an assembly. He retreats to the back of the armchair and stands scowling at me. Heavily, wearily, he leans against that solid piece of convict-made furniture. Its unadorned legs of native blackwood slide forward over the Turkmen rug, pushing it into a ripple. I stand on the other end of the rug. I feel at that moment as if *my* Lachlan is lost to me. That the man I know is broken down, dispersed and blown away; that some imposter stands before me.

157

'So it will be done then?' I ask. 'You mean to go through with the sentence? Why not simply replace the fallen blocks of stone and deprive the men of their freedom for a day or two. Issue a proclamation!'

He stares towards the blazing fire with garnet eyes. 'I must make a stand.'

'Do you realise how much you sound like ... like them?'

I leave him, flushed and unsteady on his feet.

That night the Governor's study serves once again as his lodging.

* * *

It was not the only instance I observed in Macquarie of a capricious and most unattractive rage, a willingness to exercise power in some quarter simply because the exercise of it had been thwarted elsewhere, frustrated perhaps in his own home. There was a contretemps with John Piper over the collection of excise; the latter had been a little too eager in his work.

A much graver matter still was the pursuit of retribution against the more aggressive tribes beyond the main settlement. Two companies, guided by native trackers, were sent out with a list of names and orders to either capture or kill. Among those named was Wallah, whom the settlers knew as Warren.

In the pursuit of these fugitives an entire tribe was driven to the edge of a cliff in the district of Appin, which we had named after my homeland. All chose death — leaping from the precipice — over submission. The next day a pile of crushed corpses — men, women and children — was discovered at the foot of the gorge. Fourteen natives had died. Wallah was not among them. The soldiers who returned from the massacre drank heavily, it was said, to forget the plaintive chant of the native children as they leapt to their deaths. At least one soldier took his own life, down by the shore named after Bennelong. It was a still moonlit night and I believe I heard the sharp crack of rifle fire carry up from the harbour shore as he went to the afterlife.

And yet Macquarie's better angels continued to wrestle with his demons, for it was at this time that work on Hyde Park Barrack, grandest of the buildings conceived by the Architect, began.

I do not judge my husband harshly for his incongruities. He encountered challenges to his authority at every turn. The hostility of the soldiers and the free settlers to the convicts arriving in ever increasing numbers was now echoed by the Colonial Office. Construction of the Church of St James, one of the glories of this time, was welcomed in London, but permission to build the barrack was declined. The Governor, to his great credit, had it built on the sly, informing the distant authorities only when it was too late to halt the work.

I wonder if I do not make too much of the dear man's inconsistencies, for was not Christ himself a sweet soul urging forgiveness one moment, and the very next bursting into the temple courts, overturning the tables of the money changers and blotting his own gentle legacy with the stain of righteous rage. Macquarie had changed. I also had changed, had fewer illusions about the man he was and the woman I thought myself to be.

CHAPTER TWENTY-TWO

How swiftly memories fade when distance conspires with time to dull them. Forms dissolve into chimeras, voices hush, colours fade. Already the Hyde Park Barrack seems half forgotten. Hard to believe that I — that we — fixed our dreams on such a plain structure when London could boast the colonnaded glories designed by Nash for Regent Street. But then it makes as much sense to compare the young colony's best efforts with those of the mother country's as it would to judge Windsor by the standards of Versailles.

In that distant colony, there was something valiant in the ambition to build for the betterment of the male convicts a three-storey structure of some heft, in warm local brick, trimmings of stone, and most elegantly proportioned despite its lowly purpose. Much like its architect, this was no shy building; it demanded attention! All of this for men who had not long ago mouldered on the hulks and fought for their very lives on the transports.

The Architect maintained his own firm views on the barrack. I had seen it emerge from his hand as a draft; had, in fact, approved its final articulation one afternoon in the Governor's absence — though with his express authority. My main contribution to this perfectly simple design was to suggest that its centre point align with the pinnacle of the Church of St James opposite so that these two buildings might establish a dialogue: reformation of character on one side of the street, salvation of the soul on the other.

Our interview took place not in the Governor's study but in the dining room with the lovely vista of Farm Cove; beyond it lay a blue ribbon of harbour, and beyond that the forested ramparts of Middle Head. The Architect's bearing, I remember, was a little stiff that afternoon. How excruciatingly painful was the situation we found ourselves in! We were both, I am sure, beset by confusion and guilt — the briefest of exchanges betraying our feelings had, unwittingly, inflamed them. I was sure Macquarie could sense it. How to douse — or quench — what could not even be acknowledged?

* * *

I sit at the round table in the white-walled dining room. With his back turned and his hands clasped behind him, the Architect stands before me at the bay window. He looks out, as if I were a portraitist with an easel and he the subject of my painting. He speaks to me without really speaking *to* me. From this indirect manner of address I catch only fragments of phrases: 'Exact impression ... strong proportions ... clear ...'

I am compelled to insist that he come join me.

And as he turns, I notice for the first time a few streaks of grey in his wavy hair. He apologises for his manner of address. 'Sometimes I lose even *myself* in my work ... I was saying ... saying that the instructions I have from the Governor have always been clear.'

'And those instructions are?'

'To lend dignity to a class of people that has ever been diminished; to do so by making something that both serves a purpose and delights the eye.' He takes a few steps towards me yet declines the offer of a seat. He prefers to stand with one hand in his pocket, the other turning slowly as if he were darning in thin air. 'In conversation your husband hammers this word — dignity. I perceive that it lies at the heart of his ambition: to dignify what has hitherto been regarded as dross. He is a man not lacking in natural dignity, or gravitas, himself. But ... if I may, perhaps he believes the dignity of built things reflects well on himself, too.' The Architect's grey-green eyes narrow. 'Does he — if you'll permit me — mean to nettle his superiors?'

'He certainly does nettle them, whether he intends it or not.'

I inspect the barrack on three occasions. On the first it is simply a maze of pale sandstone foundations and, above them, a few feet of red brickwork. I pay another visit when the brick walls and ceiling of the first storey have emerged from the chaos. The windows are still without panes, the doors without jambs or lintels, but the building has form and promise. That day I return to Government House with a pale dress coated in sufficient red dust stirred from the works to warrant a bleaching. I visit a third time, when it is close to completion. All that is required is a gently sloping shingled roof each side of a crowning tympanum in which a handsome clock has already been set.

Sensible of the red dust hurled by the wind I wear a dark grey — almost black — dress. On this occasion the Architect invites me up to the roof. He steps nimbly as he leads the way around clusters of workmen planing, plastering and polishing boards still beaded with sap.

When we reach the top I gasp involuntarily at the fine spreading view. The town tumbles down towards the cove. Windmills spin on the heights. Ships lie at anchor. And everything is laid out before me in folds: lightly wooded hills, the turns of the shoreline, crescents of sand at the harbour's edge, and the echoing shore to the north.

'I did not dare to think, when I set out on this journey, that I would see anything of this kind in the colony,' I say with a flat hand shading my eyes from the sun now that the wind has caught the brim of my silk bonnet and bent it back over the crown. 'It is like standing on a mountaintop. Bungaree might think it was a mountaintop.'

'You did not expect it. But you might have,' he lowers his voice, 'if we had met before; if you knew anything of me. Of my work.'

I turn sharply to face him. Looking straight ahead he avoids my gaze, though I see that he's smiling. When I turn again to appreciate the panorama he casts another look at me — I detect it from the corner of my eye. We go on like this — the speaker turning towards the listener, the listener towards the view — for some time. It is a species of self-consciousness and one to be expected. We are in strange territory as well as a strange land.

I press on, 'It must have been built at considerable cost, I expect. The Governor is nervous. He has only now, this week, written to Earl Bathurst to say the barrack is underway. And yet it is a few weeks, if my senses do not deceive me, from completion.'

'I estimate it will have cost the Government the expense of clothing and feeding the workers,' he says, joining his hands behind his broad back and spreading his feet as if he were Nelson at Trafalgar and this his Victory. 'I do not think it will exceed ten thousand pounds; a trifle compared to the sum spent on Millbank Penitentiary, which is reckoned to be upwards of half a million; and then, as the prisoners there await transportation, they die of disease, while the turnkeys wander in that ill-made labyrinth until they are lost. It costs another sixteen thousand pounds to operate, and still it never supports more prisoners than will be housed here.'

I had read of this. 'Indeed the editors of *The Times* have enjoyed the scandal of that prison's great expense and its even greater failings.'

I no longer think of myself as young, although there are times when playful instincts grip me. I have grown a little bored with this elaboration on prisons. I hear little else from my husband but the difficulties of administering an outdoor penitentiary; I have no wish to dwell on the theme today.

I step forward and, clasping the Architect's arm, turn him to face me. We have this level to ourselves, loftier than anything else in the town. None can see us from below. And a workman or overseer pursuing us up the stairs would easily be heard.

He is expecting, perhaps, some tenderness. But that is not my intention.

'I have heard said that a young rival architect, Henry Kitchen, has come out from England and that you block him at every turn. I did not think you capable of meanness.'

After a bewildered pause, he asks, 'What has he done? What can he do?' His eyebrows are drawn down, his shoulders raised. 'On the occasion of our first meeting I examined him on the subject of Gothic vaulting, specifically the ogive arch. It would appear that the word,' he sneers, 'is new to him.'

'Are you not then,' I tease, 'more than a little competitive? It seems that you must always strive to outdo what has been done, to make an impact and a mark. And now, with a young competitor in the colony, you attempt to expose his weaknesses. You men and your pride!' I press a hand against his arm.

'Steady,' he warns. 'We are far too close to the edge here for such pranks!'

'Bah! I would think we are six feet away, behind the roof's wooden frame, and you stand with your feet well apart. It would take more than the touch of a woman to topple a man accustomed to heights.'

'You forget. I have seen you in that garden of yours.' A renewed smile glides across his face. 'There is strength in those arms.'

'I consider myself armed for any eventuality.'

He laughs along with me, though not for long. 'Seriously, though,' he presses on, 'am I wrong to compete? Forget, for the moment, the subject of young Henry Kitchen. Should I not strive to do fine work here even if it is not wanted in London, difficult to execute in these conditions, and — as we both know — regarded with indifference, or even hostility, by the men of the regiment?'

The Architect leads me down the stairs and out to the gated courtyard. Brody stands conversing with a young guard at a sandstone guardhouse.

Before we reach him the Architect motions for me to pause. The ensign turns; I raise a hand to indicate that we will be a while longer. The air has stilled a little now and I put up my parasol, a fluted column of cool blue shade falling across my dark dress.

'Elizabeth,' he says, squinting in the glare. 'It was good of you to visit. Our pact — it bears fruit. And, well,' he hesitates, 'to see this building take shape. It rises — as I have — despite everything. What I am trying to say is … thank you.'

'Think nothing of it,' I return a little too quickly, one heel already pivoting in the gravel. I am anxious to flee lest Brody or any others take note of the Architect and the Governor's wife in earnest conversation. It has become a sensitive topic at the residence.

He steps forward. 'There is something else, Elizabeth. I have more to say. About … other things. In some depth. Or detail.'

'It is a letter you mean to write? You wish to correspond?'

He nods. His eyes burn at me. 'A private letter — a story.'

'Affix it to the back of your next set of drawings and have it brought to Government House next week. The Governor is touring the country ...' I hesitate. 'Things are somewhat strained between us. And so I remain at the Cove — alone.'

He stands in the glare. I face him in the shade of the parasol. And then, after an exchange of unfinished sentences, we part.

As I draw away in the Governor's carriage I feel my pulse begin to slow and to steady.

And then, a week later, his letter arrives.

CHAPTER TWENTY-THREE

My dear Elizabeth,
Many more courtiers than architects have met their deaths
at the hands of cruel and capricious rulers. Of that I'm
certain. But ART is nevertheless a dangerous business. I
have not told you about the origins of the feud between
Sanderson and me.

It started well enough, when some scoundrel on the
prison hulks with a face as purple as a swede and a nose
the texture of gruel spied me with a sketchpad on my bent
knees and a pen poised above it. We had been allowed
on deck under heavy guard for a half hour or so, to catch
some air and light, before being driven back down into the
filth and the gloom. A powerful fellow, he stood before me,
blocking the winter sunlight slanting across the Thames.

I waved a hand. 'Move on.'

He moved in sharp bird-like jerks around me, stepped
behind, and stared over my shoulder in silence as lines
receding into space suddenly fused into a recognisable
image. It was the circular Roman temple of Vesta, or at

least my imagining of it. Transfixed by this mute poetry of form, he rumbled in the voice of a man accustomed to being obeyed: 'Forget about drawing them ruins and stones and things that don't exist and instead draw me, alive — for the moment — and going out into the world on an adventure!'

I paused from my work, smacked the dirt from my trousers of convict-issue duck, and turned to him warily. 'Get down my likeness right and I mightn't thump you,' he said with a raised fist and a mean glance from a meaty eye. 'Might even save you from a beatin'.' I think this gesture was meant to charm.

He was delighted with the result, and even managed to have the sketch delivered ashore as a parting memento. He asked me the very next day for a portrait with an ocean backdrop and its subject — himself of course — with a spyglass. 'Make me a discoverer,' he demanded. I delivered that, too. And soon the taste for portraiture spread through the place with the speed of a new season fashion.

I was besieged the moment we were transferred to the Dromedary. No money came my way, but promises of recompense when fortunes are made in the New World slipped from every damned tongue. There were favours of many kinds offered. From those with a talent for force and its application came pledges of protection. If only I had invoked them at my time of greatest need!

There was to be no more of this after Captain Sanderson.

We were barely a week at sea when he had me unshackled and brought to his quarters. I rendered him *on paper much as he is in life. I am an artist, after all, not a flatterer! How could I entirely conceal that narrow angled face, the eyes deeply set beneath a tilted brow. Or the mean mouth. And yet the completed portrait was not without compassion for the possessor of these unlovely features. I portrayed them truthfully, and then I softened. I was satisfied with my efforts. Not the Captain. He fixed me with a set of soulless eyes. 'I am displeased,' he said sourly. He took a slender knife from his pocket, inserted the tip into a fingernail and proceeded to clean it. 'You will need to do better,' he said with a regal inflection. He held out a long thin hand, palm down, for me to inspect his nails. 'Clean, yes?' he asked. I said nothing but turned to leave. 'Wait!' he snapped. 'Until you are dismissed.' It was a good half an hour before I was permitted to leave his quarters.*

I returned the next day with an image best described as an idealised Sanderson. It was modelled, in truth, after a picture of Beau Brummell, resplendent in a snow-white cravat, black tailcoat and an indigo waistcoat, I had seen in a gentleman's magazine. Sanderson pronounced it good. 'A fine gentleman I do appear in this likeness,' he said with a crooked smile before dismissing me.

A month later I was recalled to Sanderson's quarters. It was late. The tropical night sky was moonless and starless. The soldier who led me stood sentry at the door. The captain, I observed, had been drinking — a half-drained goblet stood on the desk, and there was a sweet porty aroma to the cramped quarters. He motioned for me to come forward and thrust a sheet of paper at me.

'I presume,' he said with a show of long teeth, 'that you are the author of this. This ...' and he trailed off.

In the dim light I made out a vulgar caricature of a figure in uniform. The figure bore the Captain's distinctively angled features and thin moustache. It stood atop a few rocks designed to evoke a shore. On each side rose a gibbet, and from each one hanged the strangled carcass of a kangaroo, tongue lolling from its snout. Beneath the crude satire ran the words 'Captain Sanderson's Necessary Measures at the Cove.'

I had heard of harsh punishments meted out by Sanderson aboard the Dromedary and justified by him — or so it was rumoured — as 'necessary measures' to maintain discipline. Men had been flogged for insubordination, and beaten for little more than a refusal to submit to some bored marine's idle taunt. A man who returned below decks with his brow crushed by a heavy blow never regained the use of an eye.

'I may be an artist,' I replied, 'when forced by circumstances to set aside my architectural profession. But I am no fool. I have no wish to aggravate. And nor, as should be obvious, am I a draughtsman of such derisory gifts as these.' I thrust my arm out with the satire in my hand. I was anxious to be gone. 'Your enemy, sir, is a rank amateur.'

Sanderson remained seated. I am not entirely sure that he was capable of rising. He called to the soldier to lead me away, then changed his mind and commanded me to wait.

'I will have you flogged, artist, with great pleasure, great ease,' he said in a strained voice, as if the words were being

170

ground out. 'Why the cat o' nine, I have it here in the bag. Shall I let it out? Shall I let the cat out of the bag? Shall I!'

He stood unsteadily and came forward, reached out, took a handful of fabric from my poor cotton shirt, twisted it and drew me in.

'You ... have ... no idea ... do you?' he went on through heavy rancid breaths. 'I am master here. And will be out there. I shall do as I please. If I find evidence of your hand in this insult, this slander ... I will act. Why, I will flog you myself!' With this his eyes widened unnaturally.

He would not let me alone. Whenever I found myself above decks in his sight he trained those empty eyes on mine. With his right hand he enacted a pantomime of his threat — a flick of the wrist, a hand folded over an imaginary whip handle, and a knot traced in the air.

While I am certain that my first portrait failed to capture the likeness he had hoped for — could he really have considered himself a handsome man? — it cannot have been the sole cause of his animus. And the satire? He could not — not in sound mind — have mistaken it for my work. Perhaps he had concluded that I was the inspiration for it, or in some deeper animal sense that a man like me, chained in flesh yet unshackled in <u>spirit</u>, was his natural foe. It cannot have helped that I had become a minor celebrity on board. Those who maintain their station by terror are greatly unsettled by those who rise in the world without it.

I observed Sanderson once more before the incident in his quarters. We had been barely a month in the colony when Howe, the publisher, decided it was his duty to induct

171

me into the rituals of The Rocks. He was deeply learned in its ways, and rather the worse for it.

Howe was giving the lie of the land as we sat on stools at the Whaler's Arms — propped up at the bar to avoid a group of soldiers seated by an open fire. He pointed to the trapdoor behind the bar through which the publican hoisted the kegs from the cellar below. It had a far darker purpose, Howe said. Men, deep in drink, had woken to find themselves shipped to Shanghai or Canton, and well out to sea before the tincture of opiate poured into their rum had worn off. 'There'd be a tunnel beneath here,' he pointed towards the floor. 'It leads to Cockle Bay, where the merchant ships lie at anchor. You do not want to drink alone — at least drink too much alone — at this place. For you may find yourself bound and gagged and stowed aboard a ship in dire need of extra hands. The publican of the Whaler's Arms declares himself innocent of the trade. But the victims are never seen again — they can hardly be interviewed when they are half way to China.'

I noticed a figure, pressing close at the bar. Too close.

Captain Sanderson was no bear of a man. But there was menace enough for two in his sinewy frame.

'How interesting,' Sanderson hissed, placing his elbow on the bar beside my stool and bringing his head level with mine. 'The architect-forger and the shoplifting publisher. Two scoundrels toasting their golden futures with coin provided, no doubt, by the Governor himself.' He paused to take a few deep breaths, seeming greatly pleased with himself. 'And scheming,' he went on with a malevolent grin, 'to upend authority at the first opportunity. The Governor *should watch his back. And you,' I felt a sharp prod below my ribs, cold and hard — a knife handle. 'You, architect, should watch yours.'*

'I believe,' replied Howe soberly, 'that His Majesty is in a severe state of incapacitation and the throne is occupied by an unloved prince. It is no crime to speak of such things when they are spoken throughout the Empire.'

'Perhaps. The Regent is not overly popular. But one day soon he will be king,' he smiled cruelly, turning to each of us in turn. 'And then — believe me — he will be loved. It would be a simple matter for me to report you to the Colonial Office for sedition. That would be enough to deprive you of your liberty — both of you — for many a year.' Sanderson turned and wove his way back to the card table by the fire, where he took his place at the centre of a group of officers with their regimental coats placed on the backs of their seats. As they dealt him in, Howe ordered another round of drinks.

'He is right about the money,' said Howe, patting his pocket. 'A gift from the good Governor.'

For a long while I hoped that Sanderson might languish in Patagonia or some ultima Thule. I hear now he was last seen in Khurda. You know how it goes in this colony. News from elsewhere is the most precious of commodities. Now comes word fresh from a trader of an uprising in Khurda. I pray that both rumours are sound and that he is forced to regard a Nawab and his sword at close quarters, just as I was forced to look on his lash before it was laid onto me. I hope you will join me in my prayers.

Your Architect

CHAPTER TWENTY-FOUR

'Here,' I say, taking the Architect's arm as the rain sweeps in. 'I know a place.'

We have been riding in the parkland spreading east from Government House. Arthur Phillip claimed this land and set it aside for public buildings and simple pleasures, or such joys as were to be found in those lean years. In my time the sanctuary has been secured with a sandstone wall, laced with pathways and planted with native and introduced species. It has been shaped to my designs. Phillip called it his 'demesne'. My husband is apt to call it — though only between ourselves — 'Mrs Macquarie's Domain'.

It's there that my stone refuge sits on its rocky promontory. To reach it on horseback — though I prefer to walk — one takes the walled road that wraps around the Domain's southern border before swinging north in the direction of the harbour shore. An avenue of English oak trees, swamp mahogany, blackbutts and umbrella pines lines the road. Here lies the finest part of the Domain: my botanical garden. Though it has been styled by my hand, I have introduced no fantastical ornament: no statues of gods or heroes, no summerhouse decorated with fleshy putti or medallions painted with elegant frivolities after Fragonard. Nothing contrary to Nature.

We draw up abreast. He is first to dismount.

He comes with a jaunty step to take the reins and to help me down. I take the hand offered.

'Is there not something majestic about my throne on its rocky point?' I say in jest. 'I may not command — but I command a fine view.'

His eucalyptus eyes relax into a smile and he releases my hand.

Together we admire the view. From Woolloomooloo, to my right, an empty skiff, riding high in the water, heads out to Garden Island as another, weighed down with fruit and vegetables, returns.

We lead the horses to a little stone stable and return to my seat above the harbour.

It is early summer. The air is always sweet this time of year. It flies out of the limitless Pacific, picking up the scent — or so my fancy tells me — of the Windward Isles that so entranced Bougainville and Cook, along with numberless bright green islets in their equally bright blue atolls. That afternoon, quite suddenly, the wind changes direction.

We have a sou'easter, bearer of summer storms, and a keen one at that. The sky above a stand of palm and fig at the Domain's eastern fringe has purpled. Above it boils a great mass of cloud.

I take the Architect's hand to show him the place I know. After a few steps I release it to open my parasol; we must hope that it can also serve as a *parapluie*. I press it onto him so that he might do the correct thing and shelter me. I cannot always guarantee that the Architect will observe small courtesies, for he is much in his own world. A gust catches the thing and steals it like a thief; it goes

175

careening over the precipice. The Architect curses. The scene would amuse if the storm weren't gathering strength so swiftly.

I lead the way along the path, littered with rain-spattered rocks. He has the presence of mind to raise a corner of his riding coat over my bare head. Two or three steps down the side of a sandstone ledge and we are sheltered from the full force of the storm. The rain is flying sideways now. But we are protected. The trees above and around us shake, roar and whirl. I lead us further down the ledge to a cave, almost head height at the entrance, its mouth facing the harbour. He looks down at the drenched sleeves of his coat. We laugh like children.

Neither of us dares venture further. But here on the outer rim of red rock is a gallery of images: a small hand stencilled by a puff of fading white, and next along the wall a kangaroo clad in its own skeleton. Also revealed by grey light at the cave's mouth is a round fat fish embroidered with the same keen anatomical eye, as if the artist were peering through flesh. Stick figures, long and thin, mingle overhead in a dance. Some shapes, either too old or poorly done, are unrecognisable to my eye. Ghosts perhaps. Dream figures. A beast — I can at least make out a confusion of legs — that may once have walked these shores. Long, long ago.

From here a view of the harbour unfolds. A great sphere of sandstone lies a short distance away, concealing the entrance from the eyes of a curious stranger scanning these headlands from the opposing shore.

'I have asked Bungaree about this place,' I say. 'It holds some special importance. Yurong, it is called. He speaks of ferocious battles in times past between the people here and their enemies. Brody tells me that rival tribes still do battle on the level ground below at Woolloomooloo. If the cries of the warring parties are heard from the settlement, men will ride out to view the bloody melee.'

'I have heard all this too.'

'And out of delicacy had no wish to speak of it?'

'I'm afraid it is an indelicate — a savage — business.'

'But who are the savages in this story?' I remark. 'The native belligerents — or those who view their bloody quarrels as sport?'

'The way you load the question, I believe I anticipate your answer.'

'And what would yours be?'

He gives a long sigh. 'Perhaps both. I am a builder not a moralist.'

The rain drives across the harbour in sheets and eddies as if fleeing from the black clouds in pursuit. I have avoided a soaking and for that am greatly relieved, as my lemon dress is very fine and I have quite forgotten a summer shawl. Suddenly, without warning, I am gripped by a sensation not so much of fear as unease, as if I have rowed too far from shore or ridden into a dense fog. I feel as if I have strayed.

I fall silent. Withdraw.

'Elizabeth, are you unwell?'

'Yes. No, really. Quite well.'

'You have been here before?'

'I come often to this old, immensely old, place. As a child I would vanish from society. At Airds I would escape to an unused little bridge over a stream and sit, alone with my thoughts, in solitude. The habit, once formed ... is not easily broken.'

He turns, hair a little dim and damp, the shine gone from it, and thrusts his hands into his trouser pockets. His eyes are in shadow, and yet I sense that if I were to glimpse them in the light of day they might shine with wonder at the rare gift of intimacy swept in on the high wind. Here there are no prying eyes.

We enjoy our moments together. Often, alone with the viola or violoncello, I catch myself smiling as I either recall our shared words or rehearse the words we might share at our next meeting. But always, no matter how keenly he is summoned in my imagination, we stand apart like spheres in the night sky whose orbits bring them into rare alignment, though they remain on separate paths. For I am the Governor's wife, and he is the convict architect.

But now we are together, and alone, and there is no world, it seems, beyond us.

I confess some part of this to him — or attempt to. 'The Governor is so often in the countryside trying to make things right,' I say, 'that I am forced onto my books and my music for company. But often, I find, you are there with me, too, in my thoughts. Yes, it's true. We talk in my imagination. We talk of imagined worlds.'

'Imagination is the child of desire is it not,' he says, removing his riding coat and giving it a shake. 'Rarely does it conjure what is unwanted.'

With each exchange the pitch of feeling rises. Until it reaches its natural limit. Here, again, is that familiar barrier of fear.

I turn towards the entrance. He moves to follow and we stand together looking out.

The wind is coming so hard now that it shears across the water's surface and shrieks across the cave's opening.

'I would not want you to think that our bond is strong because I am weak,' I go on after a time. 'It is not the result of any frailty of temperament or lack of love or respect for my husband.'

He replies a little too quickly, 'We have grown close because the time and the place presses us into a conversation. Surely there can be nothing wrong with that. And there is no sin in an ... an alliance. Unless it threatens another pact.'

'The Governor,' I say. 'You have seen what a man he is, how deeply he cares for his people, how he is driven by a great cause. But that big heart of his! How can I best put this ... He is a very public man. His better energies are external. The inner man is subjugated to the outer. There is not much of him left for the long conversation of heart and head that is a marriage.'

There is something else more difficult to tell, though perhaps gossip has swept it to his feet.

'I think perhaps you know this already, though neither of us has spoken of it till now. I am the Governor's second wife. Jane Jarvis, his first, died of a lingering illness in the East. When Macquarie returned home from India on furlough he was looking, I believe, not so much for another woman to love as a companion for his travels. That need was very much alive in him. But I do not believe his love was extinguished by her death. He would have named half the features of the Sydney landscape after her if I had not stayed his hand. If not for *my* counsel we would have a Jarvis Point, Jarvis Street, and Jarvisfield.' I take a pause. The words, they do not come easily. 'He loves me,' I go on after a time. 'I have little doubt of it. It is a noble love but it is not —'

'I am sorry to hear,' he breaks in mercifully. His tone is kindly, though not overly mournful. He is evidently charged by the exchange of confidences, by the intimacy. He lowers his head and takes a few paces towards the rear of the cave. Soon he is engulfed by darkness. After a short while he returns: a shade at first, then a form, and finally, as he steps to within a foot of me, a man. He massages his strong jaw and says slowly, 'I dare not speak of what binds us, dare not give it a name. I am not sure that I even have a name for it.'

The next words he addresses to the cave ceiling. 'The Governor is my friend and ally. I am his. As are you. And yet we are, in some ways, one.' He breaks off, lowering his head and shaking it slowly back and forward. He remonstrates with himself. 'This tells you nothing of how I feel ...'

He looks for a place to sit and finds one. He brushes a small skull and some bones from a narrow ledge and offers me a seat. I decline the offer, motioning to my light dress, though in truth I dare not sit beside him.

'It is best that I talk around the subject,' he says, one hand inscribing a circle in the air. 'I studied no philosophy at school; a little Latin, no Greek. But from a book of myths I was given by a wealthy client I learned a tale the ancients told themselves about the origins of love. It begins in a world inhabited by gods and spirits but no men, and no women. On the face of the Earth lived our ancestors: spherical beings with four hands, four legs and two identical faces on opposite sides.'

He is much happier now, I notice, addressing the subject aslant. He cannot say what he wants to say, so he will have it said for him.

'These ancestral creatures were clever fellows, highly skilled in warfare. They could fight with swords in both hands while defending with two shields.' He makes a little pantomime, slashing with one hand, parrying with the other. 'Only the centaur could match them for speed across the ground. They grew bold. And in time they came to challenge the immortals themselves. The twelve Olympians resolved to have them lured by a trick of Athena's, captured by golden nets tossed from the heavens, and one by one cloven in two. Apollo the healer purified their wounds, forging them into the shape we possess today. And that is the origin of desire guiding us towards the person from whom we have been separated, healing the split in our nature.'

'So how then,' I inquire, 'do we recognise our perfect lost half when we see him?'

'I believe he will build a seat for you, a seat of stone. Each time you sit upon it you will recall a bridge over a sweet stream. You will feel yourself reunited with your past. And you will long to be united with him. Even if,' and here his voice falters, 'it is impossible.'

I take a step towards him. I reach out. I take his hand. And then his forearm. Slowly, very slowly, I unbutton the sleeve, folding it back on itself. I search out the serpentine scar.

'With the very first lash of the whip I raised this hand to defend myself.'

'Yes, I know.' I put two fingers to my lips and lower my head over the scar. I trace the taut raised surface with the other index finger. Gently. Gently.

And when I raise my eyes to his again, the Architect's gaze is very wide and very still.

* * *

The storm is less than half an hour spent when Brody comes for me on his bay Arab. He drops lightly to his feet and helps me into the stirrups and saddle, offering to walk back himself. Tree limbs, branches and leaves are strewn everywhere. The harbour waters have muddied. I tell him where to find the grey mare I had taken out — terrified, no doubt, in the stone stables.

Macquarie is pacing the verandah when I ride up to the house. He strides stiffly towards me, shirt damp beneath the arms and neck, as I pass the reins to a stable boy.

'Elizabeth! Where in God's name have you been?'

Later that day I feel compelled to disclose the secret of the old cave if only so that he grasps how I had endured the storm in safety and returned without a soaking. I am chastised nevertheless, my husband charging me with a 'passion for seclusion'. He is right. I cannot deny it. I have begun to retreat from the troubles of this small world to my own sanctuary: my stone chair at the edge of the harbour. To retreat there — with my secrets.

I have come to understand how a marriage, so outwardly solid, can wither over time from within. I liken it to a citadel that might resist any number of siege engines and enemy stratagems yet capitulate within the space of a month if deprived of water and sustenance. And how I yearned for the sustenance that only he, in that small world of exiles, soldiers and adventurers, could offer.

The subjects upon which the Architect conversed were those on which I had an answering interest — the very same. He was cultivated, impassioned; his wit replied to mine, his expressive eyes also. I could ask him to explain the origins of the Ionic order and he would decant his knowledge of its origins. His particular passion was design that would take from Nature — and outdo her. Mine ran rather more to Nature invested with art. He revered stone, which he could chisel and carve; I loved branch, flower and leaf, which I could train into grove, garden bed and bower.

I was warmed by his attentions — excited. And how I craved excitement.

CHAPTER TWENTY-FIVE

At Macquarie's insistence, the Architect is to take up residence at the lighthouse. I bring a glass of warm milk in preparation for bed and as I set it down on the bureau I offer a mild protest. I am careful not to press the point. But the Governor will brook no opposition.

'The lighthouse tower is a splendid monument at this point in time but that, sadly, is all it is,' he says icily from the high-backed seat behind his bureau. 'The detachment that was intended to man it — one officer and twelve men — has been dispatched to the countryside where they are sorely needed.' He pushes aside an official dispatch and an inkwell, stands his quill in its holder, and eases back into his chair.

'The lighthouse battery has been abandoned,' he goes on. 'Four cannon stand at its base, pointing vainly out to sea. But every last man has been sent to the countryside to quell the native disturbances; our sights are all trained inwards. The store room holds shot and powder, but there are no gunners to load a muzzle and light a fuse. There is nothing to be done about *that* for the present, as much as it irks me. But at least the edifice could be inhabited in order that it might serve as a beacon. There is no real work involved at present, though he will have to man the flagstaff.'

'I once knew a lighthouse keeper — for that is what you would have him become — who would beg to differ. It is lonely work.'

'You are not forbidden from visiting,' he says a little sourly, 'though you may find over time that there are fewer reasons *to* visit. Brody, on the other hand, will ride out from Government House with regular correspondence. And for fellowship there are dwellings at Camp Cove. It is a splendid fishery. The fishermen have sons and all owe favours to the Governor who has set them up there so that they may make their fortunes. Indeed, the fishermen never so much as venture out to sea.'

'He will have the company of fishermen and he will discuss ... what precisely? Nets, lines and bait? Tides and currents? Can you imagine how lonely his nights will be?'

But I have blundered. A man whose favourite book is Walton's *Angler* will never be convinced of the fruitlessness of fishing tales. And with my grousing and my advocacy, I have laid myself bare.

He shoots back, 'I do not concern myself with his nights and how wisely or well they are spent. And nor should you!'

'I only mean to ...'

'And consider,' he goes on, lacing his fingers together and cradling them behind his head. 'It will be a service to the colony. If the Government architect were to move there with his papers and pens and books and sketches, he would have nothing to restrain his dreams — his imagination. If there is a site to visit, I will call for him. In the meantime Captain Gill, our very capable engineer, will be charged with the business of construction. Gill informs me, in any event, that the Architect is wont to attend a site two days a week and then not at all for a month. His talents would be better deployed, it has for some time seemed to me, more in the conception than the realisation. If he could only give me ten more designs from the tranquillity of the lighthouse at South Head. Leave the execution to others.'

It was, of course, a form of banishment.

With a distance of some seven miles between us we resolved to correspond. It was a virtue fashioned from necessity. I believe that we set out instinctively to save one another from oblivion. Each missive was a hand extended across that queer landscape of wild bush and wind-battered scrub.

CHAPTER TWENTY-SIX

The Architect leaves the Cove on a bullock-drawn dray laden with furniture, his tools of trade and his few reference books. Most certainly his worn leather-bound copy of Palladio goes with him.

Barely a week later I write him with a sensation. It is already the talk of Sydney Town, but of course in his exile talk will reach him slowly, if it reaches him at all.

The first road across the Blue Mountains to the interior has been completed with thirty convict labourers. A rider has returned to Port Jackson, unheralded and unaccompanied, with the news. A bedraggled figure with a long ginger beard and a somewhat vulpine smile, he rides straight to Government House to inform us that the grand undertaking is complete. Jenkins is his name. He is an overseer of the work gang, having graduated from the ranks of the common felonry.

No inquiry is made as to the nature of his former crime — that would seem small-minded in the circumstances. And he is naturally disinclined to tell. A tall man, and stooped, he has the fiery look of Ezekiel who has come among the exiles to tell of the Temple. He is given a square meal in the kitchen by Mrs Ovens, which he devours, mopping every last trace of gravy with a half-loaf of bread. 'The plate was spotless,' reports our cook. 'And the noise! The man eats like a savage.'

Hawkins leads him, a little unsteady on his feet, to one of the spare servants' bedchambers. He sleeps the sleep of the dead as the grinding light of the afternoon softens into a mauve twilight.

Before nightfall Macquarie gives instructions to Miss Ringold that some coin be given him in a small purse of kangaroo hide. I cannot resist watching from the far end of the corridor. She opens the door nervously, as if feeding a morsel to a lion. A great blast of a snore propels her out. She returns to his chamber soon after with a tray bearing an entire tart of plum, a shaving apparatus, hot water and a mirror. As she emerges she notices me at my end of the corridor. I raise my shoulders questioningly and she shakes her head to indicate that the man is still insensible.

Early next morning the door to his chamber is discovered open, and the herald has vanished. Miss Ringold wakes us with the news. 'He has eaten the *entire* tart,' she says, clasping her stomach and puffing out her cheeks. 'The money has gone, and so is the blade.' I go to check. Jenkins' ginger whiskers are evidently still attached to his chin, for there is no sign of them about the basin.

Macquarie has the town searched. But Jenkins is nowhere to be found. Around midday inquiries at the turnpike reveal that he has purchased a Baker Rifle, cartridges and powder with Macquarie's gift of coin. He was last seen riding at a gallop from the turnpike, heading west in a cloud of red dust.

Blaxland, Lawson and Wentworth discovered the first passage over that formidable mountain barrier, and any citizen with horse and carriage and the stamina for such a journey will now be able to cross it. What riches might lie beyond? Jenkins must have seen something, when standing on those blue crags bathed in the setting sun, to excite him. And here lies the great difficulty with the colony's present path of expansion. The wealth of the land is a gift and a curse. I imagine Jenkins propped up on his verandah with the rifle purchased from Government money, taking aim at any man or woman, white or black, unlucky enough to venture unawares into his sights. There is his Temple — his Promised Land.

No sooner have Macquarie and Howe drafted an announcement of the news than plans are put in place for an official journey on the new westward pass.

I write to the Architect:

*I will insist that you be invited, as in former times, for your
<u>civic imagination</u> — if that gift is not so severely taxed
by your labours in the Governor's service that its powers
have waned. And then there is your unequalled company,
the absence of which I sense acutely even now. Even if
my request is denied and you are compelled to remain
behind — enslaved to your paper and your instruments —
can you not envisage, my <u>Dear Friend</u>, how quickly the
settlement will grow? Within a year townships will line
the route and the demand for your services will double —
triple. The settlements will require churches, schools, bell
towers. You may yet make your fortune in the colony!
And if by chance my request to the Governor is favourably
received, tell me you will come on the journey west, like a
faithful <u>knight</u>, for my sake alone.*

*And here is something interesting! I believe you will
have a view on it. We are told that the natives on the
rich plains beyond the mountains greatly fear a deity of*

thunder and power enthroned upon the highest peak.
The spears their sky spirit hurls are lightning bolts; his
rage stirs the storms from their mountain haunts; flood is
an instrument of his displeasure. Is there not something
familiar to us in his wrath — in his weapons of anger? We
look down on these people because they have not, like us,
built upon the land or imposed permanent settlement upon
it. Instead they roam its surface. And yet if we would only
consider their stories we might perceive how much like
our esteemed ancestors they truly are. We might recognise
ourselves in them; they in us. They have many refinements,
these people, even if a taste for elegant living is not one of
them.

It is a kind of possession — this capacity of theirs
for myth — is it not? I doubt that a British court or a
parliament would accept that the native people, long
domiciled in a place, inhabiting it with stories, have earned
the right to live out their days unopposed by us. But that is
only because the courts are ours, the parliament too.

It is a week before I have word from him. Brody delivers a large envelope. Inside is a sketch of Sydney viewed from atop the lighthouse tower. It is a fine and spacious panorama quite oblivious to the beastliness of some of the town's inhabitants and the ruinous state of the worst parts, sensitive only to the growing town in its folds of forest and water, its windmills and rising edifices. He thanks me for my letter, inquires after our health, expresses his hope that he be allowed to join the first party across the mountains. These are polite preliminaries; the kind of throat-clearing gestures made by an orator before speaking. He has a theme, and he is warming to it:

The convicts on that road gang will be commended for their sweat and their strength and their forbearance. I await my copy of the Gazette bearing the official proclamation. The Governor promised the convict labourers their freedom should they accomplish the goal. And they have earned it many times over.

If I had Howe's ear — not even a bellow from atop the lighthouse tower would reach it in my present circumstances — I would expand on this theme. I would sit with my good friend the publisher and ask him to recall that the convicts, from the time they first arrived at Jackson, have fashioned the colony in its many aspects. It would be nothing without <u>their gifts</u>. Where would Sydney town be without Howe himself? It would be a dull old place without Robinson. Lycett's pictures ornament it. Where would it be without the crafts of carpenters and joiners and the things of beauty and utility they fashion from red cedar, stringy-bark and blackbutt. We are more than muscle and bone!

I would go further still. Are not the convicts on the whole a more ingenious class than their masters? Contrast the mental energy of a titled man, who inherits a large fortune and considerable land, with the precocious enterprise of the more canny thieves! Consider the clipper, removing slivers of gold and silver from good coin, restoring the coin with a file before returning it to circulation; clip enough coin and there is gold dust sufficient to purchase a small tavern! There is a certain class of crime, I am convinced, that is merely <u>misgoverned talent</u>.

190

The Governor would surely share my sentiments, even though it might be considered impolitic to ventilate them.

If you could please convey these thoughts to Howe himself, Elizabeth, I would be most grateful. I exhort him to incorporate into his article some of these reflections — perhaps tempered and put into his vastly more subtle phrases. He may, on the other hand, wish to commission an article from me. I am known in the colony. I have a point of view. If not an article — a letter for publication? It is a worthy subject, and one that demands a hand worthy of it.

Postscript: I forgive the Governor for this punishment by exile, knowing full well the cause of it is his anxiety about our friendship. In truth the seclusion benefits me. I work well in the daylight hours; you have the results before you. But the evening wind howls monstrously and I am alone.

In my reply I write:

I have just endured a dinner with the Governor, the dyspeptic Reverend Samuel Marsden, the very superior Barron Field, and the merchant Robert Campbell. There was much talk, and all of it of the opportunities for making a fortune out of land taken, in effect, from the natives. Field will not speak of the literature he is reputed to collect because, he says, there is no one in the colony who shares his interests. It never seems to occur to him that I might. So vexing! Property is the colony's great obsession. And it is such a tedious mania.

I miss the Architect's talk about those things that bind the past to the present and the present to the future, and how they are preserved in the Grecian style — or the Gothic — or that most exceptional thing of all: a genius able to breathe the great legacy of the past into something entirely new.

There is nothing from him for two days and then:

Dear Elizabeth,
You once asked me to describe the building I would most
desire to erect in this land. I am preparing an answer in
the form of an image not of one building but many. In the
meantime, I feel I must ask you: where is the place you
would most desire to be if not here?

I reply that I do not dream of places unknown to me; only those that are known and longed for. I dream of my birthplace, of its great uplands and its waterways. I catch a stirring rhythm in that bare, mountainous landscape that can only have been produced by some mighty convulsion of Nature long ago. Of that mysterious force I was, am, and ever will be in awe.

The very next day:

I know Rome's wonders only from the views sketched by
others, and from Nolli's plan of the Eternal City. I pray
that once, once before I die, fate will permit me to walk
within the Temple of Vesta, the Baths of Caracalla, the
Pantheon and the theatre of Maecenas, to walk the cobbled
streets, shelter beneath a vault, stand for an age in the
antique squares and contemplate the passage of time not
with a poet's mind — I am no Shelley — but a builder's. By

training I know — or think I do — much of what that great
city means. It was not made by a single pagan emperor,
any single cardinal or pope; it honours many deities, not
one. It is a record of survival, long stability, and hope. But
I know nothing of how it might <u>feel</u> to stand in the aged yet
timeless city.

On a full sheet of paper I pen just the one sentence in reply.

My profound hope is that one day you shall feel it!

I seal the envelope and set it aside for Brody.

And then, a week later, comes the letter I savoured at the start
of this long night's vigil. The brief missive where he recalls our first
meeting, and I relive it through his eyes.

When I reread that letter I am permitted through the white magic
of the written word — preserved not for all time but certainly for *my*
time — to know and feel the effect I had on him at the very moment
we met. I strode into his life as the missing half to the whole he had
yearned for: a woman of like, but not identical, mind. The memory
of that formidable yet ill-fortuned man and what *he* felt ... what I
came to feel! It grieves me so much that it near blinds me with tears.

CHAPTER TWENTY-SEVEN

I wake to a bright morning, hungry for the day ahead. At this time of year the winds are high and the harbour waters shine like beaten metal beneath a brazen Antipodean sun. On such days the town seems more like an idea, or an illusion. Blink and it might disappear.

I fling back the plain navy curtains and raise the sash windows. The green scent of ocean and eucalyptus drifts in across the harbour on a northerly breeze.

Granted, it is not Canaletto's Venice. Those sumptuous views of La Serenissima are of waterways lapping at marble cobbles, statuary of bronze, gilded and coffered vaults, of wealth beyond measure. And yet there is no space to ride or run in that lavishly ornamented miracle crowded upon pylons in the lagoon. My morning view is one, rather, of promise. Here is Nature a short span beyond her state of purity.

On the promontory across the Cove is Dawes Point with its busy flagstaff. In a sweep below me are the main features of the bustling settlement. There are a dozen merchant ships at anchor, a few pleasure craft moored at the wharf, a fringe of cottages and warehouses — Campbell's most prominent — along the shore. A mess of shacks and hovels spreads across The Rocks. On a hillock above them, the terraced military hospital. And a new generation of buildings — designed to delight — from the hand of the Architect. Just below me rises the new fort at Bennelong Point, to which Brody has been billeted so that he might keep the Governor in regular contact with the men charged with the twenty-four-pounders. 'Given the power of that ordinance, and its sensitive placement, the last thing I need is trouble at the fort,' Macquarie explains. I believe it is the most romantic of all buildings at the Cove, although our critics are fond of saying that it was designed more with Elsinore than Sydney in mind. I concede that its Gothic aspect does seem a little out of place beneath a bright sky: poor weather improves it. Strange to think that the architect of the new fort, and of so much else, sits at this moment at a bench on the ground floor of the lighthouse, the tools of his most valuable trade gathered around him in company's stead.

Or so I permit myself to imagine.

Today, rounding Middle Head, is a novelty: a jaunty ketch out for a bit of sport in the sunshine. I enthuse to Macquarie, who sits slumped on his side of the bed. His hands are braced across his knees and his head is bowed; he appears like a man under sentence. He rubs his face and rises.

'It is Simeon Lord's,' he says without looking at me. 'The man is now so wealthy that he commissioned the work from two shipbuilders, brothers recruited from the shipyards of Glasgow. It is used mainly by his sons on days such as this — a pleasure craft. Can you believe? In a penitentiary at the end of the Earth!'

Stepping to his side of the bed to lay a healing hand on his heavy shoulders, I add in a peevish tone performed for his benefit, 'In my childhood a fine seaworthy vessel of its ilk was far too valuable a thing for a lark.'

'Precisely.' He rises, stiff and rusty about the hinges. 'Fishing and the transport of men and goods — arms when they were needed. Although there was a busy trade for a time in day trips from Ulva, was there not? Do you recall the autumn day both King and Queen made the journey to Staffa? It rained so heavily that the monarch, drenched to his royal bones, vowed never to return. That vessel was no larger than this one' — he flings a contemptuous hand towards the ketch — 'built for mere sport.'

'All before my time dear,' I say with a flat smile. 'My deepest impression is that the islanders thought nothing of Staffa's wonders because they were so accustomed to them; they had always *been* there.'

As Macquarie moves off towards the dressing room he gives the door jamb an unintentional nudge, seeming to tilt into it. I notice that he clears the door with greater ease than he used to. By my reckoning the cares of the colony have shaved several inches from his stature.

Over breakfast he tells me he will be away for a few days. There is trouble at Parramatta, he says. 'A papist priest is fomenting discord in the countryside with talk of Catholic rights. Or so the Reverend Marsden claims; Marsden paints him as Savonarola and Wolfe Tone in equal measure. The priest, Father McGinny, can hardly be arrested and led away in chains, but it will take what remains of my authority — and perhaps the threat of firmer measures — to encourage him back to Port Jackson. I aim to have him on the next ship home. But I fear that he will prefer the path of his creed's glamorous martyrs. An act of coercion might better suit his cause than an accommodation.'

'Not the sort of work to which I am suited,' I say. 'For I may show some sympathy for the Catholic priest. What, I often wonder, is the point of religion if it cannot better the lives of its believers. Surely this priest means only to advance his flock.'

'Even without Macarthur's multiplying sheep there are far too many flocks in this colony and all clamour for advancement: the soldiery, the emancipists, the merchants, the native born — the natives themselves. And when I attempt to advance some worthy person for the common good, there is a kerfuffle. The soldiers and the settlers will hear nothing of the eminent good sense in appointing William Redfern to the magistracy. They cling to the one tiresome objection: that he was once a convict. But they cling to it fiercely. If that kind of attitude prevails then I predict' — he shakes his head as if dousing it in icy water — 'the colony will sink back into the mire from which it first arose.'

'You are much put upon, my dear,' I say. 'Much too much!' He is heavy of heart and I struggle to raise his spirits. It is not only the untold difficulties and obstacles that he must surmount to govern this unruly colony, it is his tendency to cogitate upon his cares. It can make for a very dull household.

'You will be fine here,' he says, rising to take his leave with a rallying little jab directed at nothing but air.

I go straight to the study and take up the violoncello in a familiar embrace — there is more warmth in this instrument than in our bedchamber. I play a prelude by Couperin and though I play the piece imperfectly it stirs and awakens me, chord by sombre chord.

I pause and drum my fingers on the instrument's belly. Such solitary playing. All too often a solo part.

In the corner is a full-length mirror. I approach, not without trepidation. The form is still firm; maintained by walks through the Domain, canters on the grey across poorly kept tracks, and gardening in the early morning before the heat of the day comes on.

But the lightly freckled face that swims before me — can it really be mine? Few lines of great depth, and yet no life in the cheeks, no lustre about the eyes. Is it age? I raise my fingers, trace the border of my lips. Pleasant to the touch, these full lips. How long since they were touched with a kiss that was truly felt? I have been kissed courteously. And kissed inquisitively. But not — not for a long while — kissed with heart.

I live with a beloved, ageing man. His steady unimpassioned love was once enough. Is it still? How long before I, too, age and creak about the house, the thick blood pulsing through the veins as sluggish as a silted river?

I am not content with this situation. I strain against it. I am not for slowness, weariness and care. I am young enough to be angered by the waste of life — of my own life. The day is warm and bright and yet I shudder. A frost has fallen over me. If I do not move — move this minute — I swear I will die of a frozen heart.

I ask a servant to seek out Brody.

The ensign helps me into the side-saddle of a penny-coloured mare, hands around my waist.

'The Governor,' he inquires a little disapprovingly as he swings himself gracefully from stirrups to saddle, 'will he be expecting this?'

'Certainly not,' I answer with a flick of the reins. 'But there is no reason he should ever know.'

A few strides and he has caught me. 'But I will need to report, ma'am.'

'Report, then, that we have toured the town.'

'But if he learns from someone other than me ...?'

'Then I will say the witnesses were drunk.'

'But if it should come from someone he trusts?'

'We scarcely know anyone in the colony capable of resisting a drink before evening.'

'Not even the Reverend Marsden?'

'*Especially* not the good Reverend.'

The boy holds his ground. The wind stirs the leaves of the eucalypts into a dry whisper. 'I'm sorry to insist, ma'am. But it will have to be a brief visit. Your absence will be noted by ... others.'

We reach the juncture where the track branches down to the sheltered bay just inside the Heads, the place where Macquarie has settled the fishermen with a grant of Government land. I draw back on the reins and slow the mare. She snorts and stamps as we halt.

'I will go on alone,' I say, regarding Brody with a commanding air — my best chance of securing his loyalty. 'I take some instructions from the Governor with me,' I pat the side of my skirt.

'Very well,' he says with as low a bow as can be managed from a saddle, 'I shall pay a visit to the fishery at the cove below.' His eyes narrow and slide from mine. For a fraction of a second it looks as if he has something to add, but then he spurs the bay Arab and is away.

I ask myself what Macquarie would do if Brody were to report me, or even if he were to leave some room for doubt about my movements. Of course, it would sting him. Then I would remind him of his love for Jane Jarvis, of her place in his heart. Of his youth and its passions. And I believe he would forgive me. He would have no choice other than to forgive his architect, for to punish him for no obvious crime would be to invite scandal. It would then be left to me to manage his wounded pride, a task that would doubtless occupy me for many a day. But it would be worth it.

I do not knock at the front door but walk boldly around to the rear of the lighthouse with its large sea-sprayed windows. Yes. The Architect is there.

He sits inside at a heavy red cedar bench, expertly planed and polished to a high sheen, with a litter of drawings and designs across its surface. His torso is bare.

'Elizabeth,' he starts. 'You have caught me quite by surprise.' He makes to rise, hitching his cream trousers a little higher.

'No,' I step inside and hold out a hand imperiously. 'Please stay.'

He lays down his nib pen, slides the ink bottle forward, wipes his hands on a cloth, and rises anyway. I catch a tremor of delight and embarrassment — almost a shyness — across his broad face. But he does not turn away. He permits himself to be admired. There, I am instantly warmed. The frost, it melts away.

When I come towards him I can see that his chest and waist are not so much muscled as sculpted. He is leaner than I imagined. Perhaps, it occurs to me, he has spent too much time of late with pen and ink and not enough with chisel and stone; he has been deprived of the work that shaped his young form, work that he needs. I would recall him from his isolation and give him that work, and with it his life, but then I am not the Governor; I am only the Governor's wife.

'I took a morning swim at Camp Cove,' he says, reddening. 'The water is chill. But how it quickens the blood! I apologise for my state of near undress.'

Quickens. Yes.

I see how a light covering of fine hair spreads across his chest, swirling around his navel.

'No, it is I who should apologise for bursting in on you unannounced. I have been impulsive. But I was concerned. Your melancholic state. I fear you are too much alone, my friend. And I — well — I am ... alone without you.'

We have danced, we two — have been dancing for years. A courtly game of advances and retreats, feints and turns: a stolen look, a furtive touch, a fugitive sigh. But this time we dance together. These steps I have never learned, and never forgotten. And they belong to no ballroom.

I come closer: a small step followed by a long joyful stride full of purpose. He stands steady. Across his clean brown shoulders spreads a dusting of sea salt. It is then that I notice the welts where the lash caught him across his neck and chest. I turn him around gently; for the first time I survey, laid out before me, the full extent of his ghastly injuries. Ah! His back is cross-hatched with scars. He will never be the same.

'I'm told it could have been worse,' he offers, turning his head towards me. 'I have Gooseberry and her magic to thank.'

Stepping around to face him once more, I run my hand lightly over the scars on his shoulders. 'Does it hurt? I know I have asked before — but now that I have seen it ... entire.'

'Sometimes, yes. It is the memory that pains.'

I kiss his shoulder, his chest, tasting the salt of the sea and a pure scent that is more an absence — of liquor, of tobacco, society itself — than a presence. For he is alone with the ocean and the sea breeze at the world's end.

He retreats from the embrace. 'Elizabeth,' he says, running a hand through his thick hair from brow to crown. 'If we should be discovered.'

'There is only Brody, some way off. The Governor, he is at Parramatta.' I shake myself from my daze to protest, 'Is this man before me the very same who risked everything to challenge Sanderson? Has all your boldness fled?'

I had thrown open the blue curtains in my room this morning. I go to these other curtains now and draw them tightly, bunched and overlapping, together.

'Am I not worth the risk?' I ask, removing my bonnet, shaking out my hair.

The Architect takes my face in his hands, pulls back the rust-coloured strands from my face. He places a kiss on each cheek, another on my lightly freckled nose. 'These blue eyes,' he says, as if to himself. 'This lovely face.'

He kisses the nape of my neck. I close my eyes. He kisses the lids. I am melting into his embrace. But I grow impatient, too.

'There will be time later,' I whisper, pressing myself to him so that he may feel me. 'Time for tenderness. Not now.'

His hands reach for my flanks. I license his hands. I take them and place them where he does not dare.

Now he is alive to it.

He lifts me and takes me towards the polished cedar workbench. I place a hand on his shoulder and he sets me down before it. I turn and with one sweep of the hand send the papers and instruments to one end. I hear the small clatter of a pen as it drops to the floorboards, the dull thud of an ink bottle.

He lays me down. I brace myself on my elbows and watch without shame as he steps back.

At that moment I catch the whinnying of Brody's bay Arab above the crash of surf and the moaning of the wind at the window. The Architect's eyes widen. We spring apart, panting. I rearrange my dress.

'Time,' I cry as I bridle my hair with a clasp. 'After all this time ... *this* was no time at all.' I lean towards him, placing a hand on each bare arm. 'Pray that we have another.'

His quick green eyes are wide and bright and he seems to struggle, like one shaken awake from a brilliant dream. He turns from me — those scars! — and retreats. I open the curtains as he covers himself hastily with a linen shirt.

The unwelcome sight of the bay Arab, tethered to the lighthouse enclosure, greets me. The young ensign stands towards the ledge staring discreetly out to sea.

Brody helps me to mount before riding ahead. I shout for him to wait. He slows and when I fall in beside him, furiously flushed, I ask why he would not give me longer.

'It's as I said, ma'am. We do not want a long absence to be noted.'

'We?'

'Yes, ma'am,' he says a little sheepishly.

As we ride back at a steady trot he reveals the identity of his fiancée. It is none other than the pretty Miss Ringold. Of course her father — now I recall — is a milliner with a store on George Street: Ringold's Hats for Everyday and Evening Wear. The store was open two weeks before it was pointed out to Ringold that he had spelled 'Wear' as 'Ware' on the shopfront sign. It was promptly corrected, but not before Howe had noted the error satirically in a small column devoted to correct English usage. He went so far as to suggest that Mr Ringold's hat size must be small indeed if he had never learned to spell. A cruel taunt, as the old milliner, who hailed from Dresden, knew at least one language more than Howe, even if his English was a little infirm.

'My fiancée,' confesses Brody as he slows the horse to a walk. 'She watches us — the comings and goings. She says she harbours no suspicions. But she also tells me she thinks you very beautiful, and high-spirited to boot. And I am left in no doubt that she is fearful ...'

My blush must have deepened at that moment for he checks himself. '"A fine and *good* woman," she calls you. Fine and *good*. But she will have taken note of our time together. If a lengthy joint absence from the residence were to result in a lover's tiff, well, it would not be the first, will not be the last. But you do not, I think, want idle talk among the help. Because people will — and do — talk.'

I turn from Brody, who has managed unwittingly to raise the measure of fear and guilt in my already troubled mind, and cue the penny-coloured mare to a canter.

I return to my violoncello. I play all afternoon; I play till I am no longer able to. I play so that I might lose myself in those celestial harmonies and so guard myself from the fears and the doubts that begin to gather and thicken as Macquarie draws near. Brody's story alerts me to my own blindness — and to the danger bearing down on me. Is that why he told it?

I cannot count the times I have dreamed of realities other than the one I lived that afternoon. I close my eyes even now and I am there. I am on that table, like a farm girl in a haystack. Not yielding and passive, but braced by my elbows, arms at a tilt, ready.

The Architect, normally a man of many words, is intent and withdrawn.

He is in such haste to take me that he does not even bother to unlace my bodice — that comes later.

With the two of us straining as one for air, he reaches for my breasts. He grows strong. Yes. This now. I am near losing myself to pleasure. So near. I pull him deeper. And I hold him. Hold him there.

PART THREE

PART THREE

CHAPTER TWENTY-EIGHT

I watch as the world remakes itself around me. The century has barely begun and already it pulses fast and strong with trade, industry and invention. The telegraph devised by the brothers Chappe, and by all accounts used to great effect in the Revolutionary War, will within twenty years — I am quite certain of it — have spread across the land. I expect before my lease on this Earth is expired to send a message from Oban to London without the application of ink to paper and wax to envelope. How quickly things change!

In that colony, far away though not so long ago, signals were sent by a flag run up a staff. Arthur Phillip understood that a flagstaff was needed at South Head to communicate with ships and relay signals — the arrival of a transport or a Baltimore clipper, a ship in distress or one with hostile intent — to the settlement. The first settlers sent a work gang to clear a road to South Head by following an old native path. They were ordered to raze every last wind-bent tree on the promontory so that the signals sent from the place they named Lookout Post could be seen from Windmill Hill. In their wake smaller gangs were sent to keep up the war against Nature. Every few months they returned to shear any renewed growth to ankle height. Even today, the bluff on which the lighthouse stands, save for two lozenges of ornamental lawn, is as bare as Bungaree's tribe.

The French desired a foothold in New Holland. And Spain, fearing British designs on her prized possessions — the Philippines and Chile — also cast an anxious eye in our direction. She was believed, on the report of an English agent who had risen to a position of considerable rank within the Palacio Real, to have planned a strike on Port Jackson using a new form of incendiary cannon that would reduce the settlement to cinders. But it was the French with whom we danced that spring of 1819.

* * *

On a gusty afternoon I ask that I be allowed to visit the Architect. Macquarie acquiesces, though he insists that Brody ride with me. It is a delicate game we play. My husband cannot bring himself to concede that the Architect has been exiled in the hope that the bond between us can be broken, or at least weakened. So there are no more meetings at the stone chair, atop an unroofed building, in the Domain or on the verandah. But I am permitted to visit on urgent matters related to the building program in which we — all three of us — are invested. That afternoon I leave with a folio of sketches under my arm. As always, I am accompanied by my chaperone.

We tether the horses at the fence below the lighthouse and approach the long verandah extending between two domed pavilions on either side of the central tower. I knock on the left of two doors. There is silence but for the battering of the wind. Brody steps forward, rapping more assertively with the points of his knuckles. Still there is no answer.

We crab our way up the rise and around to the front, leaning into the wind as we go. Before us is a powerful view of a heaving sunlit sea. Brody's thick black hair spins about his crown. I tie the ribbons of my bonnet. There, with a spyglass affixed so firmly to his right eye that it looks to have been speared, is the Architect. Something out in the rolling swell, beyond the orderly rank of breakers, has him transfixed. He stands shoeless, coatless, a white shirt flying this way and that in the gale — like a crazed invalid. I can make out that serpentine scar on his forearm: still red, angry and raised. The ocean roars. Sheets of ragged surf and spray erupt from the rocks below. Atop the tower a rusty weather vane creaks and spins. A window slams against its frame.

The Architect turns around, motions busily for us to come to him. He runs his hand through his unruly hair and offers me the spyglass. There is no welcome; no thanks to us for making the journey; no sign, save a quick empty glance, of our previous intimacy. I am hurt. I prepare a rebuke. But as I step up beside him I see.

There, square sails puffed out like the cheeks of a mythical zephyr, is a French corvette flying a frayed Tricolour. She has a stiff nor'easter behind her.

'The French,' booms the Architect over the roaring surf.

I hand the glass to Brody.

'She comes in quickly. It is remarkable.' The ensign's face is consumed by a grin. 'Why, I wonder, does the captain not heave to and await the pilot? If there were to be a sudden change in the wind direction ...'

'The reef. He could be blown onto the Sow and Pigs,' chimes the Architect.

The French captain pays no heed to the harbour's hidden dangers and its fickle winds. On comes his jaunty three-master, sails plumped with that bustling nor'easter behind her.

'This Frenchman,' says Brody, turning on the spot as the visitor threads through the Heads. 'I would like to meet him.'

He hands the spyglass to me again. I observe men running the length of the deck. The sails begin to slacken. 'I think she means to slow,' I say. 'Just a little.'

The ensign turns towards the lighthouse with an agitated look. 'Apologies,' he says as he makes to leave. 'I must return to the settlement, and quickly.' There is nothing for it but to follow. I turn to the Architect with a feeble gesture — a splay of the hands. But he has already returned his attention to the ship.

The ensign and I leave for the Cove. As soon as we reach the guardhouse we part company. He descends to the town by foot as I stride alone up the path. When he returns later that afternoon I am at the pianoforte in the wood-panelled study, playing a few phrases repeatedly but quite unable to concentrate.

'The town is abuzz,' Brody says as he enters the study unannounced. 'Where to start?' He reports that the corvette is named *Uranie*, and she swept in so quickly that the garrison at the new fort was alarmed at the sudden appearance of French colours. The twenty-four-pounders were loaded; the twelve-pounders too. The artillery crew stood ready for orders. The entire garrison was mobilised. The soldiers set out for the shoreline in loose formation, muskets raised, bayonets fixed. 'There was much excitement,' says Brody. 'Your husband is at the garrison now. I should add that the Architect is pilloried for his failure to raise a signal.'

'As if the man's name could be further blackened among the soldiery,' I say, pacing the room. 'I shall explain to anyone who will listen that the blame should be apportioned three ways. We are all equally at fault.'

'A catastrophe was averted,' he goes on, 'when the French captain lowered his colours, fearing that so isolated a colony might have become overly nervous of intruders, despite a year of peace between us. What an immense relief that was!'

'Brody,' I chide. 'By my reckoning you have just narrowly escaped an early grave, riding so hard to a garrison aroused from its stupor and preparing to go to war. You could have been clipped by a nervous marine or, more likely, an inebriated one. How curiously events run — if the French had meant to do us harm their Tricolour might be flying from Fort Phillip this very moment. I fancy they would have allies in this place.'

'Monsieur Brody,' he says in his best approximation of a French accent, mouth puckered like a vaudeville performer.

I motion towards a chair. He accepts the offer. But no sooner is he seated than he is up again.

'They are such a contrast to us, the French,' he continues. 'If I were to spit at Dover it would almost carry to Calais on a high following wind. The French and English languages have borrowed from one another, the royal houses too. But the people seem as foreign to us as, say, the Cantonese. There are French sailors camped at Dawes Point — the Governor requested some separation between the *Uranie* and the merchant vessels at Cockle Bay — and they are speaking Latin to the ruffians of The Rocks.'

Brody delivers an exemplary report — nothing is missed. He goes so far as to surmise why the French captain, Freycinet, made such show of his arrival. It seems that he was with the expedition commanded by Nicolas Baudin in 1802; the subtly coloured jellyfish painted by one of the French artists on that voyage still hangs in the office. The French must have had their own reasons for recalling that expedition, but in the colony Baudin is chiefly remembered for his encounter with Matthew Flinders on the *Investigator*, the two explorers colliding along a stretch of barren and unknown coast, as gentlemen might do when taking an afternoon stroll.

Brody returns to the seat offered to him, though he sits like a patron of the theatre with a front-row seat for a tragedy, bent forward, arms crossed. 'Freycinet is a fine mariner and seems to know the coast well,' he continues. 'Knows our own waterway well. Consulted his own charts and saw no reason to bother the pilot. This, in any event, is the talk.'

Up once again he springs. 'Ah,' he says, snaring an afterthought. 'And here is the best of it. Freycinet has brought his wife, Rose, on the journey, had her stowed aboard, secreted away in a cabin fashioned by shipyard carpenters under his instructions. Her hair was cropped short like a deck hand, and she came aboard dressed as one. All of it against instructions from the French court. Why, his Rose is said to move about the ship as if she belongs at sea, much to the displeasure of some old salts. Her hair is now grown, of course. John Piper, who was the first to greet them on behalf of the Crown, says there is a great stillness in her black eyes, a great deal of life in her bow-shaped mouth, and that all in all she is an enticing beauty.'

We strive to divert ourselves with all available means from our true situation — as a mere offcast of European society affixed to an unknowable vastness at the world's end. But we are in some way merely biding time. Waiting. Novelty and excitement come from the sea. And so it is with the arrival of Freycinet and his Rose.

Of course, I sense a rival for the attentions of the men whose company is worth keeping. There are so few pretty women in the town. Well, there are beauties — but scarcely any of virtue. The settlement, on the other hand, is rent by rivalries. I resolve at once that our French guests will not be the cause of further division. If Rose Freycinet is keen for friendship, well, I am for it too.

Brody is standing with his hands behind his back, his breathing a little shallow, a look of exhaustion on his young face with its cherubic dimples. I have seen him dismount after a six-mile gallop over rough terrain but I have never seen him look so weary, and at the same time so exultant.

'It seems the French captain is no different to an Englishman,' I remark, 'except that he is more knowledgeable in the ways of the world. A man should never leave a young wife at home when setting out on a long voyage, if it can be helped. Who in his right mind would leave behind such a Rose to be picked by another? And if she is all for the adventure — why not? Besides, this Freycinet is a bold enough seaman to hold no fears for his command.'

The ensign has been staring absently out the window with the irregular panes.

'You have not been listening this past minute, Brody. I have been saying' — he snaps to attention — 'that the French in my view are not so very different from us. Not, at least, intellectually. Morally, though? Perhaps. Our Church is very bleak. The French I think are ... more like the Irish in their attachment to pleasure. But how much of the Irish gaiety is drink?'

'I wouldn't rightly know, ma'am, though of course I am Irish as you know. Try as I may, I can remember few pleasures from a childhood in Connemara.'

Brody shoulders so much responsibility that I sometimes forget his youth.

213

CHAPTER TWENTY-NINE

As light fades, I summon the Governor's trap and make my way, uninvited, to the military barrack. I sense a foreign presence in the streets and alleys. It is as if there has been a shift in the town's geometry; something is out of place, subtly altered. Despite the gathering dusk there are more people out than usual, and the townsfolk are better dressed — as if for show. Where has this colour come from? Where has it been? I detect a current of excitement, and what seems to be a suspension of normal labour. There has been drinking on the streets, a thing normally forbidden by Macquarie till after dark.

A small function is underway at the regimental headquarters, a two-storey sandstone building with large windows, described by the Architect as Palladian. These are always spotlessly clean, thanks to the convict labour expended on their maintenance.

Macquarie turns sharply when my name is announced at the door. Resplendent in regimental dress, as I'd expected, he stands directly beneath a magnificent chandelier, a glass of claret in his hand and a flush to his cheeks.

'Elizabeth,' he says. 'I thought you would be gardening, or reading, or sketching out a new adornment for the town.' He turns beaming to a ruck of soldiers, as if anticipating their affectionate laughter.

The Governor moves off hastily to fetch *la fameuse Rose*. Justly famous, I have to concede. She has long, heavy black hair, a small triangular chin, shapely lips glossed blood red, and an equatorial tint much too deep for the salons of the Palais Royal.

'Mrs Freycinet,' says Macquarie, inclining a little towards the newcomer. 'My wife, Elizabeth.'

She reaches out and looks searchingly into my eyes. Without returning her gaze directly I reach for her hand. She rests hers in mine. I am unnerved to find it is like shaking a paw — the hand is still gloved.

'My wife,' Macquarie goes on, 'says she has been reading a French novel about a princess.'

'*La Princesse de Clèves*,' I say. 'The most sober love story I have ever encountered.'

Rose Freycinet gives a little pucker of surprise. '*En France toutes les ecolières* ...' She pauses, a little frustrated with herself. 'In France,' she goes on in strongly accented and quite deliberate English, 'this is the novel all schoolgirls — you say schoolgirls? — must read.'

Her speech may be stilted but her movements are languid and assured. Her hands move about freely, rattling her many-hued bracelets. A dress of aubergine-coloured silk divided by a ladder of pearly buttons hugs her hips, and from her long neck hangs a silver chain with an inscribed gold pendant resting on the swell above her neckline. She has a gypsy look. If I were to place a wager on her deep ancestry, I would say ... Catalan. Or Sicilian.

The French captain detaches himself from a group — a mingling of some of his men and some of ours — to join us. His pepper-and-salt hair is short, fashionably pushed forward, and clipped to reveal the ears. His eyes are dark, cheekbones high.

'A great pleasure,' he enthuses in more fluent English than his wife's. His full, cherry red lips are rather self-consciously mobile, as if newly acquired. 'We have been marvelling, all of us, at the fine city you have managed to build. And from such poor beginnings! It was not much to look at when I first saw it almost twenty years ago. But it will very soon, I'm sure, become a fine European city. My draughtsman, Arago, asked as we took in the sights of the harbour if our best architects had not committed crimes in London and come to the colony as' — he stirs the air with his hands — 'convicts.'

'*Mais vous nous flattez, monsieur,*' I say. With this little flourish of my schoolgirl French, the Captain seems unsure whether to use his mother tongue, or the language of his hosts, and so he uses both.

'*Pas du tout,*' he demurs with a half step towards me. 'We are quite envious. It could have all' — he spreads an arm — 'been ours. If Bougainville had been able to penetrate the *Grande Barrière de Corail* he would have beaten Cook to the trophy *et voilà*, I might have one day welcomed you to these shores! If La Pérouse had sailed to Botany Bay *avec plus de vitesse* he would have arrived before your first fleet and pfff!' — he opens his hands as though releasing a dove from his grasp — '*Qui sait ce qui* ... Who knows what could have happened?' He steps back, with an expression of mild chagrin.

'Our architect,' the Governor says in a tone of forced bonhomie, 'has a fresh idea for a new building every hour. It is not your architects we need, it's your idle hands to quarry, carry and dress the stone.'

A fellow officer joins Macquarie, apologising profusely yet demanding his attention. They move off together.

'So you are not concerned then, about the Commissioner?' Freycinet inquires. He adopts a conspiratorial tone. Rose, wearing a fixed smile, watches on.

'The Commissioner?'

'Bah! Of course. You have *not* been told. It's as I thought.' He turns to his wife with a troubled expression, drops his shoulders and head an inch or two, flaps a hand excitedly to bring her closer in, addressing her as she comes near in rapid French.

She takes my arm and we move, the three of us, towards the corner of the room. Several sets of inquisitive eyes follow us. A finger is pointed from the midst of a group of soldiers and a waiter follows bearing glasses of wine and punch.

Freycinet and I each take a glass of wine and Rose, removing her gloves, chooses the punch.

She takes a sip and her eyelids flutter. 'This *ponch*.' She shakes her head. 'It is very strong.'

'Regimental strength,' I say. 'Mostly rum and gin. A touch of fruit juice to make it respectable.'

We pause beside the large window and gaze onto a darkening view of the garrison's barren parade ground. I catch the highlights of our reflection in the glass. 'We encountered him in Rio de Janeiro,' offers the French captain. 'Not in person, of course. But we, or rather Rose, discovered through some of our agents, that he comes to Port Jackson with a commission to inquire into the workings of the colony. I should warn you — it is not a friendly commission.'

And with that he strides off.

With small gestures and an almost imperceptible nod, Rose draws me closer. 'He desires to put an end to what he calls a "war",' she says in French, her almond-shaped eyes widening. 'We believe that he means to provoke one. Be careful! Be alert!' As if to perform the motions of vigilance she looks sharply over her left shoulder, then her right.

In Rose I perceive a like mind and spirit, and she, I believe, detects an ally in me. She speaks her mind, as I do. Holds her head equally high. Was she chastised, as I was in my young years, for her fiery spirit? I am certain of it. And if Macquarie had announced his intention to sail the world on an adventure then I too, I like to think, would have stowed myself on board.

And yet she is vastly more skilled in the arts of deception — this Rose. Freycinet has acquired both a wife and a spy for his long voyage. Masking her purpose with a smile, she throws her head back and laughs.

'This Commissioner believes,' she continues calmly, 'that there are two classes of people here: the rabble and the upright, he calls them. The Governor, he claims, is on the side of the rabble. The Commissioner comes to ensure that the upright prevail, and in doing so —' She breaks off. Once more she takes in her surroundings nervously. 'He means,' she continues in a secretive whisper, 'to injure your husband. He calls him a radical. Yes, he does. Says it openly.' A small nod. 'But you are fortunate, no? This man is very boastful. Even in the port of Rio he makes his intentions known to the French consul. Fool!'

My eyelids, I am aware, have been blinking rapidly. My mind has come to a halt. Surely my features betray my bafflement.

Rose cocks her head and looks at me quizzically. One fine strand of her hair has detached itself and come to rest on her thickly painted lips like a crack in a painted portrait. She takes it between her fingers — there is a flash of red nail polish — and sweeps it back into place. She draws herself up and gives a solemn bow as if to say, 'There. I have played my part.'

'I know nothing of this,' I return after an agitated pause, hands clasped so tightly together that it pains the joints. 'Nor does the

Governor; I am his confidante as well as his wife. You had best tell him, and quickly.'

Freycinet weaves around groups of uniformed officers, arranged in ornamental circles, to rejoin us. He has replenished his glass. 'Have you told her,' he asks Rose, his lip curling, 'the Commissioner's name?'

'It is John Bigge,' she says.

He muffles a laugh with a sip of claret, takes another, and looks around. 'And you know — this is the most delightful thing — he is very, very small.' His laughter ends in an asinine snort, which draws a curt look from Rose.

Elsewhere in the room conversation stops and heads turn. We, all three of us, adopt blank surprised expressions. After an awkward moment of silent disapproval, the hum renews.

Freycinet pauses to take another sip from a glass that seems too meagre for his thirst. He sighs a little too loudly, and drinks rather too deeply. 'Depending on the force of the trade winds,' he says, 'Bigge may be here any day.'

'Please, then,' I entreat him. 'Inform the Governor — immediately.'

I trace Freycinet's path through the crowd towards Macquarie. There is a conference between them. I believe I detect the precise moment the news is delivered. Even from a distance of several yards I note a tightening of the eyes, a slackening of the cheeks and the liquefaction of Macquarie's normally impeccable social smile. It is followed, just as quickly, by a partial recovery.

Soon afterwards I am asked if I might play a tune at the regimental piano that is only ever used for bawdy drinking songs. I arrange myself on a seat before the keys, focus my thoughts on a Haydn sonata. As I begin to play I catch sight of Freycinet and

Macquarie departing the scene together. For a beat I pause with hands raised above the keys, quite overwhelmed by the pace of events, before collecting myself.

It is not the most musically educated audience I have performed for. But I am surprised how quickly I manage to disperse it with my poor playing. I desire something tempestuous: the *Appassionata*. In this rush of motion, I crave a rush of *emotion*.

CHAPTER THIRTY

The day after Freycinet's arrival I set out for the Domain in the
trap. I seem to feel so many things at once — excitement and
remorse, guilt and promise, conviction and fear, mostly fear — that
I scarcely feel anything at all. I seek the air out here; the reviving
air of solitude. And what of these rumours? If they prove true, and
we have an enemy stalking us under British colours, what can be
done to avert catastrophe? But perhaps my fears attach themselves
to a fiction unworthy of the time I indulge it. The French would
love nothing more, says Macquarie, than to plant a thorn in
Britain's flank and sail gaily home to their monarch. As a young
man he helped to drive Napoleon from Egypt and he still believes
they fight by their own rules, that they are tricky, overly subtle and
Janus-faced. I am not so sure. What rules do we obey in our fight
with the natives?

Drawing up to my stone seat, I unpack a nest of cushions from
the trap — deep blue fringed with crimson and gold lace. I arrange
them about me. I sit, inhale, take in the view.

* * *

Unbidden comes a line of verse, or perhaps a mere fragment of a line: 'She did lie in her pavilion — cloth-of-gold, of tissue.' Shakespeare, I think. The Egyptian tragedy? It calls to me from the past. But the past — how strongly present it is at this moment. I am here on the isle of Mull, a woman of forty, hair falling loosely over the shawl wrapped around my shoulders. Set before me is an orderly book of octavo sheets, a file of Antipodean mementos, and beside them a steel pen, ink and blotter. And I am a woman in her mid-thirties seated on a rocky plinth in the Antipodes beneath a spreading fig tree, plumping up my cushions. And here I am, twelve again. I'm perched on the little bridge above the glassy stream on the Airds estate, feet dangling in the cool liquid air. I am all three. The same blood. The same soul. But would the two younger selves recognise me, a memoirist beset by her sorrows, awaiting the dawn and whatever it is that the dawn might bring?

I take a candle and pick away the guttering to release the pale fading light. I swing it in an arc to illuminate the walls. Here is a sketched portrait of Bungaree, in three-quarter profile, drawn by an expert hand; beside it is an oil of my husband, more naively done; and there the Architect's fantasia of buildings from all ages and places rising from the forested coves and promontories of Port Jackson.

The stone chair. What was I feeling that day? What did I see? I kept no diary; my memory and my mementos help to orient and steer me as I journey between two hemispheres and two lives. Without them I am lost.

* * *

I am tilting back my head, untying my cap and shaking out my hair. I gaze up at the arabesque of oily leaves from the embowering fig tree.

Gone are yesterday's blue–white breakers. The insistent, impetuous wind has lost its force.

I am fortunate to call this bluff my own — only too aware that my lease upon it is for a brief span — and to watch this New World at work. In my time here I have watched it grow.

For an incalculable age — millennia, maybe more — this place belonged to another people and their dreams are set out like a glowing grammar upon the wall of the cave below. A stencilled hand in its cloud of ochre declares, 'Me. I am.' And also, 'Mine this place.' The kangaroo trussed up in its own skeleton is primal magic and also a deity: 'Come to me great spirits of prey, I call upon you!'

I take out my novel and place it face down on the bench. The Princess will have to wait. I am too distracted even for diversion.

Behind me, a clatter of hooves. I leap to my feet, turn to face the intrusion. Towards me come two horses, rasping hard. Brody rides the bay Arab and there is a visitor on a powerful chestnut stallion. I tie up my hair and put on my cap.

Brody comes forward as the figure behind him dismounts in a tangle. Here is a man who once rode confidently and well but no longer rides often. My guess is that he boasted of his riding prowess before the stallion was saddled for him, and confessed to Brody on the ride that he had slightly exaggerated. If he had been honest at the start they would have saddled him a gelding.

'Monsieur Arago — from the Freycinet expedition,' Brody beams as he approaches with long strides before executing a sharp pivot and motioning to his guest. The visitor follows, bow-legged and a little pained. He rubs his side, lifts a leg and shakes it. Before he has a chance to speak, Brody speaks for him. 'Did you know they are circumnavigating the world? We catch them on their run home.'

223

The visitor removes a deep green hat — gaucho style, I have seen its type before — from a head of thick curls darkened with perspiration. He takes my hand, pressing, almost caressing, with light fingers. And then, with an open expression across broad, high-coloured cheeks that have not seen a shaving blade for several days: '*Enchanté*. A pleasure to meet you, madam. Arago — Jacques.' Unlike his captain, the *Uranie*'s draughtsman wears his hair long over the nape of the neck. It recedes from a strong face defined by a beetling brow and a heavy, slightly simian, upper lip.

'I have just been explaining to Monsieur Brody' — he turns to the lad and holds out a hand as if supporting a tray of drinks — 'that Port Jackson is a great surprise. A joy. I am charmed. We were told to expect a prison, very grim. One of the inner circles of an' — he clicks his fingers to spur his mind — '*enfer terrestre*. A hell on Earth. But the spirit is lighter here — more hopeful — than many of the free ports we have put into on our voyage. Although it is certainly warm enough today for hell.' He loosens his damp neck cloth as he smiles and then, not satisfied, unties it.

Brody breaks in excitedly, 'After a fortnight at Jackson they sail for home. The Governor and I plan to make the most of their company — they have so many stories to tell, tales of the Sandwich Islands, of Guam, Hawaii, New Guinea, the oceans, the strange creatures of the sea, the even stranger inhabitants of land. I felt you would like to hear these tales … of adventures.' The ensign's Irish brogue is more noticeable when heard in a duet with Arago's liquidly accented English.

The visitor, who has been staring at his shoes during Brody's narration, raises his head with a flashing smile. He has forty years behind him, I would guess. But most certainly he *believes* himself to be a man of twenty-five.

'May I trouble you first for the whereabouts of a fresh spring?' he looks about, shading his eyes. 'I have ridden in this heat for an hour. I have thirst. And the water — I have just realised — it is all gone.' He cuts me the look of a small helpless boy. He must consider it charming.

'Here,' I say, taking a bottle of fresh water from a basket beside me. 'But there is only one glass.'

'I would be so ... very ... grateful, madam. Please, you first.'

I drink a half glass, refill it to the top and offer it to him.

'The storms crash into these headlands with the ferocity of Mongol hordes,' I say as he sips from the glass, not forgetting his table manners, even though there is no table and the chair is of stone. 'They bring good rainwater to a dry land. But the Tank Stream is fouled. For a fresh spring you will have to ride to Queen's Wharf, just below the old hospital. Now if I am able to direct you to the source of good water, Monsieur Arago, are you perhaps able to reciprocate with good wine?'

'Ah, wine,' he says with a smile and a sleepy nod. 'I have drunk enough good wine on board the *Uranie* to last a lifetime — we were especially well provisioned in that regard. But there have been many times at sea when there was barely water enough for life itself. My mouth felt like the inside of a cheap leather purse.' He pokes out his tongue, crosses his eyes and drops the corners of his mouth.

Arago would shine brightly in any company. Is there a queen who would not want him at court?

'You were saying — the colony is a surprise. I know that I was surprised, on my first day. But you, I think, had different expectations. What, if I may ask, were they?'

'Difficult to say,' replies Arago with the confident air of a Frenchman who has lived at one time among English speakers.

'It was never expressed. Not openly. We deliberately chose to visit a society — perhaps the world's first — entirely dedicated to the rehabilitation of malefactors.' He rolls the word out slowly as if savouring it. 'Freycinet gave a very good report,' he goes on after a pause. 'But almost twenty years has passed since his first visit with Baudin. I wondered if the English since that time had built a Château d'If on the shore of a shark-infested ocean. But I see instead that you have built for pleasure.'

'Not entirely ... But you have noticed Captain Piper's villa.'

'Yes. And a fine lighthouse with a tapering column. A pretty fort. And this, er, large castle,' he turns, scans the settlement, picking out the castellated stables with a forefinger. 'The horses sleep in a palace while the Governor and his fine lady make do with a cottage. That, if you will excuse me, is as upside down as the seasons in this country.'

'A very large and well-appointed cottage, if I may correct you.'

'Yes, a cottage orné.'

'In any event the plan is to unify all the parts. Make the building coherent. In time ...' I detect an earnestness in my tone, and break off. He has not come all this way to hear of my plans for the residence.

'May I,' Arago says motioning towards the seat.

'Apologies, I am so often alone here that I begin to think of it as my exclusive domain. Which it is, in part.'

'It seems,' he goes on, 'even after this brief stay, that England's felons have reason to prefer a life at Port Jackson, despite its hardships, to one at home. The cold and damp of an English winter — that alone is reason to wish for transportation. No?'

I incline my head a little towards him. 'It is certainly not missed, the cold.'

226

'There are, I am sure, many indignities such as these' — he swipes the air — '*mouches*. But there is much to hope for in a new country under the rule of law, even if you have come to it as one disowned by the land of your birth. As a place of correction it barely serves. It is a place, rather, of liberation.' His mouth and cheeks inflate into a grin that collapses as if punctured when it goes unanswered.

'In France,' he continues, 'we killed a king and his queen, and then we killed their killers, and we do not forget to kill one another. We have bathed in blood. All so that we could begin again. But the remaking was not done. We have restored the monarch. It is very ... boring.' He places a heavy accent on the second syllable, which has the strange effect of making a word designed to express tedium sound almost jaunty. 'Ah, but the remaking,' he goes on, 'is being done here. *Voici la vraie révolution.*'

I wave a chiding finger at Arago. 'Well sir, you may speak your mind with me for I am,' I turn from the harbour and look at him a little fiercely, 'of the same view. But you must take care not to put it about too widely.'

'For the fear that I might ... what? Seriously. *C'est vraiment ...* It is really true. There is a mild yet reasonable Governor. He believes in his heart in the ... the rehabilitation of the convict. A jail has fathered a settlement. And that settlement will one day soon be a city. Before too long there will be a nation; a fine one, perhaps. *Pourquoi pas.*'

'You have more confidence than me, my good sir. The Governor is criticised strongly at home by wealthy men who believe the convicts are treated a little too well.'

'Too well. Or ... perhaps well enough to embarrass those who would treat them poorly? A criminal, almost by definition, forfeits his rights as a human. In most places.'

'I know only that the Government in Britain will not sit idly by in the face of criticism from titled men and those of means.' I pause at the intrusion of a memory — a dispatch from Bathurst cataloguing these complaints. 'In point of fact it will not,' I go on, 'even permit itself to be accused of meekness, for it is the Government of the powerful. And you say yourself — at least your captain and his charming wife seem quite certain — that there is a Commissioner on his way to address the situation.'

'Very true. He is to have an inquiry, but he has already made up his mind. He is, on the other hand, an Englishman. He is not a monster. France has produced a Robespierre and a Bonaparte within one generation. Here in this colony you have not, I note, enslaved your native population, as we might have done.'

'This, surely, was the crime of an earlier age,' I remark in a combative tone. Arago recoils, just a little, as if he had received a knock on the jaw. I go on. 'Britain has abolished the slave trade and within a few years it will be stamped out across the Empire. Meanwhile Dawes, who was a famous friend of the natives here' — I point to the promontory named after him — 'fights for the cause from Antigua.'

'Ah, but we French are very clever. The trade was declared illegal, then legal again. The business itself has redoubled everywhere sugar is grown. Voices are raised in protest, and tears are shed in pity. But the profits climb. We have some two hundred ships in Le Havre dedicated to that ugly trade, and another hundred in Nantes alone. Believe me, madam, if it were the Tricolour and not the Jack planted on these shores — a fact that I, as a Frenchman, naturally regret — the natives here would not roam free. The leg irons used to transport the convicts would be fastened, on the return journey, around the ankles of native slaves. They would serve the sugar plantations of Martinique.'

'You speak with strong conviction, sir.'

'I am proud of my country in many respects, but not all. Why we have just this morning met with Monsieur Bunga ... Bunga ...'

'Bungaree.'

'A great, as you English say, character. He told us Sydney was his — his domain. His! Well, King Bungaree would be serving the Governor's table if La Pérouse had not been so, er ...?'

'Tardy. Very close to the French.'

'Tardy,' he says with a shrug. '*Tardif*. Yes, you are right. Bungaree would not be cooking a big fish over a fire, attended by his queens, as described by my friend Brody. How delightful! No. He would be pressed into service. Enslaved. Shipped away never to be seen by his family again.'

* * *

I have a signed copy of Arago's *Voyage Autour du Monde* bearing a scrawled dedication. It reached me on Mull — quite how he knew where to find me after Macquarie's death I do not know. Ah, but perhaps I do. In any event, it comes with a note to say I am fondly remembered. And there is an invitation to lunch — in Bordeaux.

In his chapter on Port Jackson, Arago wrote of magnificent hotels; majestic mansions; houses of extraordinary taste and elegance; fountains ornamented with sculptures worthy of the chisel of Europe's best artists; spacious and airy apartments; rich furniture; horses and carriages of the greatest elegance; and immense storehouses. On and on it went.

He singled out John Piper's harbourside mansion and in his recollection extended it by several floors in height and in span until it became a veritable Fontainebleau. He fancied he had been transported to one of Europe's finest cities, because he wished so fiercely to be home. He smiled at the settlement, and the settlement returned his smile. He was adored in the colony — by me as much as anyone else — for his gay talk and his endless treasury of traveller's tales. He sought the company of those who found him sophisticated, and in return he attributed sophistication to them.

I know full well what he did and didn't witness in Sydney, how he sugared what he saw and what, as he sat in his cabin with his journal on the voyage home, was phrased to give texture to the narrative or balance to a sentence. If Arago had been an historian he would — he confessed this to me himself — have made Antony the victor at Actium in order to spice the tale.

I find it difficult, even now, to get Arago's measure. I came to know him well enough in that brief time, and found him delightfully candid, generous and gay. But he was far too liberal, I thought, with his enthusiasms. Arago's aim was to gain renown as the discoverer of an Antipodean Utopia, and in so doing to finance his next round of travels. But, of course, if he had given the right words to the evil that was afoot — the evil of which Freycinet had warned — it would have seemed no sort of Utopia at all.

CHAPTER THIRTY-ONE

Overnight there is a change. Before bedtime — Macquarie is already asleep, mouth open — I catch the soft crunch of thunder far away. I open the curtains of the bedchamber as a thick fork of lightning cleaves the night sky to the north. I finish my sad novel by the light of a bedside lamp and, though I remind myself it is *only* a novel, a mere fancy, it strikes me as such a true falsehood.

Dawn brings a lid of grey cloud, heavy and unvarying, from the north. The grey-green harbour is dull, flat and lifeless. Around mid-morning the waters are needled with rain, and then the shower, like everything else in this inert monsoonal weather, gives up — exhausted. It is not unpleasant; in fact the syrupy air out of the north is sweetly caressing when it stirs itself into a breeze. But there is little sleep to be had when the breeze drops at night.

In the summer months we women who have the wardrobe and the help will go through several changes of clothes a day, if only to rid ourselves of the unsightly perspiration stains that attach themselves like limpets to the underarms and the lower back. The men on the chain gangs suffer badly. The pace of work slows. And the skin of every Port Jackson citizen — man and woman, fettered and free —

takes on the damp sheen of a tree frog. Ah, the democracy of high summer humidity! Even grey glare does nothing to reduce the risk of sunburn, as I learned in my first year.

'I adore it,' says Arago as we leave the sloping lawn of Government House. He is fanning himself vigorously with a misshapen grey fedora as I open a floral parasol. His hat once, I can tell, had crisp lines. But that was before it was crumpled in his fist. 'For me — for one who will never return to this latitude — there is a scent on the air of this place and no other ... It tells me that I am far from home. It reminds me of my adventure. One day, when I am old and lame and ... *aveugle* ... *Comment dit-on?*'

'Blind.'

'When I am blind ... thank you,' he tilts his head, 'I will long for it.'

'You are quite sure that scent on the air is not the kilns, the abattoir, the putrefying mess that clots the Tank Stream?' I ask. I have become a little arch with this man. It is his charm that provokes me.

'That perhaps,' he concedes. 'All that. And the dozen or so species of eucalypt, the tranquil air of the harbour mixed with the breeze that spins the windmills on either side of the Cove.' He sweeps a hand from Dawes Point to Woolloomooloo. 'Though I would not call that,' he raises a finger, 'cloud. It is more of a false ceiling. I find it hard to believe there is sun, moon and stars beyond it.'

'More like an ocean of rain just waiting to fall.'

'There was some this morning but then' — he makes a fist and snaps it open — 'pschew! It is gone.'

'Pschew.' I purse my lips. 'The word is foreign to me. Is it French?'

'You are fond of teasing, madam, making fun. Undercutting.' There is a courtly lengthening of the neck, straightening of the back. 'I am a Romantic. You must allow ... some space.'

'Yes, of course. A Romantic must roam. But truly! You are a Frenchman whose English has more polish than the Governor's. They will think you a spy.'

'I have been spying on you this morning — that crime I will confess to. The maintenance of that garden, which I believe you undertake yourself — to your great credit — has allowed you to maintain a ... a fine robust form. You possess, madam, and I hope you will permit it' — he leans towards me without breaking stride, lowering his voice — 'the form of Venus and the wit of Madame de Staël.'

I beat the air with my fan. 'I am relieved the likeness is to her mind not her countenance, for she was reputed to be plain.'

'To a woman, ugly perhaps. To a man: *jolie-laide*. And yet she had more lovers than many a beauty. One for the morning, another the afternoon, and then the evening ...' He gestures breezily.

I am sure Arago enjoys the sight of my flushed cheeks, for he cannot keep his eyes from me as I stroll beside him beneath my parasol.

We pause before the low stone fence and turn to look back at Government House. A more humble dwelling than John Piper's villa at Eliza Point, it surely seems, to our visitor.

Arago tells how he has spent the early morning wandering the gardens, admiring the harbour. The guards opened the gate and let him enter: they had no orders to do so, but his charm evidently served as a passport to the grounds. He lingered for some time on the wicker chair beneath the canopy of our Norfolk pine. The tree's shape reminds him, he says, of the Vesuvian ash cloud described by Pliny. There is something about this generation of men. The Architect has it too — the classicising disease.

'Shall we walk?' Arago extends his right arm.

I take it. 'We shall.'

'Excellent. A mariner spends too much time at sea. He is driven here and there by the power of the breeze. He is its servant; it is his. But God made us with legs — not sails. And the muscles of locomotion, they tend to wither without use. I am sure you noticed me at the stirrups — not the most elegant dismount.'

As we stroll from Government House down the hill to Macquarie Place, I indicate a small public garden, triangular in shape, into which I have set a water fountain; and in the process I detach myself from Arago's arm. I explain that the Architect's designs for this park were a trifle extravagant when first conceived, but even in this more modest form — Doric columns supporting an entablature and frieze — they still give us a fountain such as one might have found in Edinburgh or London.

'Or Paris,' Arago adds.

Lending further distinction is an Egyptian obelisk of nicely dressed sandstone, completed but for the inscriptions that will give distances to the main settlements: Parramatta, Botany Bay, Windsor, Pitt Town. It was the Architect who had first suggested this small adornment. Macquarie began by rebuffing him. Privately, though, he was charmed by the idea. It persisted. Eventually Macquarie, without bothering to tell Bathurst in advance, asked for it to be done. And so we have a small pleasure garden near the Cove, facing the fine homes of judges Bent and Field.

Further to the west, the two main streets of the town join. On the right rises the sober, red-brick male orphan school; on the left the high walls and wooden gates — essential to deter theft in a colony of thieves — of the lumber yard.

'We stand now on the main street — George Street named after the King.'

'The mad king,' Arago says, casting me a pleading look as if asking permission to mock.

'So it is said,' I confess in a quiet voice. 'In the words of a fine young poet: "Old, mad, blind, despised, and dying."'

'To the right is The Rocks,' I change the subject. 'Our ... entertainment district. To the left, further up, is the military barrack. At the outer limits of the settlement, along the road to Parramatta after it crosses Brickfield Hill, stands a Gothic tollgate. One of my finest things, even if it has been called a "fugacious toy" by some choleric critic in the *Gazette* who believes it will not withstand the next winter storm.'

Ten years have passed since I first strolled out with Brody along this path through the town. There is still much squalor. And crime. And suffering. New South Wales, after all, remains a penal colony. But the town of Sydney has such a pleasing aspect now. It prospers and grows. And its flowering is an argument, by my reckoning, with the age. It speaks a truth: that the lowly, the stunted and the poor will grow tall and strong if conditions are right. Villains are made not born, and they can be unmade. But it is an argument that men such as Lord Liverpool are determined to silence — certainly to ignore. This is, it would seem, the reason for Commissioner Bigge's impending visit. The conclusion of his inquiry, says the rather unfit Frenchman beside me, is foregone.

'Have we walked enough?' complains Arago, fanning himself with his fedora.

'A little more. I have yet to show you the finest parts of the town. From the water, on your arrival, you viewed the Gothic keep at Bennelong Point. On the western side of the harbour the fortification is answered by the Dawes Point battery, named Fort Phillip after our first Governor. But further on here' — I turn around — 'visible only in glimpses from Government House, rears the castellated stable that you admired yesterday. To the south, a little inland, rises the pinnacled chapel of St James, across from it the three-storey male convict barracks, both of them forming a gateway to the handsome promenade of Hyde Park. All but one of the buildings in that direction — the Rum Hospital — are from designs drawn up by the Architect and myself. His forms have answered the call of my ideas.' I check myself. 'Though of course he has ideas of his own.'

'Why the Rum Hospital?' he asks. 'For heavy drinkers? If such a principle were adopted in France we would have an *Hôpital du Vin* in every town. A fine idea.'

'It was the rum trade that financed the construction,' I explain. 'But that,' I screw up my face to conceal my amusement, 'I think you already know.'

'I have spent only a few days in the colony and already I have heard of the Architect's convalescence in that hospital,' Arago says with a sympathetic smile and a softness in his round eyes. 'I have heard, too, of the assault that sent him there. I would have thought a society such as this needed its architects living, not dead.'

I take a breath. 'He did nothing.' I feel a jolt of anger and my heart kicks mulishly at my ribs. 'Nothing to bring it on.'

A surge of memory. In an instant I am inundated. I tell myself there is no need for guilt, or shame. I raise my chin and give my parasol a merry twirl to mask my feelings.

'Come now, Mrs Macquarie. That's more like it. Cheer up. The story endears your architect enormously to us. We think his — your — achievement extraordinary. Rose Freycinet thinks him a hero for even provoking the man — Sanderson was it? To endure such vicious abuse! To then take the man to court in a garrison town! To brave the "barren fields" of justice — yes, we have had some sport with that ourselves!'

I offer the kindly Arago a smile of gratitude.

I had wondered about the balance of things between such strong personalities: Freycinet and Rose, and Arago as well. All three were recording their impressions with an eye to publication. 'Is it true,' I ask, 'that not one but three books about the voyage of the *Uranie* will contend for the attention of the French public?'

'It is a surprise to even *me*,' he says, raising both hands in a gesture of surrender. 'I, at least, announced my ambitions beforehand. I draw and I write. Draw and write. And talk. I do little else — it is my work. And yet Madame Freycinet passes me on the deck as we approach Rio de Janeiro and pretends that I am a novice who comes late to the business of drawing and writing. *Moi*!'

A theatrical sigh, a pause, and he goes on sourly. 'She tells me she is putting down her own impressions. Freycinet too. I did not believe when I agreed to accompany him that I would be so long aboard a ship of scribes.'

'It seems,' I put in, 'that where we English send out men with muskets, you French arm your corvettes with quills.'

'*C'est ça*,' he says wearily, his fedora crumpled in his fist. '*C'est vraiment ça.*'

Later that evening a rider comes to the house with a gift from Arago in a clean white satchel: a sketch that he has had made of Bungaree in three-quarter profile, needing only a frame to make a perfect souvenir, and a good Rhône wine, 'to be enjoyed immediately,' insists the inscription. It is signed by Arago, 'With gratitude.'

We Scots take some pride in our filial bond with the French, even if there are times we would like to disown it. We are raised on the memory of the beautiful Mary, ripened to brilliant womanhood at the court of the French king, and cut down by an English queen.

Macquarie takes the bottle as one cradles an infant, lovingly. Passing his hand over the heraldic crest embossed on the bottle, he asks, 'Shall we drink it now?' He answers his own question. 'We shall.'

The only sound sweeter than a cork released from its prison of green glass, I think at times like this, is the release of wine from the neck and the slow liquid pulse as it empties: pleasure taken in advance.

On this last contented, uncomplicated night the moon is near full. Its brilliance is tempered by cloud, which has broken up a little on the evening breeze. And the cloud itself, backlit by the moon, is dappled with an eerie luminescence.

Just outside the Heads is a strange unknown ship. Many, later, claimed to have seen it that night: the pilots, a few fisherman, and Bungaree himself. Some say that ghostly barque, rising and falling over the light swell but never moving, looked for all the world like a dead bird — long dead — on a funeral bier.

The next morning Bigge delays his entry to the harbour by several hours. Rowers from his three-master come ashore at dawn with official news of his commission and, in addition, a request for a thirteen-gun salute. Pleading a shortage of powder, Macquarie instructs the garrison at Dawes Point to fire just four.

CHAPTER THIRTY-TWO

He possessed an honest face — round, ruddy and open — disarmingly at odds with his nature. And on reflection he behaved truly, though at the same time viciously: a rather paradoxical thing. For is not fidelity a virtue? It is a fact, however, that the service he rendered to the King was repugnant to me. And for Macquarie, it was catastrophic.

Even at such a distance from his sources of power, Bigge was skilled in its use: a true Machiavel. He moved through the colony like a character acting out a part in a plot already written for him — and scripted most adroitly — rather than a man like any other struggling to craft the mess of life to his designs.

Freycinet, on account of his previous acquaintance with both the colony and Bigge, had, I think, his measure. If the two had been in one another's company for very much longer there might have been a resumption of Anglo–French hostilities in this far corner of the globe.

The Commissioner wasted merely a day, not even that, before seeking allies of his own disposition. Then again perhaps it was *they*, given advance notice from Whitehall — a courtesy denied the

Governor and me — who sought him out. He was soon to be seen riding a black Arab stallion, the finest mount in the colony. It was the property of John Macarthur, the wealthiest, most wilful and cunning of the propertied classes.

Trim and athletic, Bigge was nevertheless — yes, Freycinet had been right — very small. He stood perhaps a head shorter than me, making him five foot four or, to be generous, five; and seemed a mere hand puppet beside Macquarie. Impeccably dressed, he swept his thinning hair forward. The fashion, I believe, was inspired by busts of Tiberius. How contradictory is this age of ours. Blenkinsop invents the steam locomotive, and a Roman emperor inspires a new coif.

The Governor had been summoned to meet the Commissioner — a rude reversal of roles and already an inauspicious one — aboard his ship the *Cerberus*. Macquarie never spoke of it. Events sped us forward too quickly. But it must have pained him greatly to be rowed out to his judge and jury, his inquisitor, in full view of the settlement.

As no suitable quarters were immediately available to Bigge, there was nothing for it but to acquiesce to his demands. It took the better part of a day to prise Barron Field from his fine sandstone terrace overlooking the obelisk and fountain, and to relocate him to an apartment on the second storey of the castellated stable. If not for its excellent view of Farm Cove, the harbour and the Domain, I doubt he would have complied. With this accomplished, Bigge came ashore like a conquering hero. Once installed in the Chief Justice's terrace he set about provisioning his home as if he meant to stay for an age, ordering enough soap to necessitate an urgent shipment. The final touch was a permanent military guard at the door, for reasons of personal security: a dramatic splash of scarlet. 'Is it not, after all, a city of scoundrels, papists and desperadoes,' he was overheard to declare by way of explanation. 'And am I not the declared enemy of that scum?'

The remainder of the Governor's day was spent in furious activity, all of it defensive: meetings with allies and inspections of the barracks and fortifications, accounting for the progress of public works. My husband behaved as a man might before an important interview, running a brush over his coat to ensure no blemish was visible. He needn't have bothered. If there was some gain in the matter Bigge would have proclaimed an unsightly discolouring on the lapel of a coat straight from the tailor, and his supporters would have crowed that they had seen it there, too.

Macquarie rode home briefly around lunchtime — I heard the percussive beat of hooves before I saw him — to warn me and bestir me to action. The raincloud of the previous day had moved inland. It was a hot dry day on the coast with a bitter scent on the air. I remember it as the odour of fear, though it was more than likely a forest fire lit by the natives deep in the interior. How much more vivid are my memories when I reach into my treasury and lay my hands upon one of the few things — a letter, a clipping, a shred of bark — that survived the journey with me from my past.

* * *

'Quickly now!' Macquarie cries sharply from a few yards away as if I were a domestic. 'A function will be held tonight at the residence — a joint welcome for Bigge and Freycinet, a table for eleven.' He comes forward in a determined mood, his footfall heavy. 'I thought it politic,' he adds, 'in the circumstances.'

'A not inconsiderable imposition at such short notice,' I reply as he strides through the door.

He delivers his instructions for the evening to Hawkins, pounds down the hall to his study, and after some time reappears on the verandah where he pauses briefly to view the town — his town, as he sees it — before plunging again into the white day.

There is time enough to ask, 'How was your meeting with the Commissioner?'

'Civil,' is all he says.

He leaves clutching a thick roll of papers tied with a red ribbon. I have the pantry and the cellar raided, a fire lit so that it will collapse into a pile of coals by nightfall, and a few extra servants appropriated from John Piper.

Brody arrives shortly afterwards with a flat parcel in wrapping the colour of pastry, his eyes uncharacteristically anxious as he searches mine.

'Are you well?' he inquires.

'Yes, quite. A little on edge with these ... events. The wheel of providence, it spins rather wildly. And you?'

'I have only once been so unnerved and that was under fire from a Spanish raider.'

I do not envy the lad. He has been sent to find Bungaree, if at all possible. To ensure that he is sober — and to insist that he remain so. The native king is to attend the evening's function in a white shirt and a fresh pair of trousers, without the admiral's uniform to which he is so deeply attached. This was Macquarie's firm request, although the terms of it may have been laid down by Bigge. There will be a reward — a side of beef and a hogshead of ale — as an inducement.

The summer sun arcs gracefully towards the Blue Mountains. Why, I wonder, could a more imaginative name not be found for this low granite cordillera, now pierced by a road opening up the rich pastures beyond; no mountain when seen from a distance is anything other than blue, unless of course it is snow-capped.

I flee to my garden. When I return the dining table has been set. The kitchen is a scene of ferocious activity. I am desperately tired of my fellow man. If only I could steal away to that stone bridge over the icy stream and disappear without anyone noticing.

I sit instead on the wicker chair beneath the towering Norfolk pine — as lofty as Macquarie's lighthouse and perhaps taller — with its spreading arms like the spokes of a vast arboreal wheel. I catch the raucous screech of a sulphur-crested cockatoo, and an answering cry from its mate. From somewhere in a nearby copse of native trees I hear a melodious toot: deep and hollow and liquid. It sounds like a creature of enormous size, but eventually I catch sight of it: a dowdy black bird on long thin legs with a hooked beak. The imposter!

The lawn, freshly cut at midday despite the heat, gives off its fresh vegetal scent. A family of plump black swans waddles up from the small ornamental lake. They keep to the centre of the sandy paths as if they are the domain's true gentry and we are merely minions.

What do I, knowing these quite magical creatures, make of their absence from Genesis? Did our Maker's gaze not extend to the Antipodes? Did God conceive of this as some other world beyond His kingdom, to be ruled by inscrutable laws? The more one ventures into the world, the more one doubts the literal truth of the Hebraic faith, for it is a narrow creed and the Earth is large.

These thoughts in turn recall the Inner Hebrides and its leaf of ash, oak, willow and elder; the bullfinch, blackbird and all the seabirds — tern, eider, gannet, cormorant. I desire at that moment to leave and never return. I suppose it is my own spacious childhood with its rare liberties that I long for. I feel cramped in this role.

Hastening back to the residence, still in my long-sleeved morning dress, I notice we have a visitor. William Redfern, thin-lipped and scholarly, sits slumped on a verandah chair like a man in a slough of despond.

'What can be the matter, William?' I ask, approaching gently, hoping not to startle the man in such a delicate state. 'This poor soul before me, he looks so grey of cheek and red of eye that I am tempted to call for you, knowing there is no better surgeon in the colony.'

He gives a pained laugh.

'To what do I owe the honour then?'

He lowers his head. I sink to a crouch before him. 'It is not the Architect?' I cry, fearing some fresh indignity — or worse.

'No, no,' he shakes his head of fine hair, 'not the Architect.'

'What then? I feared, for a moment, that you had come directly from the hospital.'

'It is the welcome party tonight, Mrs Macquarie.' He gives a resolute shake of the head. 'I cannot attend.'

I draw up a wicker chair — the chair that *he* would have offered if he were not so discombobulated — and sit.

'But you are ill. Of course, I see it.'

'Not ill. Troubled.'

'How so?'

'The Commissioner,' he answers heavily with a heave of the shoulders. 'Bigge. Are you aware he called for me within an hour of his installation at the Judge's residence? And with malicious intent. He did not need treatment. Of course he made some show of it when I entered, complaining of dyspepsia on account of all his trials. His trials! Huh!'

'I'm sorry, I —'

244

'No, I am. I truly …' He scowls and shakes his head once more. 'I'm sorry for us all. You must make every effort to disarm the man. Immediately, before it is too late. He is a danger to you.'

'Do go on then, if it is pressing.' I lean forward so that he might lower his voice.

He looks away, and for a brief moment I permit myself to hope that he might keep his own counsel. But then he turns to face me with a determined expression, and says, 'I found myself drawn into the Judge's study. All was prepared there. Bigge offered me a seat on the other side of the desk from him. He looked at me blankly for perhaps a minute, saying not a word. There was a knock at the door, and in walked a secretary with a large open volume in one hand and a quill in the other. His name was Thomas Scott. It was only with Scott's arrival that the wax figurine before me stirred.

'"You are the same William Redfern whose name the Governor has advanced for a position in the magistracy?" Bigge inquired in a judicial tone. I felt as if I had been arraigned for sentencing.

'He went on without my answering: "The same William Redfern who was convicted of treason?" There was a quiver of the lip, a twitch of the nose, a shallow look from a set of hateful eyes.

'He meant,' Redfern goes on wildly, 'to threaten me with the crime for which I was transported, though I was little more than a child. The beast!'

He leans towards me, quite flushed. 'I don't know if you are aware of the circumstances, Mrs Macquarie. Shall I tell you the story that he already knew?'

'Do go on,' I say, after an anxious glance along the verandah. I hear the sound of preparation in the kitchen, the short heavy strides of Mrs Ovens, and smell the savoury scent of baking meats and the sweet-sour aroma of unlidded pickle jars.

'I was a young surgeon's apprentice on the HMS *Standard* when its crew, along with those of sixteen other Royal Navy ships, rose up against its officers. The vessel was not at sea; it lay peaceably at the Nore anchorage in the Thames estuary. And the action was not a full-blooded mutiny. It was a maritime strike for better food and pay. Bigge knows all this, of course. But he wanted it from me. Will you hear me out? Shall I go on?'

It is not the right time for such tales, but I have little choice — I am deeply indebted to this good man. I settle into my chair. 'Most certainly, William.' Gazing into the surgeon's eyes, enormous and glinting behind his oval-framed spectacles, I see that the redness at the rims has spread to the whites. 'Some tea? Water?'

'Water, please.' He removes his spectacles, wiping them fussily with a cloth extracted from his plain black vest.

I call for the maid.

'The sailors, as I was saying, asked only that a certain number of men on every ship be allowed to see friends and family on coming into harbour, that they be paid money owing to them before going to sea. And also that the prizes of war be distributed more evenly among the men and not seized by the Captain.' He looks towards the harbour, a sheet of diamonds under the bright sun, and blinks once or twice into the light.

'It began as a protest for better conditions,' he says returning his glasses to his nose, 'and no different in its essentials from any such action on land. When it was ignored, the leaders faced a choice: either step down and lose the initiative, or press on. A decision was made to blockade the Thames; a catastrophe, as it turned out. The protest was brutally put down. The ringleaders — all thirty of them — were hanged.'

The maid arrives with a mug of fresh water, which I offer to the visitor. 'But what was your part in all of this?'

'Nothing of any consequence. I simply urged the men, as one boat after another abandoned the blockade, to be united among themselves or risk defeat.'

'A trivial matter I would have thought.'

'Not in the eyes of the admiralty.' He drains the mug.

'I believed for weeks on end that I would hang, too. I spent that time in the condemned cells close to the gallows. From there I caught the last words — mostly tearful prayers and laments, sometimes curses raised boldly to the heavens — before the sharp clank of the trapdoor, the utterly helpless shuffle of feet presaging the fall, and the terrible tune of the noose and rope bearing the dead weight. I was reprieved on the very day I was to climb the scaffold, but only after an interview with a priest who assured me that my sins would be forgiven by a merciful god. What sins? I inquired. "All those committed, and all contemplated," he said. Contemplated! The sin I contemplated at that moment was strangulation of a priest. I have never so much as set foot in a church since.

'The reprieve was followed by a sentence to transportation for fourteen years. Then came a few months on the hulks. The voyage out was a greater trial than the condemned cells. I emerged looking more like a shade than a man. I had been perpetually busy caring for the sick and the dying. My skills were noted by the Captain, and communicated at the first muster ashore. And from that moment my restoration began. I flourished under Bligh, and then Foveaux, and in your husband I found a friend. Some time ago — perhaps you are unaware of this — the Governor put my name forward for the magistracy.'

'I am aware, yes. And Bigge will have none of it?'

'He is in furious opposition. I will never forget what he told me: "The crime for which you, William Redfern, were transported ..." — note how he avoided the honorific due to me by virtue of long training and service — "that crime is unparalleled in naval history." Ha! "Unparalleled," he says. Such dreadful cant and nonsense! And he declared, furthermore, that there will be no emancipist magistrates in the colony. This is what he said — or words to the same effect: "The Governor will withdraw his application on your behalf, or I will have his commission withdrawn."'

The recounting of this horrid tale seems to lance a boil and improve Redfern's demeanour. He is one of those men for whom the talking cure is better than the solace of the bottle. But his mind is quite made up. 'I simply cannot — will not — share a table with that damned malicious imp.'

The cursing seems an even better cure than the talking. And when I rise he does too, much restored.

'It is a dreadful turn of events,' I say as we walk along the verandah towards the steps. 'We had been warned of Bigge's malevolence. And we are prepared for battle. But, his pomposity aside, this is the first real sign of it. I assume that he is aware Macquarie has made it a principle of his administration that the sins of the past are forgiven, and one is judged only by the deeds of the present.'

'I remember when I was called to treat the Architect,' he smiles grimly. 'It is the same principle at work. They dismantle a man in stages. The first is the ruination of his closest allies.'

I perceive a hammering of the heart and a sickness in the pit of my stomach, though not the kind for which the good doctor has any remedy. Regaining my composure, I tell him that while I understand the reasons for his absence I will not convey them to the Governor until he himself has recovered from the insult of Bigge's arrival. 'This is what I *will* tell him,' I promise. 'You are ill — too ill for company. A touch of grippe, contracted in all likelihood from a patient. A professional hazard.'

'Once again, I am sorry,' Redfern says placing his hat on his head of fine hair and adjusting it. 'But I simply cannot ...'

I resolve to make light of the matter and, leaning towards Redfern, I whisper, 'Perhaps Bigge was right after all. You are a born mutineer! For you, sir, have scuppered my dinner party.'

He recoils a little and regards me quizzically. His lips move. There is the mere twitch of a smile.

'I am sorry to joke, William. I did not mean to make light of your ...' I shrug my shoulders.

At last he offers up a smile. 'No offence taken, madam. Laughter is as good a salve as any in the circumstances. As a matter of fact I am rather grateful. It puts me in mind of a story that arrives with Bigge and comes from the surgeon of the *Cerberus*.' He leans towards me conspiratorially and begins in a bright tone, 'It appears that our Commissioner, during a recent term in Trinidad righting some wrong on behalf of the Colonial Office, took his horse out one morning to exercise on the beach — you may have seen how fond he is of riding. He was some miles from Port of Spain when his mount, which he had been riding at a leisurely canter as he enjoyed the sea vistas, was struck and concussed by a coconut.' He pauses, eyes shining mischievously. 'Can you believe it? If the trajectory of the fall had been a little different we might not have to deal with him.

'For some time the Commissioner was pinioned by the stricken beast. When the natives finally came to his aid they discovered that his left leg, though not broken, had been badly hurt. Bigge was taken to the local witchdoctor, a statuesque native woman of ravishing beauty. The horse, rendered lame by the fall, was shot.

'Bigge returned the next day in a carriage, limping badly. Over the next few weeks he insisted that no one other than his native doctor minister to him. She visited every day, locked herself with the Commissioner in his room, aiding him in his recuperation. Well, after several weeks of this treatment Bigge pronounced himself cured. But the witchdoctor, she continued to pay weekly visits. Just to check on his progress, mind. And for this she was rewarded with payment from Bigge himself.

'After several months one of the Creole merchants, a man whose trade takes him to the many small villages about the island, came forward with important information. The witch was both woman and man; or, rather, was a man who took the part of a woman for ceremonial reasons connected with her — er, his — doctoring. When informed of this Bigge insisted on his innocence and promptly broke off the arrangement. But there are those in the Commissioner's household who maintain that he did know, and that this aspect of his cure was one he greatly enjoyed. A chambermaid is not easily deceived in such matters.'

Redfern lowers one foot onto the steps, leaving the other on the verandah. He places his hat on his head and makes ready to leave. His eyes are still red but there is a hard glint of satisfaction to them now.

'It is a fine story, William. But please — *please* — ensure that it does not make the pages of the *Sydney Gazette*. Promise me. If Howe so much as hears a whisper, well, there is no telling where he will go with it. We do not want to defame the man!'

I can understand why Redfern has held the story in reserve, decanting it only when taking his leave. From anyone else I would judge it distastefully risqué. But I am happy to give the surgeon his head — to allow him this small revenge.

I recall the advice Octavio Jewkes gave me on my first morning at the Cove: never believe what a man here tells you about his past. It is doubly true of a man telling you of a declared enemy's past. And yet ... I do not doubt that there is *something* in this tale.

If true — and if I am honest — it would rather cool my ill will towards the man, which presently runs hot. Bigge would then be more contradictory, more complex — more human — than the fanatic among us.

CHAPTER THIRTY-THREE

In the shadowed corner of my room of memories stands a lovely pine chest with handles of faded vermilion modelled on the waratah. Each of its five drawers is stencilled with a species of bird native to the Great Southern Land: a gallery of kookaburras decorates the top drawer; the emu, earthbound beneath its thatch of feathers, the second; the crimson rosella graces the third; the warbling magpie the fourth; while the fifth celebrates the glorious rose-breasted cockatoo. It's in this, the fifth drawer, that I find four spare candles lying loose beside a brass candleholder encrusted with wax. As soon as the dawn breaks I will search the butler's former quarters for the box of spares. It will be, by my reckoning, another hour.

My body is anchored to this island where my cold husband lies. But my mind soars to the other, as if in a dream. I regret nothing from my time there, and yet I lament so much. I feel most acutely the absence of so many Antipodean oddities from my life. It used, so often, to amuse. How preposterous a thing is an emu, a kookaburra's laugh, a magpie's chortle, a lumbering wombat, a sleepy koala. Even the kangaroo! Eccentrics — all of them. I miss the infinite space of land, sea and sky. The illusion of freedom, even though there was little of it in my role. My stone seat. The scent of eucalyptus. And a set of lively leaf-green eyes.

I returned to my homeland for my husband's burial, riding in a carriage at the head of the funeral cortège as it wound its way through the streets of London. It was mid-summer; almost a year ago today. Death brought to Macquarie the dignity he was denied in his last years: a number of dukes, earls and lords joined the procession to the London docks for the journey by ship to Mull. Word was sent ahead to prepare the chancel of Iona Abbey — the ravaged roof of the nave lay open to the elements — and to assemble as many friends and relatives as could make the journey. Macquarie, despite his later indignities, ended his life with the rank of Major General; few of Ulva's sons had risen or ventured so far.

* * *

On the day of the funeral a clear sky glorifies the scattered isles and islets, like so many fallen stars. Duruga: I hear Bungaree say the word and recall his fluttering voice.

Ben More — imperious and unchanged as men and women live and die — rears serenely over the island. I wake to my first morning of widowhood on Mull and take a walk in the grounds of the house at Gruline. There is no wind; everything is hushed, just as it had been on the morning he proposed to me long ago.

Macquarie lies in state beneath the roof of what I had imagined would one day be a keeper's cottage. The Campbell clan — brothers and sisters, nephews and nieces — gathers around to cushion my fall. But my mourning has scarcely begun when they disperse again to Oban, Inverness, Glasgow — there are even cousins at Kirkwall living among the descendants of the Vikings. Death is so commonplace in these battered isles that the bereaved are no sooner revived, soothed, and fortified by kin than they are farewelled and left alone with their sorrows.

Some six months after my clan departs the island, my butler does, too. 'I cannot live on promissory notes alone, madam,' he says. 'I hope you understand. Or will come to understand.' He is a big-chested fellow, with a neck oozing over his collar, colourless hair and small stiff eyes, all of which give him a porcine appearance. He informs me of his departure with his hat in one hand, his heavy portmanteau in the other, and a carriage waiting at the gate. 'I know the economy of this household better than anyone,' he adds in his supercilious way. 'Your reserves run low. The funeral was costly enough. And the chapel you are building to house your husband's *glorious*' — do I detect a satirical note? — 'remains will drain you of every last shilling. Why, the house here is so draughty that in a high wind it is all I can do to keep the candles and the fires alight at night!'

I cannot say that he was wrong in any of his assessments, though it was most certainly wrong of him to make off with a candelabrum and God knows what else in that heavy portmanteau. He crunched along the path to his carriage with his weight thrown to one side so that he could carry the thing.

The closest Campbell to me, my sister Margaret, lives but ten miles away in a house with a view of the Ulva Sound. After the wake she pressed her hand onto mine and promised to call regularly. Through the summer and autumn she pays several visits and on the days I repay the favour I cannot help but look, even when there is no clearing in the clouds, towards Ulva. In winter Margaret leaves the house for London. The islands are too hard, she says. She prefers the lights of the city. And so I spend the dark months — the winter months — alone. Alone, but not quite.

One morning in early December I wake a little after dawn to find a crust of frost upon the lawn and icicles bearding the eaves. A few frozen copper leaves still cling resolutely to the boughs. Everything looks as if it has been fashioned from coloured glass. From the kitchen window I spy the familiar figure of a buck. Head bent to the ground on his splendid tawny neck, he is demolishing a carrot top in the kitchen garden.

The deer seems too thin for early winter, so I let him breakfast on my carrots. After a time I feel it better to discourage him, for his own good. If the footman happens to wake this early, which is unlikely, he will chance a shot — and there is no telling what he might hit. I put on my coat and hat and open the door. The cold air sluices past me into the house as I step outside. The deer is so engrossed that at first he seems insensible to my presence. But he picks up the scent within seconds — raising his head dreamily like a pauper smelling a square meal. Then he has me in his sights. Holding those splendidly arboreal antlers aloft, he regards me with the same arrogant air I encountered on the mountains more than half a lifetime ago. But on this occasion I am no stranger to his upland realm; he is an intruder in mine. Three sharp claps of the hands — the closest sound I can make to rifle shot — and he turns, leaps gracefully and crashes through the bare woods in search of cover.

These recollections — how tyrannical they become with the approach of dawn. They are all out of order. And yet they will not be denied! I search for the way back, which is also the way forward. Where did I leave off? Ah yes! The welcome dinner.

CHAPTER THIRTY-FOUR

John Piper is the first to arrive. When his name is announced by Hawkins I am still flying about the house with bare arms and an apron about my waist. I come to the front door with damp hands, drawing my hair back behind my ears to offer the Captain my cheek. It is kissed with enthusiasm and a somewhat tart, vinous waft. I wonder if, toasting the good life at his harbourside villa, he has not made a head start.

'I appear to be early,' Piper apologises, taking his gold watch from the pocket of a handsome frockcoat, crimson with black lapels, and regards it quizzically.

'Not at all,' I say. 'The others are late.' I draw a slow, deep breath, for Piper is a good half an hour awry. 'Let me take you to the Governor,' I urge. 'He is consulting his records.'

'I can well understand his haste!' trumpets Piper. 'Bigge will soon be running a cold eye over every line of the accounts. He has been here less than a day and I have already received word that he would like to see mine. Damned unpleasant business! Quite unnecessary.'

Piper is tall — almost as tall as Macquarie — with handsome mutton-chop whiskers and, above them, a thatch of dark, thinning hair. He does not bother, as do many with this affliction, to lay a pomaded thatch over a shining scalp. And it is much to his credit. I always find that a man who comports himself with few cares for such minor imperfections of physique stands a very good chance that they will go unnoticed by a lady; at the very least, will be excused. Self-assurance, for a man, is the greatest of all cosmetics.

I lead him to the office, where the Governor is engrossed in his cares. I knock and stand at the open door, holding out an arm to bar Piper. The documents tied with the red ribbon that he left with in the morning, they returned with him barely an hour ago and lie across his desk. My eyes fall on the curious scroll. 'Oh, yes,' he says. 'A list of public works completed in my time.' I linger in silence to draw him out. 'Copied by Howe for safe-keeping,' he goes on in a contained manner. 'I thought it prudent.'

Depositing Piper in the office, I take one last fretful tour of the household before retiring to dress.

Over the course of the next half hour most of the guests arrive in fading light. The breeze has swung around and now comes with great verve out of the Pacific. It bears a sweet, humid shimmer and a light scent of the sea. Being a lively gust, it drains some of the heat from that white day. Spirits rise as the temperature falls. The Antipodean sun, as it sets towards the low mountains, plunges into a reef of parakeet-coloured cloud bordered with gold inlay.

Captain Freycinet and his wife, Rose, arrive arm in arm. The Architect, in a sober black coat and bone-white neck cloth, arrives with them. He has no French but it seems not to matter — the three look to be perfectly at ease. No doubt he is utterly charmed by her liquid accent; certainly, he regards her raptly. I find myself touching the nape of my neck — where he had kissed me. That fire seems to have subsided for want of oxygen but is not, I think, extinguished.

Rose, deep in conversation with her two chaperones, has her back to me. She wears a bold dress of magnificent red silk in a cut that seems more Latin — South American perhaps — than European. In aspect she looks not unlike a hibiscus, or some other exotic species. Rather more constrained is her husband's dress — nankeen trousers tucked into fine riding boots that look as if they had never so much as glimpsed a stirrup, a chocolate brown coat and cinnamon waistcoat. I wonder if he is not, with his intense black eyes, refined nose and full, expressive mouth, the most attractive of the men. Perhaps he is, though not the most attractive to *me*.

The Architect looks very fine in his sombre hues. Macquarie cuts a more dramatic figure in regimental dress that seems ever hopeful of a triumph: high-collared red coat, gold epaulets and black riding trousers with scarlet piping. He is sharing a glass of wine with Piper, gesticulating towards the township.

The Freycinets approach with kisses, compliments and pleasantries about the weather. I ask the French captain about the likely length of his stay.

'Oooooh,' he says with a confounded look. He closes his eyes as if turning over the question, opens them and shrugs his shoulders. '*Ça dépend*,' he says, looking to his wife.

It seems a simple enough query. But it has prompted some unspoken complexity.

Turning to less conjectural questions I gesture towards Freycinet's coat.

'You do not wear uniform to formal engagements on land?' I ask.

'Not if I don't wish to,' Freycinet replies with a restless social gaze that spins about the company.

'For your husband,' says Rose as she leans forward, 'it is, perhaps, important ... you know ... to show,' and here she draws herself up, squares her bare shoulders and puckers her pretty, painted mouth. 'But for us. Boof! Not really.'

Placing a firm hand on my arm, Rose leans forward to ask if 'ponch' is served. I shake my head. '*Dommage*,' is all she says.

With the arrival of Commissioner Bigge I go to join my husband. Bigge is accompanied by his private secretary, Scott, who is significantly taller; he bows and offers a few bland courtesies as he is introduced, but otherwise seems sour and put out. I am privately chagrined that his name is not Little, for would they not have made a grand comic duo!

'I bring apologies from John Macarthur,' says Bigge, offering a limp ambivalent hand to Macquarie. 'He has felt compelled to decline the invitation on account of some rural emergency or other at the Cowpastures.'

'A native raid, I wonder?' I can see Macquarie is not so much concerned for Macarthur as fearful of renewed hostilities so close to town.

'He was not specific. But I doubt anything quite so dramatic. His letter, which was delivered to me in the late afternoon, simply mentions the necessity of remaining overnight on the farm.'

'Still. It is strange that the rejection did not come directly to me,' Macquarie splutters in a wounded tone. 'As of course the invitation had come from my office.' Honestly, I believe his hide thins with age.

He raises a hand to one of the servants from Piper's villa, who scuttles over. The young man is rather plump and his black coat and trousers, clearly on loan, are too tight.

Bigge seems to pick up the scent of frailty. 'That he should prefer the company of ten thousand sheep to this sparkling group,' he says with a mocking laugh. 'Strange indeed.' He will not look Macquarie directly in the eye, or at least not for long.

The night is coming on now and the Governor draws the group to him in his office to toast the representatives of two European kingdoms now at peace. Glasses are charged, raised and drained, although the toast, I note, fails to arouse any great feelings of bonhomie. Except for a new triptych of the growing town that moves from the civic to the bucolic in one sweeping panorama, the paintings on the walls of this room have not changed since the days of Foveaux: a testament to his good taste. Scott, I see, has broken off from the company to study the Baudin expedition jellyfish. The Freycinets come to join him beside this iridescent watercolour. Ignoring Scott, they talk animatedly in French. From where I am standing I catch only the artist's name: Lesueur. I make a note to inquire later, if there is time, what they know of him.

The doors to the dining room have been drawn back and the beautiful polished redwood dining table has been set with a forest of wine glasses and cream candles. Macquarie and I, arm in arm, lead the way from the office, back through the reception room, to the dining room. It is a festive sight. Blue and white are the colours of the plates; the borders are of gold. The colour scheme is reversed on the serving dishes with their oriental gilt filigree and borders of Delft blue. As we enter, the servants are spreading the places noisily to compensate for Macarthur's absence.

'So now we are nine,' I say. Turning to count the guests I note with alarm the absence of one more. 'Or, rather, eight.'

'Bungaree!' says the Governor.

Leaving the dining room, I stride hurriedly with Macquarie to the verandah. The last gleam of sunlight has bled from the day. We have a clear silvery night beneath a fat floating moon. Bungaree is present, though he has not joined the party. Something has detained him at the fence. A guard should have warned us, but there are none at the guardhouse — they have all been dragooned to the kitchen. I have spied even Brody carrying a tray of drinks.

I note with relief that Bungaree has dispensed with his regalia. A minor victory! He stands at the fence with his white shirt and black trousers plunging to bare feet, like a poor country preacher. Behind him stands Gooseberry, wearing an enamel necklace, and further back from her, cloaked in the night, stand several other members of the tribe, silent, statue-still, their beautiful eyes huge and unblinking.

'Come,' I motion to Bungaree. I rush fussily down the path towards him. The Governor stays behind at the verandah.

'Bungaree's mob too?'

'No, *of course* not.' My voice has tightened now.

'They stay here then.'

'No. Bring them inside the wall, if you must. The servants will take care of them. Feed them.'

'And bull?'

'I will have some prepared for you.'

A victorious grin and he comes forward. His people turn to one another and settle on the lawn, chattering cheerfully. I envy them at this moment, for there is no telling what will be said over dinner between a tipsy naval officer, a cruel commissioner, a flamboyant Frenchman and his spirited wife. To say nothing of an opinionated — and oddly distant — architect. No telling if the party will end as it has begun — with a fragile accord — or how long it will last.

CHAPTER THIRTY-FIVE

When we return to the room with Bungaree the conversation has already struck up and I can hear Bigge's mild Midlands voice purring away. The guests rise to greet the new arrival — Bigge and Scott somewhat reluctantly. The room's walls are a subdued white; a decorative antidote, I pray, for the evening's explosive potential. In the western corner — the direction of the mountains and whatever lies beyond — stands a heavy rosewood serving table. Its polished top gleams like glass and in its very centre, like a capstone, is a scalloped white soup tureen with lion's head handles. A tower of plates stands to one side. Facing east, towards the ocean, is the generous bay window that in daylight frames a view of the Domain. From here I can usually make out my stone chair on its hummock beside the harbour, and all the gentle folds in the landscape as it retreats from the kitchen gardens towards Farm Cove, and then to the shore.

I lead Bungaree, who has for the moment lost his liquid ease of movement and walks with uncharacteristically short stiff strides, to his place on my left. Macquarie is on my right. Beside him sits Rose, then Freycinet and the Architect, who has been quiet this past hour. Then there is Scott, and next to him Bigge, followed by John Piper. It is Piper who prods the conversation back to its starting point as the pumpkin soup is served from the white tureen.

'We were just hearing of the Commissioner's family background and his education — Oxford. Profession — the law. He has conducted inquiries on behalf of the Prince Regent into the colonies of Trinidad and South Africa. And he comes now, he admits, to right matters in the colony.'

Macquarie's gaze fixes itself on the mid-point of the table. The muscles at his jawline pulse and twitch. He takes a spoonful of soup.

'By that,' Piper goes on over the clinking of spoons on plates, 'I assume you mean our attempts to conciliate the native population, the most distinguished member of which' — he flaps a hand at Bungaree — 'is here with us tonight.'

Bungaree shifts in his chair and makes as if to speak, though Piper presses on.

'The aim is civilisation,' he declares. 'But now it seems open war has broken out. Damned nasty business, what! Like many long wars of the past it is impossible to tell where this one begins. The first cause was likely a trivial thing: the theft of a woman, native or European —'

Rose laughs unpleasantly.

'John Piper,' I interject. 'You should know better. That is hardly a trivial matter.'

Piper throws up his hands in mock submission. 'Now, now,' he says, offering a coy look to me and then Rose. 'I merely mean to say ...' — he pauses to gather his thoughts and hurries on — 'that a crime that need not have drawn blood — but a crime nevertheless —

has had the most grave, and sanguinary, consequences.' He takes a deep breath, mops his brow, and is about to continue when he pauses again for a sip of wine.

'John,' I say. 'The soup. It is getting cold.'

'Nothing gets cold in this infernal climate,' Piper roars. He takes a spoonful and makes a purse-lipped 'Mmm' of appreciation. 'Damn fine, Mrs Ovens!' he says with a twist towards the kitchen. 'Now as I see it ...' He gives a leathery cough. 'Ex-cuse me. As I was saying. Was saying ... Oh yes. The natives had not seen an enclosure in their lives until our arrival. Their ancestors do not even possess a word for it. They spy a flock of grazing sheep and think, "What ho! Dinner." Lamb must be quite a delicacy after' — he pauses, lips quivering with delight — 'goanna. Haw-haw. What ho!' He looks around imploringly. There is a polite chortle from Bigge and Scott. I place a hand on Bungaree's forearm.

After another nervous cough, Piper continues, 'Yes. Well. The settlers, believing in many cases that they are entitled to *extreme* measures to protect hard-won property, have and will shoot, in their turn, those they believe guilty of theft. They would not ordinarily, of course, kill a white man — even a bushranger — in retaliation for the loss of a sheep. But they see the natives as little more than pests. I am sorry' — the hands are raised once again — 'but this is how things stand.'

Scott reaches for his glass and takes a long, slow sip. Those with full glasses follow him and those who have already drained theirs motion to the servants for more. Piper presses on, 'Some of the natives, particularly those from the richer areas inland — I presume they are a prouder, fierce race — have retaliated by raiding homes, laying waste, leaving no one alive. It is a dreadful situation. I fear somewhat for the future.'

As two servants pick their way around the table removing the soup bowls, Bigge opens his small mouth to speak. Closes it. Opens it again, like a fish gasping for air. 'As a matter of fact,' he says finally, 'my commission is rather broader than this, as you say, grave situation that will in any event resolve itself with military victory over the hostile natives. No, my brief encompasses *every* aspect of colonial life.' He moves his hands over his thighs before folding them, leaning back in his chair with a thin smile — just a gash.

'Then you will help to put an end to these dreadful divisions?' asks Piper as he takes a beef pie from a plate passed around by Hawkins. Adding a dollop of pale horseradish, he shovels it into his mouth as if stoking a fire. 'Mmm, very good.' He points to the horseradish in its silver bowl. 'Excellent in fact,' he says through a mouthful. He swallows. Goes on. 'Not too watery. Freshly made. Mrs Ovens. You have struck gold with her. Can I perhaps borrow —'

Bigge breaks in, 'Most certainly the ending of social divisions, which have been fomented — quite possibly — by the elevation of one class over others. An end to public waste. No more unnecessary extravagance. These kinds of things.'

'All endings then,' says the Architect with a narrowing of those green eyes. 'I mean ending things. Cutting, banning. *Banishing*. No beginnings. You have nothing new or generous to offer us.'

'To the contrary. The beginning of great things. A new kind of future for men like Macarthur, who has sadly been detained in the country.'

Bigge raises a glass and the others follow; Macquarie's is the last glass raised. 'To a prosperous future!' toasts the Commissioner.

'God Save the King!' declaims the Governor powerfully.

'God Save the King!' echoes the company.

I feel compelled to ask, 'You foresee a future based around multitudes of ruminants: sheep and cattle? An agricultural colony serving the Empire?'

'On the export of wool — most certainly.'

'I am an outsider here,' says Rose. 'But I have seen much of the world. More, I would guess, than many of you *wise* gentlemen.' She inclines her head towards her husband, who murmurs in French. They both smile. 'I have,' she goes on, 'my own perspective.' She leans forward, training her gaze on Bigge directly across from her.

'You must allow us, then, to see things with your pretty eyes,' says Piper, taking a thirsty sip from his glass.

'Wool, yes. *Pourquoi pas?*' she says with a falling intonation. 'Your English mills want wool and a growing country needs a source of wealth as a growing child needs *nourriture*. I wonder, however, about the source of this hostility towards the state. The state built the colony. It still does.' Turning to her left she gives me a lingering, affectionate look, takes a delicate sip of wine, leaving on the glass a lipstick print like a pressed flower. 'This meal. Your quarters. Provided by the Government.' She returns a hard gaze on Bigge. 'The state — it cannot be all bad.'

'But *my* government,' he says flatly, 'has no wish to continue its support.' Scott nods, then nods again.

'Will you allow me to continue?' asks Rose. Without waiting for an answer, she goes on. 'The smoky huts witnessed here a decade ago by my husband have been replaced by many fine buildings: spacious, beautifully proportioned and finished in stone or brick. Why, Captain Piper here lives in a paradise on the waterfront. Can it be true that he fires shots from four brass cannon to announce the start of his Saturday night revels?'

Piper throws back his head. 'True enough,' he concedes. 'True enough.' Then he comes forward, elbows on the table. 'Your intelligence, madam, is excellent.'

Says Rose, 'Have you noticed the pride that the freed take in their little cottages with their well-ordered gardens? Take a poor seed, plant it in fresh soil. How it grows!'

Macquarie permits himself a contented smile and a few simple words. 'So young,' he says with a dark base note. 'And green. But already straight and tall.' He turns to me, and I notice the pouches in his jowls where once there had been a plane of firm jaw.

Glasses are raised. But the salute is aborted by Bigge, who shakes an upbraiding hand at the company.

'That is all very well,' he crows. 'But I come here as the agent of a king not a jolly gardener. And the King cares not a jot for the health of the colony, so long as it serves its purpose. Sydney was, is, and will be for some time to come, a place of correction. It is a jail in part; in another part a source of labour for an economy that will in time serve the Empire most ably. I am not entirely sure what end it serves now. Perhaps the ambitions of the good Governor and his wife.'

'Damned harsh,' says Piper.

Rose takes a deep breath. Macquarie makes to rise. Looking at each in turn, I spread my hands and lower them slowly to the table. The large, sweet-natured servant in the tight borrowed coat stands behind Bigge with an expression of murderous rage. The Commissioner is fortunate, it occurs to me, that the young man is nowhere near the carving knife.

'If. I. May,' Macquarie breaks in. My husband has no wish to say anything that could be recorded by Scott and used against him. But his reticence has its limits. 'I cannot let this rest. I have shared some

267

brief words. You must now permit me to speak at length.' He regards each man, each woman, in turn. 'Your opinion, Commissioner,' he continues, 'is really no different from that of Macarthur. And others of his kind. I will avoid the subject of politics and say only that I have known many convicts. I have freed hundreds. Perhaps thousands. Few among them have reoffended.' He speaks to his hands, placed on the table straight before him, avoiding Bigge's eyes. I slip my own hand beneath the table and let it rest on his thigh. 'The felons have been reformed by the system of rewards and punishments,' he shoots me a quick look. 'The chief reward being what they so fiercely desire —'

'And that is?' Bigge interrupts in a high tone.

Macquarie shifts his gaze from his hands and trains his eyes on Bigge. 'Their freedom, sir! They have risen up. Some have made fortunes. I see that you would like to keep them down in the world: I cannot believe' — he shifts in his seat — 'that you truly mean it. It is very — I must say — un-Christian. But of course you have more time in the colony. We may yet separate you from your prejudice.'

'Well, now,' says the Architect abruptly. 'You are dining, Commissioner Bigge, with a criminal tonight.' There is silence but for the unnerving scrape of a knife edge on china. 'And I wonder that you have not dined with a number when you have eaten at the halls of the wealthy, though no magistrate will bring them to trial.'

'Outrageous,' fires Bigge. 'You have no right to malign —'

Macquarie holds up his hand to silence Bigge. The Commissioner, remarkably, backs off.

'I see no reason,' the Architect goes on, 'why this city might not one day be London's equal, or at least her rival. You know I have plans for a Chinese pagoda at Newcastle — a lighthouse.' He will not smile at me, though I know he wishes to.

'A Chinese pagoda at Newcastle?' snorts Piper. 'Capital! A lavish touch or two never harmed —'

'Your ambition,' says Bigge, nodding pointedly with every word. 'It ... is ... quite ... over ... weening ... And overwhelming. If not for the clemency of our monarch you would have swung on the gibbet. You have only recently been granted your full pardon — with the completion of the convict barrack, I believe. And yet you assume such liberties.'

'Commissioner Bigge,' says Macquarie, shielding his architect from blows directed at him. 'I wonder if you have noticed the fine craft that has gone into the making of your rosewood chair tonight. I possess two of these. I sit here in one; you have the other. When you have a moment observe the exquisite blind fretwork on the panels; I believe it rivals the carvings on some of your best English church choirs. The finials and arches are in imitation of a Gothic chapel. My crest — I hope you will excuse this touch of vanity — crowns the entire ensemble.'

'As a matter of fact I did observe the work. You were fortunate to be able to bring such impressive pieces out from home.' A yielding nod in the Governor's direction. 'Are they newly arrived?'

'No, but they are fashioned by two new *arrivals*: the convicts John Webster and William Temple.'

Bigge rises slowly from his chair. His napkin drops to the floor. 'Well in that case, Governor Macquarie, it is my great pleasure to rest my behind upon your convict chair. One always aims' — he turns to Scott with a triumphant smile — 'to keep the felons down.' He bares a row of neat white teeth, motions to Hawkins to retrieve his napkin, and plants himself back on his chair. I return his smile in the joyless spirit in which it was offered, feeling just a scintilla of regard for the man's self-possession.

As Bigge eases back into his chair, Piper's hand shoots up as if catching a passing projectile. 'I almost forgot,' he says reaching into his pocket with a crumpling sound. 'How damnably vacant of me.'

All eyes fall upon him as he takes out a folded square of paper bearing the faint impress of print, places it on the table and unfolds it. 'For those who have not seen,' he says mischievously, 'I bring the latest *Gazette*.' He holds the paper by a corner and displays it like an exhibit. 'From Howe himself. We, er, spent some hours together this afternoon — a social call from our publisher and he came with an advance copy. Well, well,' he smiles tenderly at the page, 'it features a most interesting ode from our own poet laureate, Mr Massey Robinson.'

He turns to Bigge. 'Sir, you will have to bear up for this — stay cheerful. Remain stoical. Howe is in the habit of publishing, from time to time, jolly little satires about the state of things. This one, it seems, has been inspired by your visit.'

* * *

John Piper, a little worse for wear that night, left behind his copy of the *Gazette*, allowing me to seize it as a souvenir for my little treasury. I found it the next day in the kitchen — my guess is that Hawkins had been reading it before retiring for the evening. Of course the Governor most certainly contributed to Robinson's squib; had at the very least approved it. I wonder if he didn't orchestrate the dinner precisely so it could be read to Bigge. Over time, with repeated readings, the creases that it bore that night have deepened into furrows. I am attentive to the object's fragile state as I open it beneath the pale candlelight. How oratorical Piper sounded that night as he cleared his throat, leapt unsteadily to his feet, and then, with majestic voice, read:

Happy the convict, farewelling all care,
Some ripe Sydney land he has found;
Content to breathe the pure sweet air,
Of wide New World, clean fresh ground.

His herds bring forth milk, wheat sways in his fields,
From his flock comes a splendid attire.
In summer his forests supply him with shade,
In winter he gives thanks for the fire.

Blessed he is in soul, body and mind,
In sunshine his years slide gently away.
Happy, that is, til it grieves him to find,
His Governor besieged, beleaguered — at bay.

The soldiers, the free, the wealthy and such,
No friends of the poor convict, the currency too.
Have allies on high — virtues not overly much —
In Whitehall that over-loud, overfed zoo.

So gather around me, I summon good folk,
Macquarie, your friend, needs your loyalty now.
Britain's unfortunates, released from the yoke
Raise spades, shake chains, shake ploughs!

Drive foes from these shores as you were once driven,
The enemies of all we have done, we have given.
Those who once heard the gavel: we build and we dig,
Let us farewell a Commissioner not very big.

* * *

As Piper returns to his seat the company — or a goodly portion of it — erupts. 'An insult,' cries Scott, red-faced, as he thumps the table. 'Under the guise of —'

'Bravo,' roars Freycinet across him, tossing back his fine head.

The Architect cries out to Piper, who merely shrugs noncommittally, sticks out his lower lip, and says, 'Printed already, this afternoon I believe ...'

Bungaree's teeth flash brilliantly as he shakes his head in delight, slaps his thighs as if drumming out a beat, and repeats several times, 'Commissioner not very big!'

Macquarie slowly raises his hands, then he claps them together before him. Silence returns to the table. Bigge shifts a little in his chair and says, with redoubled hauteur, 'Why should I take notice of some verses composed by a criminal. They are a foreign language — they mean nothing to me.'

'Well put, sir,' says Piper. 'Good riposte!'

'And yet,' Bigge goes on with a crooked smile. 'A recommendation from me to his Majesty and, pffff,' he throws out his hands. 'No more *Gazette*!'

Rose, leaning behind Macquarie, taps me on the arm and says, with shining eyes, 'Do you know your Molière? *"Un homme sage est au-dessus de toutes les injures qu'on lui peut dire."*'

'English, please,' barks Scott in her direction.

I turn towards Bungaree, who seems to be eyeing the Governor's gilded coat with covetous eyes.

At this moment three servants emerge from the kitchen with platters of duck, goose and lamb, together with a pink crumbed ham. Following behind, like minions, are red ceramic boats of gravy, round black bowls of apple sauce, and others of capers. Placed in the centre of the table is a large serving of pickled vegetables and another of boiled carrots and potatoes: not a fine meal but a hearty one.

From that moment the conversation takes a lighter turn, dying down altogether at the heart of the feasting. For a time the only sounds are grunts of appreciation, the tap and scrape of knives and forks on plates, of wine poured from bottle to glass and from glass into gullet: a medley of sounds that, if one were listening intently beyond the doors yet had no idea of the activity within, might make dining seem a less attractive activity than it actually is.

As the evening wears on, and a heavy wine from La Malgue replaces the rosato, the range of conversation expands. We hear Bungaree's impersonations of the Governor, as well as Foveaux and Bligh. He could even do a passable Matthew Flinders, having accompanied the explorer on his circumnavigation of the continent.

'Then we have met before, I think,' says Freycinet, leaning towards the native excitedly. 'I was a junior officer in the Baudin expedition. I think ... I remember ...' — he raises a finger — 'the day we met Flinders. Yes of course — I *do* remember! You were the interpreter. We envied Flinders having the use of your services; there were times when we badly needed them. Bungaree — you must be very old. That was almost twenty years ago and you seem not to have aged.'

'Gooseberry magic,' replies Bungaree to a round of applause from the men and two sets of lowered eyes beneath long lashes.

'Seriously now, Bungaree,' Freycinet goes on. 'You share the table tonight with representatives of two European powers. You have the ear of the Governor and of the man who, it seems, has been sent out to ... scrutinise his good work.'

'But you ...' begins Bigge.

Freycinet snaps forward in his seat. 'Do not interrupt, sir,' he glowers. 'Do you take us all for fools?'

The Commissioner recoils sharply, as if fearing for his person, even though I have placed the Architect and Scott between him and Freycinet. The Frenchman addresses him directly, as if they were the only two in the room. 'Rio de Janeiro is a busy port but you would have been wise to inquire a little of the ships flying European colours. If so you would have discovered that the *Uranie* was bound for Port Jackson and you might *not* have spoken out so freely about your plans and your prejudices to *tout le monde*.'

Bigge, reddening conspicuously, his mouth set into a rictus, consults with Scott in low tones. Without turning my head, I let my eyes slide to the faces of each guest to gauge the mood of the table. My husband, I notice, also surveys the company. The Architect is staring absently at the glossy black window as if he means to escape at the first opportunity. The Freycinets conspire in low tones. Bungaree prods a picked-over bird with his fork, gazing deeply into the carcass as if searching for omens there.

Resuming his conversation with Bungaree, Freycinet presses, 'Surely your people, they remember a time before we Europeans. What exactly *do* they recall?'

'We are happier then,' Bungaree says, lifting his gaze from the bird and smiling serenely. 'Everything belonged to everybody. Nobody belonged to nothing. There were no walls ...' He picks up the napkin, wipes his hands and returns it to his lap.

'That was our great happy time,' he goes on, swaying a little in his seat. 'We followed the fish, the kangaroo, picked oyster and mussel from the rocks, gathered food from the bush. Now we come to the town to beg for white man's bread and grog. Our women sleep with your men, and they change. There is some bad spirit in that business.'

Bungaree casts a pained look towards Macquarie, and then me. There are points of light in his velvety eyes. He shakes his head. Looks down at his plate.

Piper says, 'Do go on, Bungaree. I for one accepted this invitation not realising it would prove to be a veritable symposium. But now that it has become one you must have your say and we must listen intently. We are all, are we not, your guests in one way or another.'

Bungaree hesitates. He looks to the Governor not so much for approval as courage.

'We were free,' he goes on in a low voice. 'But you have made us like your ...' — he points to the door of the dining room — 'your servants. Your slaves. Only the Sky spirit Baayami has power to make a man a slave.' And then, after a pause, 'Are you great spirits? Or are you demons who steal the spirits of the healthy and return them sick and dying? We are sick — and we are dying.'

'And a terrible situation it is,' says Piper. 'But we have cleared the land. Created wealth from it. And now we feed a growing population. Progress — my good man.'

'Is the land yours to take the wealth from? I know that you will not go away, and you will not be beaten by our spears and our sticks. Do you know our name for you? It is *your* word. Musket. I will not raise my spear against you. I am for peace. But if you stay, you must promise to be good spirits. Not bad.'

Scott, with the expression of a man who has reached for an orange and unwittingly bitten into a lemon, says, 'Surely our French friends have been giving the natives volumes of Rousseau to imbibe?'

'I think you will find Rousseau was Swiss, not French, though he thought and wrote in French,' returns Freycinet. He swirls his wine in his glass, but does not raise it to his lips. 'And I doubt you have read a word of him in French or any other tongue.'

'Well, well! Another taunt, what!' Piper bellows, before raising his glass and draining it.

'If I can add something,' Freycinet goes on, looking in both directions for approval — not a given, necessarily, as the evening is drawing on. 'To be honest I do not take this talk of lost native innocence overly seriously. I believe I know this race a little better than most, having seen much of the natives of New Holland in 1802 — and since that time I have seen *les indigènes* of many places, all subtly different. I recall their murderous melees. You witness them here at the Cove. They have become gladiatorial sport — entertainment? I would much prefer a life of culture to life in a state of Nature. Life in a state of Nature is short.'

Bigge and Scott exchange a quizzical glance. Piper suppresses a yawn.

'What I mean to say,' Freycinet goes on, 'is that I would rather the services of a ship's surgeon than a sorceress — no disrespect to Gooseberry.'

A few murmurs of assent.

'But our native friend is getting, I think, at another idea of innocence. The native people here — if I may, Bungaree? — seem content with the little they have. They are no more noble than we Europeans. But I think they are, or were, happier.'

'Only do not stand between Bungaree and a bicorne,' snorts Piper, stirring up a round of uncertain laughter.

The Architect, who has been drumming the table with the heavy end of his bread knife, breaks in. 'If we have found another Eden at this place — and what better place — then how do we retell the story in Genesis?' he asks.

'It is not your story to retell,' says Bigge. 'It belongs to the Holy Father.'

'Bear with me awhile ...' The drumming continues. 'This land is richly forested. Its oceans teem with fish. The air is good. The climate kind. It is a Garden of Eden. Can innocence, once lost, be regained here? And goodness? It is a jail, of course, but of a peculiar kind. A jail that began as a place of exile. And yet it is a jail that promises a new beginning.'

'Your point being ...?' says Piper.

'My point? I am not so sure if I have a point. It is late ... There is just this. America was founded by men and women in whom the fire of faith burned brightly. Sydney Cove was settled by sinners. From which of the two New Worlds will the better world grow? I sometimes wonder.'

'A question,' I am forced to interject, 'that has no immediate answer. None that we can possibly give. Although it is interesting conjecture.'

'And what of your view, Elizabeth,' says Rose reaching a hand across the table. 'You have been the perfect hostess. But you do have a view, do you not?'

Ordinarily, I would not allow myself to be drawn on such a sensitive subject in official company. But if Bungaree can speak so candidly — I do not pretend for a moment it was easy for him — then I shall too. 'For myself, and speaking only for myself,' I begin, turning towards the Governor, 'I have never been able to conceive that there was justice and equity on the part of we Europeans in seizing lands desired by us when others have a much stronger — at least older — claim. Do the natives possess it? Can they unroll a title deed? No. But it matters naught — they inhabit it. I should think the noblest course of action would be to offer some generous terms to the natives. We are wealthier than they, and yet all we give them are trinkets.'

I turn to face Bungaree, but his eyes are downcast and he says not a word.

John Piper, a little deep in drink though never less than genial, breaks in. 'Very well said. Bravo to all! A very philosophical night. Speakers of three nations: the English, the French and the, er, Indian. Most illuminating. Now on a lighter note, I am in the possession of some curious gossip from the town. It seems that Campbell that old rascal —'

'Will you excuse me,' asks an appropriately roseate Rose Freycinet, flushed with excitement. 'Or us. I have a feeling the conversation will soon take a colourful turn. Mrs Macquarie and I prefer more sober diversions. We would like to take a walk on the verandah.'

'Not to worry,' says Piper. 'Don't concern your pretty heads. Look here,' he leans forward. 'I am also in the possession of some very fine cheroots. Now back to the Campbell business ...'

CHAPTER THIRTY-SIX

Rose leads me with a rustle of skirts down the half-lit corridor. On the way I notice that a picture — a still life of many-coloured fish native to these parts — hangs askew on the wall. Someone must have shouldered it, a little drunkenly, while on a secretive reconnaissance.

My sense of disorientation only deepens when we step into the soft night air.

Rose tugs at my sleeve and we hurry on.

In no time at all we have skipped down the stairs of the verandah and left the garden behind. We set out towards the Domain along a sandy path by the light of the fat moon. Rose leads the way. Bats chatter — uproariously — in the figs.

Turning back, almost tripping in the process, I catch sight of a guard in a snow-white shirt recently released from serving duties and, in the darkness, the swelling glow of tobacco alight in his pipe bowl. He tilts sideways as he follows our movements along the winding path. But he dares not pursue.

'Rose,' I hiss. 'What on *Earth* is going on?'

She stops as the harbour comes shimmering and magnificent into view. 'Look,' she says. 'What do you see?'

'Very little,' I reply as the moon is swallowed up by storm clouds. We continue along at a slower pace.

'Yanadah,' I say.

'Yana …?'

'Native word for moon.'

I let my eyes linger on her gypsy face in its frame of black hair. There is just enough light to catch the swivel of her eyes as they reach for a thought.

'Strange,' she says. '*La lune*. The moon. Those two words — so close. And then, what was it? Yanadah. So distant.'

'Distant like this place.'

'Yes, of course,' she says in an urgent tone, as if dismissing something from her thoughts. 'But we must not delay.' She reaches out with both hands. She cups my face. A bold gesture. A bold woman. Slowly, she turns my head towards the harbour's entrance. Then she steps back.

'Look again. What do you see?'

'I see the garden, the near shore, the far shore, the inky harbour between. Some ships anchored there. Your own, the *Uranie*, lying at anchor towards the Heads.'

'And where were we several days ago? Dawes Point.'

'Something is afoot!'

'The *Uranie* makes ready to sail,' she says excitedly. 'I have reason to fear. Listen carefully to what I have to say …'

My unsettled mind spins.

'Freycinet will inform John Piper by morning. He will explain that we are anxious to avoid the trade winds. And we are anxious for ourselves. I am speaking about the presence of Commissioner Bigge.'

I withdraw and shake my head.

'Yes, Bigge. As we talk here in darkness and seclusion plans are being made by evil men to harm your husband. And your architect — I am sorry, but he is finished! Bigge — it is a wonder he did not make an announcement tonight — plans to have him prosecuted on charges of misusing public funds.'

'What public funds?'

'That I do not know. Perhaps' — she flutters her hand impatiently as if I were detaining her on a trivial matter — 'the barrack.'

'But he had no access to funds. He was merely the architect. This is just another way of needling the Governor. And how, in any event, do you know all this?'

'Our suspicions were aroused in Rio. Since then we have purchased many ears about the colony. Bigge, though small, speaks,' and here she drops to a whisper, 'very, very loudly. I wonder, Elizabeth,' she takes my hand again, 'if we do not have more agents in this town than you. The Irish would rise up in an instant if we were to return with three more ships.'

I withdraw from her grasp. 'I think you flatter yourself. It may lead you to overstep. Remember Ireland in 1798. I say this as a friend.'

'They talk here of Vinegar Hill; I say this in the same spirit. But listen. There is little time.' She comes forward. 'Elizabeth, if your husband does not resign he *will* be removed. You must find a way of urging him, using all your womanly skill, towards the former course.'

'It is unconscionable. He offered his resignation two, maybe three, years ago. His request was denied by Bathurst. Surely they were not planning, all those years ago, to send out a commissioner in order to publicly demean him — and to diminish his cause?'

I will never know the answer to that question and I no longer care. The effect was the same, whether it was contrived or not.

The clouds untangle themselves from the moon. The waterway silvers.

I usher Rose forward to the sandstone refuge — my chair — and we sit together.

It is here that I learn of the plan — initiated by which party I know not — to stow the Architect aboard the *Uranie*, to transport him by stealth from the colony. I wonder, even now, at the audacity of it.

'But it is preposterous,' I burst out. 'No ship is allowed to leave this harbour without a Government vessel beside it, and a prior inspection, to ensure that nothing of this kind occurs. There is talk aplenty of men kidnapped from The Rocks and forced into service on traders heading north. But honestly I believe it is a myth.'

She raises her hand and says coolly, 'You must lower your voice.'

I nod in compliance. She goes on, 'You forget that I joined Freycinet this way. Or perhaps you do not know. I thought Arago made some mention ...' She shakes her hands. 'No matter. You see my husband had a small compartment built for me on the *Uranie*, hidden from sight. I came aboard at Le Havre in men's clothing, disguised as a cabin boy. I spent the better part of the day in that small though perfectly comfortable space — as large as a maid's chamber — and showed myself only when we were well at sea. You should have seen the faces,' she smiles a little conceitedly. 'The men — they looked as if they had seen a goddess step from the heavens.'

'And this is where you would stow the Architect?'

'There is *nowhere* else. Your English soldiers will give the *Uranie* a cursory inspection at dawn. They may well have heard the story of how I came on board, but they will not think to interrogate our men as they have no French. And if they were to ask — if they have heard my story — we will take them to the cook's storeroom and say, *voilà*, it has been converted to this use.'

'And he is willing — ready to take on the risk? The Architect.'

'Quite willing. You heard the tenor of the conversation tonight. Even if your husband and you were to escape official censure, *he* will not. He will be placed under arrest tomorrow or the day after. Suppose he is reprieved — he will be fortunate to see out his days in obscurity on a parcel of poor land among mosquitos and hostile natives. There will be no more work for him of an architectural nature. He will wish himself dead.'

'But if he is caught attempting an escape, what then?' I ask. 'You say he is to be tried. Would he in addition be charged with resisting arrest?'

'Perhaps you underestimate the man. Is it not the case that if he had lost against Sanderson he would have been as good as dead?'

'And what of the risk to you?'

'One that we are prepared to take. We think the man a hero! Freycinet would dearly love to offer passage to you and the Governor as well,' she goes on quickly, 'but there is room for only one in the secret compartment. He believes you have a story to tell that will awaken the world. Remember, he was here in 1802. He cannot believe how far the lowly have risen. Christ, he believes, would have been on the side of the convicts.'

The Son of God. Where is he now, I ask myself.

'The only practical risk, we are convinced, will come when he is rowed early in the morning from the cove just inside the Heads. We must pray that none of the fishermen witness the departure. But to guard against it Arago has purchased fresh fish from these men today and paid with six bottles of calvados. There will be no fishing from that place tomorrow.'

I look out to the black waters lapping at the rocks below. Three, perhaps four, lamps aboard the *Uranie* cast ribbons of light rippling towards us. I am quite speechless.

I feel the ache of his absence even though he is most vividly present. On the eve of our separation it occurs to me, with as much certainty as I have about anything in my upended life, that I have loved him; loved him for years. It is only with the imminence of his loss that I feel free to use the word.

'You mentioned on the night we met that you were reading *The Princess of Clèves*. Have you finished it?' Rose inquires.

'Just last night.'

'What did it say to you at the very end?'

'I'm not so sure ... There has been so much incident of late in my own life. A sad end, certainly — resignation. Failure. Failure of love.'

'At school in France we were taught that it was a novel about the struggle between duty and love. But I think it talks to each heart about generosity ... the generosity of *true* love. A love that renounces possession. That loves in solitude.'

We fall silent. And then, with a sigh, I raise myself wearily from my stone chair at the end of the Earth. I offer her a hand. She shakes her head.

'No need for gallantry here,' she says. 'We are not at the court of Henry II.'

'Rose,' I come closer. 'A favour?'

'Anything you ask.'

'Later tonight I will give you a letter for the Architect. It will list the names he needs to contact if he is to make his way to safety. Your destination is Marseilles is it not? Or Le Havre?'

'First, Marseilles.'

'Better there, a commercial port. Le Havre, I am told, groans under officialdom.'

'Very well. He leaves us at Marseilles.'

'And yet a hundred ships from all the world come to that port each day. On them will be adventurers aplenty keen to take advantage of the reward that will ever be on the Architect's head. If he flees the colony on the eve of his arrest, even on spurious charges, he can never return to his homeland. Bigge is clever: he will have him pursued for resisting arrest. France will not serve well as a permanent sanctuary. He has no friends there — barely speaks the language. But I know a place. My homeland will throw its arms around him.'

There is a heavy footfall and the soft crunch of leaf and twig underfoot. I spin around to catch sight of another mop of raven hair, this much shorter, and an echoing splash of crimson.

'Mrs Macquarie?'

I know the voice.

'Brody.'

'Madam.' A sober bow of greeting. 'Mrs Freycinet.' Another. 'The evening is ending well enough. No more disputes or jousts.'

'What of Bigge and Scott?' I ask as we pick our way back to the house.

'They departed shortly after you, the Commissioner seeming slightly agitated after something Monsieur Freycinet said to him in a low voice. I was too far away to hear distinctly but it sounded like a mild inquiry about his health after some incident in Trinidad. Surprising that it should elicit such a frosty response.'

The Architect, he reports, also sought an early night. 'He says he has some distance to travel on the morrow.' I cut Rose a quick knowing look.

'Bungaree returned to his tribe carrying a basket of leftovers and some bottles. Captain Piper, I think perhaps, tries too hard to shine: there was at least one joke you were both fortunate to avoid. The Captain, Monsieur Freycinet and the Governor are taking brandy and smoking cheroots in the office. They are all three quite jolly but they have sent me to look for the "two beauties", as they put it.'

We walk back briskly through the gardens.

I long for sleep. I fear that the days ahead — the months — will be the unhappiest I have ever known. But there is one more thing I need to do.

Within plain sight of the residence I give a little tug at Brody's sleeve.

'When I am home, Brody, Madame Freycinet will go first to the office to join the men. I will tarry in my room. Shortly afterwards I will join the gentlemen and you will leave us. There will be a letter — pray that I have time to seal it — inserted into the leaves of the sheet music at the pianoforte. Meanwhile in the laundry, freshly washed, you will find a white satchel. It came yesterday with a gift from Monsieur Arago. I will need you to slip the letter inside the satchel, and convey them both to Madame Freycinet at the moment you accompany her and her husband to the boat that will take them to their ship. Before you leave them for the fort, make sure they are aware it is a gift from me for the traveller. Do you hear: *the traveller*.'

He nods gravely.

'When the time comes you must act swiftly: the letter to the satchel, the satchel to the Freycinets.'

And it was done.

CHAPTER THIRTY-SEVEN

Soon after dawn there is a heavy knock at the front door. I am already awake, frozen with dread. I rouse Macquarie and we go to the door together in our dressing gowns. Hawkins arrives presently in his butler's livery, hair neatly combed and parted in the centre. Piper, unshaven and a little the worse for wear, has come in the company of a guard to relate the news of Freycinet's sudden departure.

I let the men go together to the office and return to the bedroom but I linger in the hallway long enough to catch a fragment of their talk. Says Piper, 'I was informed an hour before dawn and I have been awake since then with arrangements. I thought it best not to disturb you.'

'I'm glad you didn't ... So last night's welcome party was in fact a farewell.'

'I am not particularly surprised after the events of last night. I swear that Freycinet sent all his squibs at Bigge knowing that he would not be around for the consequences.'

'Thought he might fire his cannon and be gone,' murmurs Macquarie in his husky early morning voice. 'Very French.'

Anxious that he might have left a parting letter of deep sentiment for me — among a file of sketches, or leafed into his copy of Palladio — I make an excuse to visit the lighthouse.

Arago, I tell Macquarie, has left in my possession a few panoramas of the town sketched from the observatory. 'He begged me to deliver them when he was gone to the man he called the "demiurge of Sydney's marvels — the creator". That can only be one man. Of course I had no idea his departure was … imminent!'

I ride off hastily with Brody to deliver an empty folio. If I had waited any longer the Governor might have grown curious about these drawings of Arago's and asked to see them. But I can rely, I wager, on his ruminations over the events of the week to keep his suspicions at bay.

The Architect, as I expected, is gone; his most treasured possessions, among them his Palladio, have vanished with him. His fantasia of buildings drawn from the Old World and imagined afresh in the new — an Ottoman minaret, a Norman keep, a Chinese pagoda and a red and white striped lighthouse — it lies on his workbench wrapped hastily in copies of the *Gazette* and tied with a hat ribbon as if for a birthday.

There are no tender parting words for me. I step outside, shade my eyes from the sun, and fill my lungs with the pure, wild air.

* * *

I bear the news, with an expression of feigned surprise and shock, back to the residence. It is widely assumed among the townsfolk that the Architect has made his escape with Freycinet, but the theory is impossible to prove — or to disprove. Rumour swells to fill the void left by mystery. Howe prints an article several days later, in which he conjectures that the Architect rowed to Georges Head and there joined Bungaree's tribe. Some say he leapt off the cliffs in anguish, leaving behind an empty bottle of rum and a sketch for a mausoleum styled after Halicarnassus to be erected in his memory at the Heads so that visitors for time immemorial would know his story and weep. This tale persists even after news spreads of Bigge's intention to have the Architect arrested for embezzling public funds.

Enraged by the escape of his quarry, Bigge cannot bring himself even to communicate with the Governor. He sails for Hobart just as soon as the *Cerberus* is manned and provisioned. Some say he flees in the hope that Freycinet, with his keen memories of 1802, will take the southerly route home and might, if he is as easily diverted from his course as his predecessors, be intercepted in the waters of Van Diemen's Land.

Bigge returns several months later to renew his investigations into the state of the colony, though we are never again on speaking terms.

And then a year later, with Macquarie's health failing, we leave at last for home. The Governor and I tour the towns he has established in the west, as well as Newcastle to the north. 'That damned Chinese pagoda will have to wait,' he laughs grimly as we return to Jackson. Robinson publishes a rather tortuous ode to the 'brave Scot from Mull whose rule never was dull'.

Each night in the week before leaving we stand close together on the verandah of Government House and regard the rising town as if it were a beloved infant. I walk out alone to my chair hewn by the Architect from the harbour sandstone. I sit on the cool seat and breathe deeply as memories break upon me. Will I miss this place? Most certainly. Will I long for it? No. My life here is over; my work done. Brody comes out to meet me as I stroll across the Domain and up the rise to the residence.

'You must, when you return home, come visit,' I say. 'At Mull we are closer to Belfast than Edinburgh. You Irish sent us your priests. Surely you could make the short sea voyage.'

'I doubt I will return home now,' he says with a smile that pierces regret like sunshine glimpsed through cloud. 'Perhaps my old ma, she will take the journey if she is strong enough.'

Have I been strong enough?

Will I be?

On the day before our departure we go by barge across the harbour to Georges Head. All has been organised by Barney Williams: the journey, a feast for the natives — even some grog. Bungaree and around fifteen of his people come down from their village to farewell us in a slow procession. There is much wailing from Gooseberry and the women, who have clipped their hair and stained their bodies with red ochre. Wearing splendid adornments of tooth and bone, they dance in a circle around us, waving smoking sticks.

And then, with great solemnity, the departing Governor presents Bungaree with a red and gold bundle: the uniform that he will never wear again.

CHAPTER THIRTY-EIGHT

I finish my long night's vigil with two fresh candles, ecclesiastically white. The house lies in darkness save for this bedchamber alight with memory. Any moment now the golden light of dawn will catch the crest of Ben More. Already I have caught its herald in a trill of birdsong.

I sat myself down here not so much to write Macquarie's eulogy, as to *prepare* myself to write it. I did not expect to relive the story of our lives. But that is what, it seems, I have done.

I loved my husband, most assuredly. And he loved me. Yet an earlier perhaps even more powerful love had claimed him. Although she died long ago I do not believe that he ever stopped loving her, poor spectre that she is. Poor Jane Jarvis.

And my pact with the Architect — a man closer to my age and more attuned to my dreams, who is part of my conversation even when he is not by my side to converse with. Is that love? Was it? Did I feel it long before I named it? Or did I give it that name only to console myself when it was near lost to me?

I could not have imagined two more different men: the solid and the quicksilver, the ruler and the artist. I needed both braided into my life. Just as, I suppose, I am nourished by the Antipodes and the Hebrides at the extreme ends of the Earth.

There was a love between both men, a fraternal, often strained, yet abiding bond that set limits on the Architect. He could so easily have played the part of Lancelot to my Guinevere, yet he managed to tame his affections and his natural boldness so that he was always my loving accomplice and not my lover, though there was a time when I wished — and dreamed most vividly — that he were both.

And the Governor, who could easily have banished his rival, dismissed him from his service; he refused to do so. He was the Architect's ally, and the Architect was his. My husband smelled smoke and decided, out of some loving kindness that may have been in part paternal, to contain the fire rather than extinguish it. Even if the Architect was banished to his lighthouse, I was free to visit now and then in the company of Brody. And so things went on in this manner. A fine balance. A delicate web. Until one man left me. And then another. And now I am alone.

I return to the bureau with a clear head. The storm has passed. The gale of memory is spent. The fine public words for Macquarie — I see and hear them clearly now — are ready. Words for a life.

I pick up my steel pen:

HERE IN THE HOPE OF A GLORIOUS RESURRECTION

LIE THE REMAINS OF THE LATE

MAJOR GENERAL LACHLAN MACQUARIE

OF JARVISFIELD

WHO WAS BORN 31ST JANUARY, 1761

AND DIED AT LONDON ON THE 1ST OF JULY, 1824

THE PRIVATE VIRTUES AND AMIABLE DISPOSITION

WITH WHICH HE WAS ENDOWED

RENDERED HIM AT ONCE A MOST BELOVED HUSBAND,

FATHER AND MASTER, AND A MOST ENDEARING FRIEND.

HE ENTERED THE ARMY AT THE AGE OF FIFTEEN

AND THROUGHOUT THE PERIOD OF 47 YEARS

SPENT IN THE PUBLIC SERVICE

WAS UNIFORMLY CHARACTERISED

BY ANIMATED ZEAL FOR HIS PROFESSION, ACTIVE BENEVOLENCE,

AND GENEROSITY WHICH KNEW NO BOUNDS.

HE WAS APPOINTED GOVERNOR OF NEW SOUTH WALES A.D. 1809

AND FOR TWELVE YEARS FULFILLED THE DUTIES OF THAT STATION

WITH EMINENT ABILITY AND SUCCESS.

HIS SERVICES IN THAT CAPACITY

HAVE JUSTLY ATTACHED A LASTING HONOUR TO HIS NAME.

THE WISDOM, LIBERALITY, AND BENEVOLENCE

OF ALL THE MEASURES OF HIS ADMINISTRATION,

HIS RESPECT FOR THE ORDINANCES OF RELIGION

AND THE READY ASSISTANCE WHICH HE GAVE

TO EVERY CHARITABLE INSTITUTION,

THE UNWEARIED ASSIDUITY WITH WHICH HE SOUGHT TO PROMOTE

THE WELFARE OF ALL CLASSES OF THE COMMUNITY,

THE RAPID IMPROVEMENT OF THE COLONY UNDER HIS AUSPICES,

AND THE HIGH ESTIMATION IN WHICH BOTH HIS CHARACTER

AND GOVERNMENT WERE HELD

RENDERED HIM TRULY DESERVING THE APPELLATION

BY WHICH HE HAS BEEN DISTINGUISHED

THE FATHER OF AUSTRALIA.

CHAPTER THIRTY-NINE

I had no communication with the Architect after his escape. I received no word, not even through the loyal Brody. And I sent none. But then, almost a year ago, I wrote to him from London with news of his old Governor's death.

Macquarie and I had been visiting the capital in an attempt to restore his reputation in influential circles after the catastrophe of Bigge's report. An interview with the Prince Regent had been promised, on account of Macquarie's long and distinguished defence of the Crown. No such interview was forthcoming. A champion was sought; someone to petition on our behalf. None came forward. Bathurst did agree to a meeting, but was not prepared to publicly defend the thing that mattered most to Macquarie: his reputation. The career soldier had aimed in the latter period of his life to make his mark with something more than a sabre. And he had done so. But with Bigge's calumnies so widely put about, all seemed lost.

Macquarie had been ailing for two years before his death, and in truth had not enjoyed good health for a long while; I suspect that some equatorial debilitation from his early years of service in India conspired with his labours at Sydney Cove to weaken his constitution. But he would — I am convinced of it — have lived another decade if it were not for the injury to his pride. To demean such a man — and so publicly! — was to poison his soul.

They killed him, Commissioner Bigge and his kind; this I will always believe. Labelled a humanist and a liberal in an age of vicious conservatism, he was disgraced. How did Bigge put it: 'The most effective way to the heart of the Governor — and to his table — is to have been sentenced at the Old Bailey. Only declare yourself to be a free man, unstained by crime, and he will turn his back.'

If I had armies at my command I would send out ten thousand men to avenge my husband. If I were a character in a Greek tragedy I would plunge a dagger into Bigge's heart and scream 'Aiieeeeee' as it went in.

* * *

I wrote to the Architect again from Gruline, to tell him of my return. I sent the letter, as I had done once before, via the boatman, an old family friend and the only messenger we could both trust in our treacherous circumstances. I was not ready to see him. It was not the time. But in the summer, I promised, that was when we would meet. I asked him to leave a message for me with the boatman by the last Monday of June, when I would retrieve it myself, weather permitting.

On our last evening together at the Cove I had slipped my letter to the Architect — a farewell and a plan for escape — into a white satchel, the one that had held a gift of Rhône wine from Arago. Once back on Mull I had time enough to sew a white cotton satchel much like the one that had served us both so well that evening. I planned to place a gift for the boatman in it — some peaches or a handful of cherries if they were ripened by then — and he would return it to me with a letter from the Architect.

The cottage the boatman selected for the Architect at Ormaig was little more than a shell. It was in need of a new roof, strengthened walls and a sitting room. He would have time to rebuild. The labour might do him good, I thought, but I begged him to continue to work with paper, to sketch his dreams.

'In the meantime,' I wrote, 'Survive!'

In time you will become again — I am certain of it — what you were meant to be. The Architect. Today you dream of what you might build. But tomorrow — or the tomorrow after — you will begin once again to build your dreams. Though perhaps not on the islands. It may be time for another journey.

It is my intention, so long as a decent price can be obtained for some parcel of the estate, to undertake the Grand Tour that you always desired. Will you accompany me on some small part of it? To Rome, at least!

Of course you will.

CHAPTER FORTY

In the marbled file of mementos lies his unopened letter with my name written upon it in his beautiful hand. I took it from the milk-white bag with the cherry stains, just as soon as I returned from Ulva. I resolved to deny myself the pleasure of its contents for one night: I had denied myself so long, a few more hours should be easy enough to endure. Once or twice in the course of this long night of reverie I have caught myself reaching for the letter. But I needed, first, to attend to the past and to honour a most honourable man.

Now, in this perfect moment, I have made my peace with the past. It is time to conjure a future. The right time.

I open the letter.

My dear Elizabeth,
In the still hour before dawn I stood before a mirror, my
face lit by a lamp set at a tilt on a porcelain sink. Across
my back and arms — unknown to all but you and William
Redfern — spreads a lattice of red scourge marks and the
scar that looks for all the world like a serpent — you once
told me this! — soldered onto the skin.

*I cannot afford to have that scar discussed in the streets
of Tobermory. A blaze of gossip might be the end of me.
So I wear my shirtsleeves fastened over the wrists — a
little too long for ordinary wear. I clasp them tight with
a set of silver cufflinks fashioned in Batavia and given to
me by a Frenchman as a parting gift. His name is Arago.
He asked me, when we were next in communication, to be
remembered to you.*

*Are you asleep? I wonder. Do you, alone now in the
house at Gruline, sleep at all? I doubt it very much. I
suspect you are with me: awake for the dawn.*

*So we are to meet. We are in high summer and it dawns
bright. It has been a long absence, achingly long and full of
uncertainty. I will be ready for you when you come.*

*I hear the complaining cry of gulls and the slow regular
pulse of the waves below. The broken cottage in which
you had me installed at Ormaig, I have restored not to its
former glory — it had none to begin with. But I have made
it a home.*

*The sea is a constant companion on this islet, as it was
at the lighthouse. Even on still days when the swell subsides
into a pool of molten metal the ocean's animal presence is
sensed through the breathing silence. I would miss it if fate
were to bear me away.*

*Elizabeth, your first letter arrived twelve months
ago from London. On my way here I followed the trail
you laid out — from Marseilles on a brig flying French
colours to Ajaccio, Cadiz and Porto, and from there by
steamboat to Calais before the crossing to Dublin, thence
to Glasgow.*

298

*I have no notion of how you managed to explain
the need for complete secrecy — and mine is a perilous
secret! — to those Campbells young and old who came so
valiantly to my aid. But I fancy they might have enjoyed
the adventure — providing me with a new identity and
transporting me by coach to Oban and from there by
boat under a moonlit sky to Ulva — if only to vex the
English.*

*The man to whom I have entrusted this letter — the
boatman, your friend — will move south to Loch Fyne.
He is of an age when the work wearies him, and desires to
return to the place of his birth. There he will continue to
enjoy the Campbell's excellent patronage. He and his wife
move from the boathouse tonight. Everything has been
arranged.*

*I send his fond farewells through this letter. He would
have farewelled you himself but he thought — we both
thought — it for the best if you read of these arrangements
in privacy. He alone has been entrusted with the secret
of our lives at Sydney Cove, and a friendship has sprung
up between us. He has spoken of you often, without once
mentioning your name. Instead he calls you 'Mrs M'.*

*So you see Mrs M — I am to be the new boatman. At
least for a time.*

You will find me much altered.

*I am now a man of settled rhythms — the physical
work has helped — and a modest degree of self-mastery.
Over time I have prevailed over the chaos that put me in
chains and sent me into exile. I am too old for another
banishment. Though not too old for another journey.*

*If you truly mean to sell some portion of the estate —
and a decent price can be got for it — well, yes, let us away
to Rome!*

*In the meantime I will be there, on the Ulva side of
the channel, waiting for you. You need only call for the
boatman, and I will come.*

CHAPTER FORTY-ONE

Ah, there it is. The footman returns from his revels. He makes himself supper — at this hour! I believe the lad tries to be quiet — he tries. But in his state! It sounds as if the buck has bounded into the larder and upended everything — pots and pans, cups and saucers — with his antlers. The footman's time has come, I think. It is time.

The wind outside is a mere sigh. Another fair day beckons. It has been a long wakeful night, and my thoughts grow ragged. But this I know: I will go back to tiny Ulva, to Ulva facing the sea. I will call again to the boatman. And he will come to me.

We will walk together to the high point of the island. There we will catch the echoes between the New World so very old, and the Old World made new to us.

POSTSCRIPT

Lachlan Macquarie, Ulva born, served as the Governor of New South Wales from 1810 to 1821. He left the colony in February 1822, never to return. Commissioner John Thomas Bigge arrived to review the state of the colony in September 1819; two months before, a French corvette *Uranie*, commanded by Louis Freycinet, arrived at Port Jackson. The French were sympathetic to Macquarie, as their journals reveal. Bigge was hostile. The most damaging findings of Bigge's three-volume report — a report highly critical of Macquarie's 'pro-emancipist' policy, his building program and his leniency towards convicts — were made public in stages from 1822. Bigge also recommended that Macquarie's architect, Francis Greenway, be sacked. Macquarie's successor, Governor Darling, dutifully had Greenway dismissed. The Bigge report has been described as a 'political disaster' for Macquarie, who was forced to fight, in failing health, for his reputation. The ageing Macquarie regarded it as 'vile' and 'insidious'. In July 1824, a year after Bigge's final report was tabled, he died, a broken man, in London. His wife, Elizabeth, took his body back to his estate on Mull, where it lies today behind the moving eulogy reproduced in the previous pages.

AUTHOR'S NOTE

Early one morning in the winter of 2015, an hour or so before dawn, I stirred from a fitful jet-lagged sleep, prodded by a clear and high-toned voice: a woman's voice.

'I paid the boatman with a bag of fresh cherries this morning,' she said. 'I picked them myself from the sloping orchard beside Loch Bà.' I woke suddenly, half expecting the owner of the voice to be standing beside me. But she had vanished with my dreams.

I went downstairs and made coffee with her words — the tone a little mournful, yet sensible and matter-of-fact — in my head. Then I went to my computer, turned on my desk lamp, and began to listen again, in the expectant mode of a fisherman awaiting a bite, as the dawn came on. What more, I wondered, might she have to say?

The voice belonged, I realised soon enough, to Elizabeth Macquarie. Mrs Macquarie's famous 'chair' is a stone bench crafted from a sandstone outcrop on a promontory offering fine views of Sydney Opera House, with the cheering single arch of the Harbour Bridge behind it. It's the spot from which untold wedding shots are taken. I had never, naturally, heard Mrs Macquarie's voice, and I never would hear it, and yet I felt, somehow, that I knew it.

Only days earlier I'd returned from the Isle of Mull, in the Inner Hebrides of Scotland, and there I'd visited the small slate-roofed stone mausoleum erected to Elizabeth's husband, Governor Lachlan Macquarie, Australia's fifth — and most progressive — colonial ruler. Afterwards I'd stolen a peek at their former home. The next day I took a boat to Lachlan's birthplace of Ulva, further to the west of Mull, barely a hundred metres across a narrow channel. In glorious spring weather I walked the islet alone.

I knew the story of the Macquaries, their journey to Australia, and the pained circumstances of their return — Macquarie sick and dying, his reputation in tatters. I'd already written a small book about the drama of their last years in Sydney (*The First Dismissal*, Penguin Specials 2014). And I'd been thinking, my entire time on Mull, about their lives. Tragic lives, if we are to judge them by Sophocles's injunction: 'Call no man happy until he is dead.' I felt these melancholic notes acutely on the island, for it is, despite its rugged beauty, an elegiac kind of place. Stand on one of its high points, look down upon the folds of forest, pasture and gorse tumbling to the vivid white sand beaches that border the boisterous Atlantic and you will, if you have an ear for such things, catch the mournful strains of a Celtic lament.

When I returned to Sydney I was struck, with a contrary kind of power, by the triumph of the Macquaries. It was as if the tragedy had burnt away under the piercing Sydney sun. Hyde Park Barracks, the inner city church of St James and the suburban church of St Matthew; the lighthouse at South Head; the castellated Government House stables (now Sydney Conservatorium of Music), so out of place in their own time, and even, a little, in ours; the small obelisk and fountain at Macquarie Place — these foundation stones of a civilisation built from a prison at the end of the Earth, and many more Macquarie-era buildings lost to the wrecking ball of time, were designed and built by the convict architect Francis Greenway.

The defining policy of Macquarie's term as Governor was the emancipation of convicts, like Greenway, with talent and promise; and the elevation, by extension, of the convict community. Greenway was the emblem of Macquarie's ideals. And they were revolutionary, by world standards, in both intent and effect. They are not, however, of mere historical importance. In a world where the gap between rich and poor is widening almost everywhere, the idea of a society founded on the twin principles of redemption and elevation, a society established by a criminal underclass banished to an unknown land as far as it was possible to travel from home, hearth and kin — well, that is an idea worth reflecting upon. It was not always the dominant idea in the colony's early years, but it was rarely out of mind. Macquarie made it his guiding principle. There was nothing in his previous life as a career soldier, so far as I can see, to suggest that he would take what was, for the times, a radical turn; if there had been, he would most assuredly not have been appointed. He was the first colonial governor to popularise the word 'Australia' — in many ways he invented the idea of Australia.

Australians have largely failed to appreciate the moral force of their society's creation, so blinkered are they by the shame of it, by the convict stain. It is a peculiar Australian condition — let's call it Australgia — to belong to a society that does not truly belong to itself. France knew Liberty as a slogan. Early Australia experienced it as a lived and felt reality, as a release, *en masse*, into freedom from penal servitude. Lachlan Macquarie was the great liberator of the colony's early years.

Elizabeth Macquarie's story, backlit by this political tale, began to take shape, to unspool from her spectral voice with its mysterious incantation about a sloping orchard, a boatman and a loch named Bà. The story could not be told, I soon realised, without braiding it together with the voices of both Macquarie and Greenway. All three, in fact, share the same tragic parabola of rising and falling fortunes. And so, I resolved, on the morning I woke with the voice of Mrs Macquarie sharper than anything else in my drowsy pre-caffeinated mind — ringing, quite literally, in my ears — to write this story. It is Elizabeth Macquarie's story. And it is Lachlan Macquarie's. And that of the man I call the Architect: Francis Greenway. It is also, in many ways, mine. This needs a word or two of explanation.

A work of fiction, as anyone who has ever laboured over this exacting literary form will understand, is a big undertaking. Poetry is no longer written over an epic span. Literary fiction remains the only truly epic art, outdistancing — at least textually — even long-arc television. From its lone practitioners it requires, at the end of the day, a touch of obsession, or at least obsessive drive. There are no collaborative writers' rooms to spur the novelist along. It is lonely work. *Mrs M* would probably not have been written if I hadn't, in my early twenties, found myself ensnared in a love triangle that echoed the predicament of my three main fictional protagonists. The relationship was an obsessive attraction that burst into flame during a process of creative collaboration, and the memory of it latched onto the story of Elizabeth, Macquarie and the Architect at an early stage of its gestation.

Perhaps this attempt to graft a personal story onto a public one could be considered the quintessential authorial vanity. But I think this criticism, which I have naturally anticipated, misunderstands the creative compulsion that sends its charge through the art of fiction and brings it to life. The drive to create and shape fictional narrative is more often than not autobiographical at heart. The voice that spoke to me that morning was merely a key turning in a lock; in order to push that door open and step forward, I needed something else to propel me. My own memories — or perhaps more the feelings provoked by those memories — gave me that impetus. They got me moving, and kept me going. This is how I came to write about real historical figures, with emotional lives that kept time with the rhythm of my own heart.

But there is another story here, the essential truth of which has not been sacrificed to the fancies of fiction: it is the political, perhaps even philosophical, story, foreshadowed earlier. Lachlan Macquarie's rule was marked by what came to be seen as a 'pro-emancipist' policy favourable to convicts. The Governor responded to what he felt was the convict settlement's innate desire for freedom, and he felt just as deeply its inherent human worth. The Tory administration of Robert Jenkinson, 2nd Earl of Liverpool, saw this as a dangerous path, at odds with the punitive purpose of the original colony, and it dispatched a commissioner, John Thomas Bigge, to inquire into Macquarie's governorship. It wanted a hostile report, and a hostile report — in fact three reports — it received. It did not need to make these reports public. But it did. Macquarie was shamed.

Commissioner Bigge's stay in Sydney was marked by one telling exchange with Macquarie, in which the Governor counselled the man who would be his judge and jury in language bearing the unmistakable stamp of the age of revolution. 'Avert the blow you appear to be too much inclined to inflict on these unhappy beings,' Macquarie pleaded with Bigge, 'and let the souls now in being, as well as millions yet unborn, bless the day on which you landed on their shores and gave them (when they deserve it) what you so much admire — Freedom!' The Governor's plea went unheeded. Bigge's reports crushed Macquarie. He died a year after the last volume was published, still fighting to clear his name.

That this is an unhappy true story should be obvious from my brief telling of it. I hope the reader will forgive me for wishing — and giving — a much happier ending to the story than Elizabeth and the Architect enjoyed in life. Greenway died on poor mosquito-infested land in the Hunter Valley and was buried in an unmarked grave. I've searched for his remains; they cannot be found. Most probably they never will be. I could do nothing much for the Governor, at least not within the confines of my story; but I could at least celebrate, though not without some equivocation, his memory.

In many ways what I have done with *Mrs M*, though I did not set out with this intention, is to transplant a story that was true to me — that I had experienced — into history. I have threaded this story into a historical tale that accords, in its broad outlines, with the records. The personal, in this way, animates the political; the political fixes and deepens the personal. The real Elizabeth Macquarie had a son, Lachlan, who died on Mull. The Architect, Francis Greenway, was married with children. There is no evidence of a relationship between Elizabeth and the Architect that crossed the boundary of a pragmatic alliance, nor did they come out on the same ship. Greenway designed and built the lighthouse at South Head, but he was never exiled there. He was lashed by a Captain Sanderson, whom he took to court, but in less dramatic circumstances than are told in *Mrs M*; certainly, with less profound consequences. For in my story this is the event that crystalises the affection Elizabeth Macquarie feels for her architect. Every writer of historical fiction makes his own pact with the written record. Tolstoy's *War and Peace* is, as its author confessed, 'what the author wished to express and was able to express in that form in which it is expressed'. Of course *Mrs M* is no *War and Peace*, but it is similarly unbound by convention. It is less a work of historical fiction, I like to think, and more an imagined history.

There are two other works in the shadows that deserve to be spotlit and introduced. The first, from the classical age, is Euripides' *Helen*. This play, which obeys none of the conventions of its time — it is neither tragedy nor comedy but a curious mixture of the two — subverts the famous story of Helen of Troy as told in Homer's *Iliad*. In Euripides' retelling a kind of body double ventures to Troy with the pretty Trojan prince named Paris. The real Helen washes up in Egypt, where she sits out the war. To the Greeks of the classical period this upending of myth would have had an almost sacrilegious quality: the Homeric myths had the force of history and religion combined. The subversion, for Euripides, has a point: he is out to challenge the glorious myths of war and he starts by messing with the most glorious martial myth of all: the siege of Troy. As my Elizabeth began to develop, and to take on a form clearly at odds with the historical record, I returned to Euripides' *Helen* time and again for sustenance. My subversion of the real also has a political point: to draw attention to the idealism of the Macquarie years and the reaction these ideals of criminal redemption and sub-proletarian betterment provoked from a quite vicious Tory Government.

The other work is Robert Hughes's *The Fatal Shore* and it played a very different role. As a youngish reporter I wrote a lengthy magazine profile on Hughes, and came for a period within his orbit. His talent was enormous, his cultural contribution, too. But I'm not sure that he felt himself obliged, when writing that work of popular history, to present a vision of early colonial Australia in accord with historical reality. His notion of the prison settlement at Sydney Cove as the world's first 'gulag' was informed, I sometimes think, by an imagination fed on the Satanic visions of Francisco Goya (Hughes would later write a splendid book about the artist). It is certainly at odds with the reality of the earliest years, when convicts were told after the first muster at Sydney Cove that they could find their own lodgings and fare for themselves as long as they turned up for work at the appointed hour. Afterwards they were permitted to work for piece rates, or goods in kind. Only the worst — and particularly repeat offenders — manned the iron gangs. The sites of secondary punishment, such as Port Arthur and Moreton Island, might have been a truer reflection of the book's title. But Sydney Cove, for the vast majority of convicts who landed there — 160,000 in all — offered a path out of poverty, pollution, oppression and the bleakness of a European winter. It wasn't so much a benighted as a blessed shore.

By Macquarie's time, 1810, the policy of liberating convicts with the capacity to aid the administration almost as soon as they had set foot at Port Jackson had become so deeply entrenched that it troubled the authorities at home, so anxious were they about the potency of transportation as a deterrent. It had also begun to destabilise the military hierarchy of the colony. As a rule the men of the garrison despised the emancipated convicts, as did many of the free settlers.

When I met Hughes, in Manhattan, he insisted on cooking for a gathering of young Australian artists. I joined them at the writer's SoHo apartment. As I was the only one with an expense account, I went to buy the drinks. 'There's a little place on the corner where they have good Australian wine,' Hughes said magisterially. 'Tell them I sent you.' The suggestion was that he, though based in Manhattan, was a rather patriotic — or nostalgic — drinker. But when I told the guy behind the counter that I was looking for Australian wine, and told him my reasons, he laughed. 'Australian wine!' he said. 'Bob doesn't drink a lot of that!' There is something about this exchange that makes sense of *The Fatal Shore*; a wonderfully vivid story that is also, in some essential way, a lie.

In telling my story I learned a little about the mutability of historical fact. To portray the character of Joseph Foveaux, for example, I relied on Macquarie's reading of him, and on his reputation during his own lifetime as a capable colonial administrator. Hughes, on the other hand, portrays Foveaux in an extended passage as a sadist and moral monster. And yet his sources are accounts of life at Norfolk Island that are now regarded as, in most crucial details, sensationalist fictions uncorroborated by the historical record. For the hundreds of thousands of readers of Hughes's popular history, Foveaux is a kind of Antipodean Joseph Goebbels. It suited Hughes's narrative strategy to retail this falsehood. He was not to know, at the time of writing *The Fatal Shore*, that it was false. But we know it now. History, in this way, has its own history. The certainties of one generation — one decade — are often destabilised by the discoveries of another.

The irony, of course, is that in my argument with Hughes's vision I have focused on a socially narrow stratum of early colonial Australia, and neglected the blood and the gore, the pain and the suffering, that became the dominant metaphor for colonial Australia. Instead I tell the story of a woman who, if not an intellectual, was certainly cultivated and idealistic; in doing so, I have attempted to say something true about Australian history, or at least to challenge an abiding falsehood — the vision of the first gulag — with that of a social revolution. The moral largeness of that revolution — its true significance — has been occluded by the Satanic, Goyaesque vision of *The Fatal Shore*. The rather elaborate lies that unfold within the covers of this book are, at the end of the day, told in the service of this truth.

ACKNOWLEDGEMENTS

Aside from the many debts of gratitude owed to the living I am, of course, deeply indebted to the historical figures that live on in this story in altered form, particularly Elizabeth and Lachlan Macquarie. Michael Massey Robinson's ode to the Macquarie Lighthouse is faithfully reproduced in *Mrs M*, but the satire read aloud by John Piper is largely invention. Threaded through the speeches at the climactic welcome party are some nods to Denis Diderot's *Supplement au Voyage de Bougainville* and Nicolas Baudin's December 1802 letter to Governor King.

Thanks to Chris Maxworthy, vice president of the Australian Association for Maritime History, for help with some maritime details, and Keith Vincent Smith for advice based on his deep knowledge of Bungaree and his time. Catherine Milne, who saw both a story of the heart and a novel of ideas in *Mrs M*, has been tireless in her support: astute, sensitive and wise. And in Scott (by name and nature) Forbes I have had a sharp-eyed and knowledgeable editor: *il miglior fabbro*. Thanks also to Alex Craig whose adroit editorial coaxing helped me to transform Elizabeth from a presence in a drama to a character in the round.

A special thanks to my wife Helen Anderson, who has lived with this project for many years, through all its twists and turns. She was, as she promised she would be, my secret editorial weapon as the tale became a manuscript and then a book. Her tears at its closing page, though I suspected at times they were shed out of relief, always buoyed me when the going got tough.

Mrs M has been completed as part of a Doctorate of Creative Arts at the University of Technology Sydney, and Delia Falconer deserves a big thank you for seeing its promise earlier than anyone.